A COLD DAY IN SPELL

FATE WEAVER
BOOK SIX

REGINA WELLING

ERIN LYNN

CONTENTS

A COLD DAY IN SPELL

PROLOGUE

My eyes slid right over the dead zone that contained the house on the corner.

That was a lie.

I looked because I knew the man who lived there would be leaving for work and I could get a glimpse of him.

From somewhere inside the prison my goddess had constructed—to keep my heart protected, she claimed—my soul fluttered like a butterfly in a jar.

The goddess's gaze merely passed over my ex-boyfriend, Kin, without the barest hint of interest, even though I knew there was no way she could have misunderstood my reaction to his presence. If there wasn't a flashing heart symbol hovering above someone's head, they might as well have been invisible, as far as she was concerned.

She eased on the gas and prepared to drive away, and I was helpless to stop her. *Wait, just let me look at him for five more seconds,* I pleaded, but she didn't listen, and there was nobody but myself to blame for the conundrum I now faced. After all, I had been the one who called Alexis forth and begged her to take the reins so I could bow out, wallow in heartbreak, and bathe in self-pity.

How could I admonish her for heeding my request? For putting me right where she'd been for our whole life—trapped inside a body she couldn't control, none of her decisions truly her own. Except I did blame her. When your best friend doesn't want to go outside after a bad breakup, you let her eat her weight in Ben and Jerry's but then you drag her butt out to a club to help burn off the extra calories.

Except Alexis wasn't my best friend—she *was* me, which made the whole thing that much more complicated. When I first found out Cupid was my father, and that I was not only Lexi Balefire of the legendary Balefire witches, Keeper of the Flame, but also a half goddess, it would be an understatement to say I was thrown for a loop.

Pieces of myself I'd never known existed began to churn inside me, coalescing into an entire being I created as a way to deal with the heebie-jeebies. When I pulled out my father's bow and nocked a magical, heart-tipped arrow, I was the Goddess Alexis, in all her bleach-blond glory.

I don't know if it was my witch mojo or simply the breadth and depth of my belief in her that made Alexis real and gave her power, but now that she had it—sans broken heart—I doubted she'd ever willingly give it back. Or, that I'd have the guts to stand up and take it.

But then there stood Kin, that delicious curl dangling

further into his eyes than I'd ever seen it. Kin, with his guitar string-calloused fingers that used to send tingles down my spine whenever he touched me. Kin, who didn't even remember I existed, or that we'd been a fated match bound together by True Love's Kiss.

Except, for the first time since my nemesis, Diana Diamond's, love spell had nearly sentenced him to a lifetime of unhappiness and then stolen away every last memory of me, I felt a surge of hope that maybe the final nail in the coffin of our love hadn't been driven into place quite yet.

Hope: the harbinger of triumph, the eternal tease, and Achilles' heel all rolled into one.

Kin's eyes met mine and he smiled. The kind of smile not reserved for strangers, but rather for family and friends. He knew me.

Get a grip. The goddess running things forced my head around.

Mrs. Chatterly smiled back at Kin from across the street, and he looked right through me.

Hope is a wonderful thing for those who stand a chance. But for those of us who are doomed to walk the planet reliving the most painful moments of our lives without reprieve, it's nothing but a cruel joke.

CHAPTER

ONE

Eyes closed, senses on full alert, I gave in to the bone-vibrating pulse of bass, letting it ripple through my body and pull me into its undulating rhythm. Sweat traced a hot trail down my spine as my hips swiveled and my shoulders shimmied in time to the beat. But while I reveled in the absence of those pesky, unwelcome feelings of concern for things like the fate of the world, the universe—or perhaps the gods—decided I was needed elsewhere.

The prickle of awareness sliced across my hedonistic mood and the adrenaline it carried raced through my veins and burned off the pleasant tequila-induced buzz I'd been enjoying. For a split second, I considered ignoring the siren song, but then a whiff of something more specific set all the tiny hairs on the back of my neck to tingling attention.

Something evil lurked close enough to affect everyone in the place. Close enough to trip my trigger, and judging by the intensity of the energy that permeated my consciousness, the creature was on a mission. Suddenly contemptuous of the glazed-over expressions gracing most of the faces in the club, I began to shove my way through the crowd. The crowd shoved back, and with an annoyed flick of my wrist, I sent a blast of magic to clear a path straight down the middle.

Not a single eye met mine on the way through. As soon as my mood changed, I had ceased to exist in their cocktail-soaked world. Outside, frigid night air hit me in the face like a wall, turning the dewy moisture slicked across my back to icy pinpricks I had no choice but to ignore in the face of more pressing concerns.

The *thing* I was now stalking through a labyrinth of dark city alleys looked human enough on the outside—a beautiful specimen of a woman, if I'm being honest—but I knew there was no chewy chocolate center to her lollipop of crazy. No, the surprise inside Diana Diamond's skin was crunchy and, I suspected, tasted a lot like dung beetle.

Tonight, the self-styled Queen of Hearts had no intention of bringing two fated hearts together in True Love's Kiss like her billboards suggested. How she'd duped the entire city of Port Harbor into thinking her intentions were noble was beyond me. Diana's staunch contempt for love in any incarnation was so palpable I couldn't fathom how even a complete null would mistake it for benevolence.

I could identify with her desire to enter the temple of Olympus, and even understand her conviction that as a half-goddess, her admittance shouldn't be denied. I could even sympathize with the driving need to learn the answers to questions for which only the gods could provide explanation. Still, there was no doubt the price she expected humanity to pay for her golden ticket was far too high.

Diana plowed on through the streets, keeping to the shadows where her darkness could roil, uninhibited yet carefully hidden from the quarry she trailed. I followed her several blocks before I realized I wasn't the only one stalking the evil bringer of hate.

While the term might sound melodramatic, it was appropriate. Diana spewed dissent wherever she could. Under the guise of a professional matchmaker, her intentions were far from noble. Dark magic ensured her clients would end up in unhealthy, detrimental relationships while sapping the motivation to remove themselves with any sort of haste.

Without so much as an inkling of remorse, she preyed on the vulnerable and sentenced them to lives filled with heartache and sadness. Consuming the black evil produced by hardened hearts, using hate and hurt to kill her human soul, Diana assumed her god-born heritage would take up the empty space, allowing her access to her father's demesnes.

What would happen to the earthly realm as a result was none of her concern.

Between Diana's perfectly-manicured, blood-red fingertips flicked a tarot card I knew came complete with soul-piercing, razor-sharp edges and the ability to meddle with destiny's best-laid plans.

When she caught up to the unsuspecting woman and

took a surreptitious glance around, the look on her face sent a wave of nausea rolling through my stomach. An almost sensual desire sent what I delighted in imagining was a forked tongue flicking across her lips, and in the cloud-covered glow of moonlight, her eyes were black as sin.

She grinned and pulled her hand back to fling the card toward her victim, and I knew there was nothing I could do to stop her. But I wasn't alone. Diana's second stalker blurred out of the shadows and into the space between innocent and foe.

Time turned over on itself and it felt like the earth beneath my feet was about to open up and swallow me whole. It wouldn't have been the first time.

I am Sylvana Balefire. Daughter of Clara, mistress of a not-quite mythical god, and mother to Lexi, who happened to be standing right in Diana Diamond's line of fire.

Several thoughts raced through my brain during the infinite seconds it took for the tarot card to chart its course toward my daughter. The first, and probably least useful, was that I wouldn't have picked Lexi out of a lineup, considering the change in her appearance since the last time I'd seen her only a few short months before.

Gone was the flowing chestnut hair, the warm amber-flecked green eyes, and the softness of a heart-shaped face that looked nearly identical to my own. Now, a chin-length shock of platinum blond tipped with magenta framed angular cheekbones that slashed toward eyes the color and hardness of marble. Pink marble, no less.

Formidable was the only way to describe this Lexi, but no matter how capable she might look, my heart still leapt into my throat as Diana's weapon arced ever closer.

Even while I pondered the series of events that might have led to this kind of transformation, the part of me that had always been forced to fight without conscience for what I wanted called power into my palm as I raised my hand to hurl a binding spell in Diana's direction.

Oblivious to everything—being targeted and the fact her love life or maybe even her soul was about to be spared from grave danger—Diana's original quarry, a sweet-faced woman, continued walking toward the end of the block.

"Don't do it." In the bland tones of someone who expects to be ignored, Lexi warned Diana, but spite or desperation let the card fly anyway. It would not score; the three of us were now alone on the street, and I stepped back into the shadows ready to strike if Lexi needed me.

Without even so much as a raised eyebrow, my daughter reached behind her back and pulled a glowing golden bow and heart-tipped arrow out of nowhere. I'd seen her father do the very same thing more times than I could count, but watching Lexi claim her birthright with such nonchalance both excited me and chilled me to the bone.

The glowing ropes of my binding spell disappeared with a sizzle and a snap when Lexi's arrow erupted with black witchfire shot through with purple sparks. Grim witchfire. The kind that proved my daughter carried a measure of darkness in her soul. We all do, but I never thought Lexi's was strong enough to power the killing flame. It was possible we had more in common than I thought.

Gold and bone-white shining through black fire, the shaft of the arrow looked different than any I'd seen my lover, Lexi's father, use. Lexi took her stance as smoothly as she'd drawn the bow, as if it was second nature. When she fired, the arrow nicked Diana's index finger, pierced the tarot card, and pinned it to the wall behind her head. Lexi was safe, and she hadn't needed the protection I'd been willing to provide.

Dark hair, dark eyes, and dark fury. That was Diana when she shrieked and stared at the slow drip of shadow-darkened—or maybe black was her natural color—blood. Her hand fisted as she glared at Lexi and snarled, "Get out of my way, Balefire. You don't want to cross me."

"Oh, but I do." Smiling savagely, the woman who looked like my daughter but wasn't really, lifted a hand almost absently. Still trailing black fire, the arrow pinged out of the wall and returned to its owner. Watching Lexi pop a hip and stare at Diana while she blew out the flame...well, it made me feel proud and terrified at the same time.

Twirling the arrow between her fingers like a baton, Lexi assured Diana, "You should have left Kin alone. Going after him was your first mistake, and I'm planning to make it your last."

What on earth was she doing? Anger-fueled power shivered through the air, tightened my throat, and prickled across my body. If Diana thought she had the upper hand, she was dead wrong. Lexi's magic was strong. Stronger than mine, and I'm not bragging when I say I'm one hell of a witch.

In response, Diana threw back her head and laughed. "You're nothing but a common Fate Weaver. You'll die screaming just like the rest."

She was gone before Lexi could respond.

ALEXIS

I returned the arrow to its quiver and glared at the empty space left behind when Diana blinked out. Now that she was gone and I was in no danger of showing her anything resembling weakness, I allowed the scorn and anger I felt toward her to color my face. As the world's most powerful Fate Weaver, daughter of the god Cupid, and wielder of the Bow of Destiny, I should have been in possession of enough magical mojo to smite her right there on the spot.

Oh, and I was also, technically, Keeper of the Flame, though that honor fell on the side of my witch heritage, which meant that it was Lexi, and not me, Alexis, who controlled the Balefire magic. I know, it's kind of confusing, especially considering the witch and I shared a body if not a mind and a heart.

In the aftermath of a failed relationship, she'd divided us in half and let me take the reins. Most of the time, she huddled in her misery, bemoaning the loss of love, and left me to take care of business. Except for any time we got within a hundred yards of Diana Diamond, when she popped up and it was wildcat witch all the way. Those were the moments when I could see our potential if we ever pulled it together.

I didn't realize she was capable of enough passionate fury to pull out the killing fire, though. I wouldn't hesitate to make her use it again if I thought it would take out the threat.

Right then wasn't the time to stay focused on the division. Both sides of me wanted revenge, and it would have given me immense pleasure to send Diana Diamond straight to hades in a handbasket. No passing go, no collecting two hundred dollars. Just a one-way ticket to the underworld, where she'd never get the opportunity to realize her deepest desire and ascend to full-goddess status. Why she wanted to gain entry to Olympus was beyond me, but then again I'm mostly sane and tend to avoid places where I'm fully unwelcome.

Not only had Diana made a mockery of my life's work, she'd also beaten my witch counterpart's life into smithereens. Lexi could believe I took pleasure in her pain for as long as she felt the need to do so. If what she required was a punching bag, well, slap the word Everlast on my butt and let her take her best shot. Eventually she'd figure out that I was only trying to protect her, and maybe we could find some way to coexist that didn't involve one of us subjugating the other.

Until then, it suited me just fine to keep running interference. Even if I *could* damn Diana to hell, I couldn't be sure what would happen to the souls she'd affected so far. Her spell on Kin had been broken, and yet he still didn't remember his relationship with me—or maybe I should say us. If that was the fate of all her misdirected matches, I certainly wasn't going to be the one to drive the final nail into their coffins.

I could still feel the thrum of dark magic in my palm and knew we were playing with fire—witchfire, to be exact. Lexi's fire, but mine if I could go through her to wield it. Unless pushed to the brink, she'd never call forth the black variety, and was right to steer clear of magic that could darken her heart. I, however, had far fewer scruples, and since it seemed as though Lexi was the half that focused on matters of the heart, figured I ought to put to use whatever tools were at my disposal.

While I pondered these thoughts and imagined Diana dying a thousand deaths, something bright flashed in my peripheral vision. The hairs on the back of my neck stood on end, and even though there was nothing there when I spun around, prepared to fight, I couldn't shake the thought that someone—or some*thing*—had been watching me, just waiting for an opportunity to strike.

If it was Diana again, the woman had some nerve, and

less sense than it would take to fill a thimble. That was fine with me. When the time came, I'd find a way to use her stupidity against her.

CHAPTER

TWO

"Do I know you?"

Four simple words. Words made from knives. Knives dipped in poison to burn and sting.

"Do I know you?"

As it did every time I had a quiet moment, the memory of Kin's voice repeated like the echo of a ringing bell. Such a simple question shouldn't be able to cut a person to ribbons, but he'd left my soul in tatters and my heart a bloody relic.

I could hate him. I should hate him. I'd never hate him, though, because it wasn't his fault, but every time I heard his voice in my head, I wanted to kill Diana Diamond. She'd laughed at me as she'd torn us apart.

It didn't seem the least bit odd for Diana's laugh to follow me down a country road. Okay, maybe not the laugh, but the setting was odd. I'm not a back-to-nature kind of woman. Trees? Pretty enough, especially in the fall, or like now, with snow bending their spines into graceful curves. My comfort zone lies in the sights and sounds of the city, the solid feel of a concrete sidewalk under my boots. Man-made canyons with life threading between.

Before I could dredge up a shred of the memory of how I had come to be walking around in the middle of nowhere, I crested the hill and looked down at the steep expanse of snow-slippery road stretching out ahead.

A mental image of myself pinging from bank to bank like a human pinball elicited a shudder before logic took over. To avoid breaking a leg or worse, all I had to do was turn around and go back. Simple, really.

Except even when I ordered them, my feet refused to carry me in any other direction than forward. I could go down the treacherous hill or stand there until I froze, and still, my mind refused to supply a valid reason for being out in the wilderness alone.

We could call the Balefire.

Because magic is the solution to everything.

My inner witch spoke first; the goddess scoffed, threw up a mental a wall, and then I was Alexis.

T he last thing I needed was a bunch of useless suggestions while I reasoned out the next logical step.

Shutting down my softer half took a moment longer and more effort than I'd expected. Magic might keep me warm, but so would a bout of good, old-fashioned exercise, and since I couldn't go back, I took the first step into the fog billowing around my ankles.

Wait a second...fog? Over snow?

My heart kicked twice when I felt soft earth beneath my feet instead of ice or snow, and a burst of birdsong erupted from amid the rustling leaves.

"What the hell?" The words popped out of my mouth and my carefully constructed thought-wall toppled without a sound.

You're dreaming, you idiot. Honestly Alexis, you call yourself a goddess and you couldn't figure that one out on your own?

You know I don't dream.

But I came to that conclusion just ahead of her pointing out the obvious, and curled my lip into a snarl to respond.

The nasty comment died without a whimper as rising dread replaced annoyance.

Run.

The word echoed through my head and I wasn't sure which one of us—witch or goddess—said it, but it was good advice. With my heart pounding and the sound of galloping hooves forcing me forward, I glanced back to see what had marked me as prey even as my racing feet shredded the fog to wisps.

One hand loosely clasped around the reins and the other holding aloft a glowing lantern, the shadowed figure rode the dark horse as if it were an extension of his own body. A hood hid my attacker's face, but my imagination supplied a death mask skull, jaws flapping beneath eye sockets filled with burning embers of hellfire.

When a second rider joined the first, I would have screamed, but I didn't have the breath for it.

Dream? This was a nightmare.

I listened to Lexi and ran. Branches whipped against my skin as I raced through spaces I hoped were too small for them to follow, and yet the mare's hot breath shivered over the back of my neck. Being a witch and a demigod might assure a long life, but it doesn't make one invincible.

But could a dream kill me? It certainly felt like it at the moment, so I ran. And ran. Until the world narrowed to the impact of each heel touching down, the stretch of my arch, toes pushing me off the ground. Fear dragged the magic up to the surface, bringing the witch along with it.

The shift from goddess to witch happened between one step and the next. I was Lexi and still I ran.

My feet pounded against the ground until the voice of Alexis sliced through my mind. *Stop,* she yelled. *You stop right now.* Wait, wasn't she the one who started running? Now she wanted me to stop?

Black witchfire, a legacy from my mother, already crackled and sparked as it grew between my hands. Only dark intent could call the black fire, and the use of it would brand me a murderer if this were more than a dream and if those chasing me carried witch blood.

Better safe than turned to stone. Power flowed up

from the earth to pool in my center, where I could pick through it to pull out what I needed to alter the dark flame to purest silver. Where the black would kill, the silver would only steal the consciousness for a time. Good for stopping a foe long enough to get away.

Time turned liquid, drew out long as I turned toward the empty space under the dark hood and the nearest black horse reared. Hooves flashed, then thumped back down hard enough I felt the tremor through my shoes. But it wasn't the horse or even her rider I should have feared; it was the lantern.

"Fate Weaver." A thick voice issued from under the hood with the fetid hiss of an unearthed coffin lid popping open. "You will die screaming." He raised his arm while the second rider circled to try to cut me off. I'd heard those words before, and again they sent a chill up my spine.

Sickly green light flowed from the lantern like questing fingers or tongues ready to taste my spirit and determine if it offered feast or famine. Like an oil slick on a puddle, the light rippled and oozed close enough to draw on my energy.

A different dream from my past flowed up from my subconscious and I remembered being chased like this once before. Unfortunately, I couldn't recall what I'd done to shake my attacker last time, so I pulled out the most formidable weapon in my witch arsenal.

"Eat witchfire!" Okay, maybe it wasn't the bravest battle cry in the world, and I wasn't Miss Almighty Cool and Collected with her arrows, but there wasn't time to think up anything more epic as I took aim and wound up for the pitch.

Mine. As if she could do it better, Alexis surged forward and took control. She could say her taking over was my idea all she wanted, but I was getting a little tired of feeling like a parasite in my own body, so I held on a little longer.

S tupid witch. Her fighting the change cost precious seconds and as I reared back and used my superior aiming ability to lob the ball of flame the mare tried to dodge. Smart horse. Her rider clamped his knees in tight and gripped the reins harder, but lost his hold on the lantern when my missile struck home. His shout of pain carried the echo of thunder as I ducked past flashing hooves and leapt over the lantern to land on the snowy sidewalk right in front of my own home.

Ten steps would see me safe. I was so close I could almost taste the warmth and comfort when a searing pain slashed into my left shoulder blade. Spinning, I saw a black-nailed finger drop to dangle lifelessly from a shroud-like sleeve. I heard the echo of Diana's laugh a second time.

The second rider reined in the stallion long enough for me to draw up a second fiery silver globe and take aim, but before I could, it decided retreat was the better option and whistled at the mare.

Nipping the ring of the fallen lantern between her teeth, the mare bore her cargo away with a snort and a flick of her tail.

Round one to me. The thought fell into the fading nightmare and I slid into an uneasy sleep.

CHAPTER

THREE

An incessantly buzzing alarm dragged me awake and I spent a moment trying to work up enough spit to release my tongue from where it was stuck to the roof of my mouth. One eye slitted, I gazed up at the ceiling and tried to remember if I'd downed my weight in scotch or been hit by a truck the night before.

A stretch of sore muscles indicated it might have been both. Tossing back the duvet and hoping a shower might wash away the fatigue, I headed for the bathroom.

Mornings are my favorite time of day, if only because Lexi sleeps late and I can enjoy an hour or two without having to listen to her constant commentary on everything I do. This weird duality and the feeling of sharing a body wasn't my idea. In fact, I'd been happier when I was nothing more than an ethereal construct that could shoot the bow unseen in public.

Call me the Pinocchio of Fate Weavers—you'd be close.

Lifting a leg to step over the side of the claw-foot tub pinged at both calf and thigh muscles. Stupid archaic tub, anyway. Whoever thought it was a good idea to stew in their own filth? Give me a nice shower stall any day of the week. One with a lovely rain head and a few side jets would be my preference. All sleek and modern with some tile and a big, open entrance instead of a lousy shower curtain that always wanted to plaster itself against my backside.

The stinging burn when warm water hit my left shoulder interrupted my internal rant. What on earth had happened last night? And why couldn't I remember?

Quit thinking so hard! You woke me up. The witch was not a morning person. Not until I sated her with that first cup of coffee, anyway.

I twisted off the taps, whipped the shower curtain aside, and cheated my shoulder toward the mirror hanging on the back of the bathroom door. Centered on my shoulder blade was a dark blemish that, at this distance, looked like a small tattoo.

Giving in, I thought toward the witch. *Did we get hammered last night?* I certainly wouldn't be the first person in the world to make a drunken decision that would mark my flesh for the rest of my life.

You're an idiot, she fired back, and her tone pissed me off. *One of those riders did that to you. Us. Whatever. That was no ordinary nightmare.*

Nightmare?

Lexi sighed, and the dream came back to me in a rush.

By this time, I was standing next to the full-length and angling a hand mirror to get a better look. Not the easiest thing to do while also clutching a damp towel, but my innate desire for order wouldn't let me drop the bath sheet on the floor.

The mark, best as I could tell, was circular—maybe half again the diameter of a quarter. A ring with an intricate design inside. Looking at it backwards and sideways, I couldn't make out anything specific in the pattern.

Lexi's voice clanged inside my head. *You could ask Salem to take a picture of it with the cell phone, you know.*

That would not be happening. It wasn't my fault she'd let her familiar become way too familiar. In both his forms, the cat-man refused to respect boundaries, so I'd been forced to toss him and that fuzzy childhood relic of a beanbag chair out of the bedroom. Permanently.

Since then, I'd maintained a chilly silence and Salem kept his distance, and that was just the way I liked it.

Still, the witch had a point about using the camera, so I put away the mirror and the towel and stalked back into the bedroom to retrieve the phone from the nightstand. Two tries at getting a good shot yielded blurry results and I snorted out my frustration when the words *stubborn fool* drifted through my head. I slapped up the walls to shut her out.

Back in the bathroom, a combo of two mirrors and the phone finally netted me a decent shot, but by then, I was running late for work and needed to get dressed. A black cashmere sweater seemed the best option against sore skin, and I allowed myself the shortcut of a glamour instead of messing with hair and makeup.

Put together and satisfied my face revealed nothing of

my sleep-disturbed night, I weighed the certainty of encountering the faerie godmothers in the kitchen against not giving my other half the coffee she needed, and decided to chance the former. Though I preferred to avoid stimulants, after the night I'd had, I needed the caffeine as much as she did.

"Blueberry pancakes?" Fire faerie, Soleil, eyed me over one shoulder. Different as the four elements they represented, the godmothers would be shocked to know how similar the over-eager expressions they'd adopted since I'd taken over running the Lexi/Alexis show were.

I'd overheard more than one whispered conversation between the four of them about letting me/us work through whatever it was they perceived Lexi was going through, but so far, they'd broken type and stayed out of my business. I could see the effort was costing them, though.

Under flaming hair, frown lines traced the space between Soleil's ember eyes. "They're your favorite." Her tone wasn't quite a wheedle, but it was close. She, like the other two original godmothers, had taken to treating me like I was the victim of some strange illness. Only Vaeta, the most recent addition to the household, seemed unaffected by the new dynamic. But then, she spent half of her time flitting off on adventures with her demon boyfriend, Rhys, and the other half complaining about him.

Half of me—and I'm sure you can guess which half— longed to send them back where they belonged so I could be alone with my misery. Neither part of me had the stones to do it.

Normally, faerie godmothers stick to the shadows and only lend a hand to their witches when there's no other option. In this house, there was no baseline for normal, and all pretenses that the godmother-goddaughter relationship followed the usual rules had gone out the window long ago. Somewhere deep down, I could feel a numb sort of pain threatening to make itself known, but I didn't dare open that door for fear I'd wind up right back where I started before I allowed my goddess half to take over. Mired in pity, fear, and heartbreak. Had I been more self-aware, I'd have realized how true was the statement that wherever you go, there you are.

I hadn't eliminated the hurt. I had just taken to ignoring it, and with it, the people who cared for me the most. What they didn't realize was that as much as I appreciated their love, it was like a knife right through the heart. Every gentle hug, every comforting word shined a bright light on just how terrible I was feeling, and instead of sticking around and coping with it like an adult, I'd chosen to reject them all in the name of self-preservation.

Besides, women get dumped every day, and some of them go out and get a makeover to try and feel better. That wasn't so much different from what I had done, right?

"Is there blueberry syrup too?" I caved a little because, well, blueberry pancakes really are my favorite.

Terra, the only faerie who technically rated the

godmother title, kept her face carefully blank. "Of course, and by the way, could you pick up a gallon of milk on your way home tonight?" She wasn't fooling me with that nonsense. Terra could magic up a cow—or a herd of them—from thin air without breaking a sweat. Asking me to play errand girl was a ploy to stay apprised of my projected whereabouts after the end of my work day.

Which she confirmed by adding, "And if you're going to be late, you could call or text. It's the polite thing to do."

"If there's time, I'll try to remember." That qualified as nice, right? My business might require me to keep regular hours, but my life's work couldn't be done according to a time clock. Piercing hearts and weaving fates with the Bow of Destiny was a calling. It was *my* destiny, and I had to go where and when the people needed me. Mostly, that meant hitting the night shift and not spending a lot of time at the house.

The childish life of fantasy board games, hot tubbing, and refereeing faerie fights was a thing of the past. I was trying my best to be over it, and wished the faeries would realize that what I needed most was for them to move on from it too.

Besides, if they had any idea what went on at FootSwept these days, they'd stage another intervention.

CHAPTER

FOUR

I pressed the button on my key fob to unlock the doors of my brand-new car, not because I couldn't have done it with a mere snap of my fingers, but because I enjoyed hearing the little bee-bop noise that signaled the deactivation of the alarm. After years of walking or straddling a tiny, gutless scooter, I'd gone for the mid-sized, sport utility with the most powerful engine available and all the fanciest features. Sure, I could walk to work almost as quickly given the traffic most days, but cranking the stereo up to bass-thumping full-blast put a smile on my face.

Snow crunched beneath my tires as I backed out of the driveway, and the memory of last night's nightmare flared to life once more. I resisted the urge to scratch at the blemish that marred my left shoulder, preferring to ignore its presence until I had a better idea of what put it there and how to get rid of it.

It was rush hour, and the streets were lined with people walking from parking areas to offices. Their faces slid past like one long blur. My attention was not on their faces anyway, but aimed at the space over their heads where I might find the glowing symbol that called to my inner matchmaker.

The people might have blended together, but my archer's sight narrowed in to check for the little pink hearts that meant I would have to brave the cold, Northeastern winter air for the sake of instigating true love's kiss with a shot from my trusty living gold-tipped arrow.

Call me Cupid, but that's where you'd be wrong, I'm only his daughter.

Thankfully, no urgent matches popped up, and I made it to work in record time. I parked in the secret lot behind my building and opened the door to the new and improved FootSwept Matchmaking.

Hey, I redecorated. Sue me. Antiques and coziness might be the old Lexi's taste, but not mine. I go for art deco. Bold, bright colors mixed with white and chrome, and geometric lines. Just formal enough to keep the clients from getting too comfy, because while they're my bread and butter, my office is not a home for wayward hearts.

My receptionist, Angela, gave a brisk tap on my door. "Your ten o'clock appointment is here, Ms. Balefire." At my nod, she stepped back and held the door open wide for a timid-looking woman.

"Hello," she said. "I'm sorry I'm a little early. I was afraid I wouldn't be able to find a parking space, and then I did." Her left hand fluttered up to pat at her hair, then back down to clutch her purse strap.

"Come in, come in. Blake Cordell, I presume?" I said, waving Miss Mousy inside. Lexi would have whisked Blake into the now-defunct salon and had Flix snip and clip her like a prized poodle. All in the name of inspiring confidence. Nothing wrong with that, but my job wasn't to make her feel better, it was to get her matched to someone who would love her in any state.

"Yes, that's me." Blake confirmed, though she stuttered in such a way it made me wonder if the question had thrown her off. "I'm here to...because...I want to meet someone."

Early bird, plans ahead because she's nervous, probably doesn't get out much. I glanced down at her intake questionnaire. *Good job working with special needs children, which means she's dedicated, but probably doesn't have enough adult contact*, I thought to myself, pegging the client before she'd settled into the seat across from me.

Pasting on a smile to cover what I considered the most difficult part of my job, I reached across the table and patted her on the hand. "What are you looking for in a mate, Ms. Cordell?"

The answer made no matter to me. The second my skin made contact with hers, my gut locked in on her perfect mate. All I needed to do was follow the tug, find the guy, and set up the date. Easy, right?

"He has to like kids, and cats, and Indian food. Not be a jerk. That's about it. My needs are simple." She launched into a tale about her last relationship and I let her ramble.

As she talked, I tapped her answers into the computer so I'd have them on file.

These days, I was taking a page out of Diana Diamond's playbook and going digital, but not for the reasons you're thinking. Relying on points of compatibility had never been my method, and I saw no reason to change now. I followed my gut in the same way Lexi always had, but stopped short of dragging people out for a night on the town.

Much easier to set up a series of Friday-night blind dates, then just take a few potshots with the bow from a shadowed corner of the restaurant. More efficient, got the job done, and I was beating Diana Diamond hands down in matches made. So much so that I'd done something Lexi never would have agreed to, and now my face graced the TV late at night.

Computerized dating didn't make me better at my job, but it allowed me to keep better track of my matches, and provided me with a way to access Diana's files.

That's right, I'd turned hacker. Or Flix had—at my request. Ms. Cordell was not just a new client, she was a new client picked out of Diana's appointment book. Double score. Goddesses do not say neener neener—even when they want to.

Flix, the clever, clever man, had figured out how to get into my rival's network and access her scheduling software. He fed the names to Angela, who emailed the client with a discount coupon for a consultation with me, and seven times out of ten, we siphoned off one of Diana's victims.

A satisfying result on many levels. The lovelorn actually got matched to their proper mate, and the idea of Diana feeling the sting of my vengeance gave me a nice, warm glow. Okay, it was more like cold satisfaction, but I'd take what I could get. Lexi might prefer revenge, but I wanted justice.

After a few more questions and answers, entirely for her peace of mind, Blake got my most reassuring smile and a promise to call her the next day to set up her first date. Her last first date ever, unless I missed my guess. She left my office with a spring in her step.

With no other appointments on the schedule, I made my way through the former closet to the room where Flix worked his technological magic. Being half Fae, maybe he'd used some faerie magic as well. I never asked, and if he had a problem with my views on privacy, he never said a word. He looked at me funny from time to time, but kept his opinions where they belonged: to himself.

"Did you see the article in the Sentinel?" Flix asked as I entered. "I emailed you the link."

If I'd changed my look, it was nothing to the difference in Flix's appearance. Gone were the flowing silvery-white tresses that wouldn't have looked out of place on the cover of a romance novel. He'd gone shorter and darker. Don't get me wrong—he was still gorgeous. The man looked like he'd just rolled out of bed after a torrid night of lust and was ready for more. But that was just his baseline. Being in a committed relationship had balanced him out some.

Keeping the reason under wraps, I admitted, "I overslept and didn't have time to check my news feed this morning. What's it say?"

"That Port Harbor has become something of a mecca for singles. Sixty percent increase in the unmarried population over the past year, though I'm not sure how they came by that particular statistic. Diana took full credit for the influx."

The vein in my temple throbbed. "Shocking," I snarked.

"She made it seem like people were moving here just for the chance to maybe get an appointment with her, and that if they did, it would solve all their problems."

"Well, that's fine. Let her line them up, we'll just keep knocking them down. What have you got for me today?" Deliberately, I kept the conversation centered on business. Over the past few months, Flix had learned to do the same. We weren't talking about my personal life or watching chick flicks on the days he wasn't with Carl.

All business, all the time.

"Chad Kroger. Forty-something. Works in advertising, lost his wife two years ago and transferred here last month."

"Send a copy of the file to my phone. This one's going to be a piece of cake," I tossed over my shoulder on my way out.

I'd sent Angela home after our last appointment, so the tap on the door surprised me.

When I cracked it open, it was to see the wide blue eyes of one Mona Katz blinking back at me. The look of disbelief on her face told me I was in for a frustrating conversation.

"Lexi!" Mona cried as she stepped over the threshold and practically lunged at me. Split-second timing and a fancy little two-step put me out of reach. "What have you done? Hi, Flix," she said to his back as he found somewhere else to be. "Where is the salon? The closet? What happened to all the boots?"

Verbally incontinent, that's how I'd describe Mona. The old Lexi believed there was a tough, capable woman underneath the space-cadet exterior, but I attributed that to her soft heart and desire to only see the good in people. A luxury we could not afford anymore, given how life had treated us so far. Ever vigilant, that was my motto, and if you think it sounds harsh, well, you haven't walked a mile in my Manolos.

My internal assessment of Mona's character was cut short when I realized she wasn't alone. She beckoned to someone outside the door, and when Kin sauntered into the room, my pulse sped up to double time with the effort of keeping Lexi's emotions in check.

"Hello, Mona." I took a seat at the desk, pulled my laptop closer, and tried to look busy while avoiding making eye contact with Kin. "How are you doing at Crumb?" I asked. "You know, with the attention your cakes have been getting, I could probably find you something that pays better. There's a spot opening up at the Regent hotel. They do sixty weddings a year, at least. Interested?"

The head chef was a recent client. Not that it mattered; I was simply trying to quiet the voice of my past self, who was screaming at the top of her lungs inside me.

Mona stared at me as if I had grown a second head. "Of course not. I'm happy where I am."

"Suit yourself. What can I do for you?" One toe pushed the office chair in lazy half-circles while I eyed Mona dispassionately and concentrated on ignoring Kin. She continued to stare at me like if she looked hard enough, she'd get x-ray vision and see through to my bones.

"This is my friend Kin Clark, and I was hoping you could help him. You know, work your magic." In a sublimely surreal moment, Mona introduced me to the man who was supposed to love me for the rest of his life. Except he never would. She shot me a little eyebrow waggle that I chose to ignore.

"Hello," I finally let my gaze rest on the space just slightly above his left ear. The rules of polite society forced me to acknowledge his presence. After all, it wasn't Kin's fault his entrance had thrown me for a loop.

"Nice to meet you." Kin replied, his face reddening in what I chalked up to embarrassment. I knew visiting a matchmaker wasn't something he'd do under normal circumstances, and that Mona had probably dragged him into FootSwept kicking and screaming. I pushed all thoughts of our history deep down into my subconscious and treated him like any other stranger. It was easier than I expected, and reinforced my conviction that I was doing the right thing by trying to move on with my life.

I realized Mona had continued talking, and that her focus was trained on the changes I'd made to the office rather than my detached attitude. "And I don't want another job, I want to know what's going on with you. It looks...weird in here." She gestured to the spot where the sofa used to be. Personally, I preferred to meet clients in a more professional, *no surprises here* kind of way.

I sighed, "I redecorated. Flix was tired of doing hair, and if someone needs a little spit and polish, I send them to a spa. On their dime." My inner witch grunted at that, but I kept a firm hand on the reins. "No hard feelings, believe me. This place was due for a change. With Diana, Queen of Hearts trying to corner the matchmaking market, I thought it best to refocus my efforts. Clean up my act. And don't you worry about the boots. They're being put to good use." I held out a leather-clad foot as proof.

Mona's eyes narrowed and she searched my face for signs this was all a joke. Like I'd spent a fortune remodeling just to freak her out.

"Well, I suppose if you're happy, that's all that matters." She lied right to my face, but I let it go.

"I am. I am also, unfortunately, booked solid for the foreseeable future." I ignored the obvious as I stood up and slung my purse strap over my shoulder.

Mona stared at me and pointed to Kin like I was some kind of idiot. "Surely you can find room in your schedule to help him? He needs to find his soul mate, and you're the only one I trust to do the job. That horrid Diana Diamond gives me the creeps. There's something off about her."

Thinking how right Mona was, I sat back down, but did not commit myself to finding Kin a match.

"It's okay, Mona," He said, then turned to me, a ghost of his former grin on his lips. "I'm only here because she insisted. This is what happens when you hang around with happily married couples. They always seemed to think that no life could be complete without a relationship, and they're constantly attempting to set up their single friends—usually with disastrous results."

If he'd been anyone else, I would have said she was right to bring him to me rather than try a DIY approach, but I thoroughly wished she'd known enough to leave it alone. Kin looked like he wanted to crawl into a hole and burrow his way back home.

"I'm sorry, I'm booked." I wasn't, but I had no other choice than to pretend as though that were the case.

Mona tilted her head sideways and narrowed her eyes. "I don't know what's going on with you, Lexi, but I can see you're not yourself at the moment. It's not like you to turn away someone who needs your expertise. And besides, it will be a piece of cake. Kin is a really great guy. A musician with a good day job at the radio station, and an uncanny resemblance to Ryan Reynolds."

She played up his good points as if he weren't sitting

right next to us, and I nearly laughed when a muscle in his jaw started to twitch with the effort of not shouting at her. "He's just lonely," she continued on, oblivious, "and I know you could find him a girlfriend like that." Mona snapped her fingers and summoned an elephant the size of Texas to take up space in the room.

The formerly carefree Lexi Balefire of FootSwept Matchmaking flared to life inside my head at the mention of Kin finding someone else to love. She flooded my head with the vision of Diana Diamond laughing as her curse wiped away Kin's memory of their relationship. So powerful was the working that no one outside of Lexi's family—which included her best friend, Flix—could remember when "LexiKin" had been a thing.

If you asked me, and no one did, I would have said it was probably better that way, but Lexi disagreed. If seeing Kin raked claws over the witch's wounded heart, having to find him a new girlfriend might rip it right in half. And, if I had to clean up the resulting mess again, I'd be inclined to shoot myself with one of my own arrows.

"I'm sorry, Mona. As I said"—twice now—"I'm booked solid for the next three months. I'm sure you'll meet a nice woman long before my schedule clears up." I directed the last bit at Kin.

Keeping a pleasant but slightly cool expression on my face, I flipped my laptop closed to indicate my decision was final and waited for Mona to take the hint. The second hand on my vintage wall clock ticked away almost half a minute while she squinted at me.

I couldn't explain myself or that the only way I would ever get involved in Kin's love life was if he happened to step into my sights sporting a shiny little heart symbol above his head. Then there would be irrefutable proof he had moved on. The kind the witch who cried in my head at night couldn't ignore.

"What happened to turn you so cold? You're like a totally different person." Mona's voice interrupted my thoughts and carried a twinge of sadness, though why it would make any difference to her made no sense to me. "I don't know what's going on with you, Lexi. But I don't particularly care for this version of you."

For a second, my whole body tensed in panic, but then I realized Mona was just referring to my refusal to take on Kin as a client, and not the fact that the friend she used to know had deferred control of her mind and body to a bow-wielding goddess who might carry the same memories, but not the same reactions.

"I'm sorry you feel that way, Mona." I glanced pointedly at the clock. "But I do have to get on with my day. It really was nice to meet you, Kin."

The second Mona left, her shoulders hunched in disappointment, I promptly forgot about her visit. Of course, I should have known she wouldn't be content to let sleeping dogs lie—which Flix courteously pointed out even though it was unnecessary to do so.

"She won't let this go, you know." He chided from the doorway where he'd been eavesdropping. "She's like a hound when she gets on a scent. I told you this would happen if you let her shoehorn her way into your personal life."

"Yes, well, thank you for the information, Captain Obvious. I've got it under control, so don't worry about it." I shooed him back to work even while the little voice in my head told me I was being overly harsh.

If becoming entirely friendless was part of your plan, Alexis, it's working.

Maybe if I just ignored her, she'd shut up, but something told me I'd be a fool to bet money on it.

CHAPTER

FIVE

I need you. Bring diapers.

Serena's text dinged into my inbox as I locked the office door behind me. When had I become everyone's bloody errand girl? Pick up milk, bring diapers. Didn't they know who I was? Didn't they understand they were talking to the daughter of Cupid, the carrier of the Bow of Destiny? My job included spreading love throughout the greater Port Harbor area, not delivering fripperies to former enemies.

Feeling thoroughly put upon and misunderstood, I left the car running, tossed an anti-theft charm on it, and dodged into the drug store where I spent ten minutes staring at way too many diaper options.

"Help you find something?" A cheerful smile lit the face of the perky brunette who had stopped stocking shelves with shampoo to ask if I needed help.

I might have brushed her off, but for the symbol hovering over her head. She'd feel the sting of my arrow soon. Okay, she wouldn't, because my arrows are painless, but the intent was the same and her true love was out there, waiting. The symbol registered itself in my memory with a click and turned her to a blip on my radar so that the next time she and her intended came in close enough proximity, I'd be there to finalize the deed.

"I'm not sure what size to get," was what I admitted, but it was more than that. I felt weird standing in an aisle that supplied a product that wasn't in the cards for me to ever need for myself. Maybe if things had worked out with Kin we might have made a family. A little girl with his dimples and my eyes.

Since that was a Lexi dream and none of mine, I shoved it away with a vengeance, ignored the sigh that echoed through my head, and returned to the task at hand.

The clerk cocked her head at me and pointed toward the clearly labeled age range on the nearest package. "How old is the baby? They go by age to determine sizing."

"And that works? I mean, don't babies come in all sizes even if they're the same age? Or is it a *one size fits all* thing? Like socks." She did not want to get me started on the sloppy method for designating a three-size range for socks. Nine to eleven? Really?

Casting my mind back, I didn't want to admit I had no idea how old Kaine was now. Work, then more work, had filled the days between my nephew's dramatic birth and today. "Two or three months, maybe. Last time I saw him, he was about this big." I held my hands out to indicate a length. "That was a couple of weeks ago, I think. They're for my nephew."

She shot me a raised eyebrow that let me know I'd fallen short in the aunt department and waved toward the middle shelf before going back to work.

Grabbing three packages of various sizes and figuring one of them would do, I got in line behind a man with curly blond hair and the posture of a husband or boyfriend who did not wish to be seen buying the decidedly feminine items he'd placed on the belt. The witch swam up from the depths of our psyche and our heart skipped a beat until he turned to pay and I caught his profile.

Not Kin.

Not Kin, Lexi echoed and, ignoring my sniff of disgust at what I considered to be a whining tone, sank back down to wallow in her misery some more.

Men. Who needed them? Look what they did to a woman. Lose one and end up a fractured soul. That would never be me.

It already is. How stupid are you? At least there was some heat to Lexi's tone. It gave me hope.

I'd admit to a fine sense of irony, given romance was my stock in trade but I had no personal desire to mire myself down in it. Look what happened when it went wrong. The witch half of me was an emotional wreck and I was on my way to visit a single mother who'd ended up that way after making the horrible decision to get romantic with my idiot half-brother, Jett Striker, who was currently on the supernatural naughty list and serving time somewhere.

Serena yanked the door open before I managed more than three steps onto the porch. "It's about time you showed up." With one deft motion, she thrust a blanket-wrapped, squirming bundle of baby into my arms and nipped the bag of diapers out of my hand. "C'mon in. You can't keep a baby out in the cold too long. What are you doing just standing there?"

"But I didn't—" I tossed at her retreating back and resigned myself to going inside. My intention of dropping off the diapers and claiming I was too busy for a visit went up in a breath of powdery-soft, totally intoxicating baby-head scent.

Drawn like a moth to a flame, my gaze dropped down to meet Kaine's. "Who's a little cutie?" I cooed at him. "You are. Yes, you are." I could have stared at him all day just to watch the way his precious lips curved into a perfect O when he smiled.

Inside me, the witch stirred. *You think you're so cold, but you're no better than the rest of us. The mighty bow-hunter Alexis reduced to a baby-talking puddle of goo.*

She snorted in my head. How mortifying.

No matter how I tried to stop myself, more babble kept falling out of my mouth. "I could just eat you up. Yes, I could. In one big gulp." A chubby hand popped up to grasp my nose and Kaine's giggle slid through the last of my defenses. There was a goofy grin on my face as I planted kisses all over his rosy cheeks. Complete with smooching sounds. His laugh tickled over me and took me under.

It was the sight of the baby's mother doubled over and hooting that brought me back to my senses enough to realize something wasn't quite right.

Being pointed and laughed at rated nowhere on my list of lifelong dreams. But Serena didn't seem to care. "He got to you too." She took the baby away from me—nearly had to pry him out of my arms.

"I'll just put him down for his nap so we can talk." Serena's tone carried a hint of derision and, oddly, resignation. Minus the baby, Serena returned only moments later.

With Kaine out of my sight, it was as if the world opened up again, but the cuddly puppy feelings he'd let loose refused to completely dissipate. For a moment, I reveled in them, and I could feel Lexi's resolve to remain mired in her misery waver just a little. And then I felt her slam the metaphorical door back shut.

If you're fine with missing out on the good in order to avoid the bad, stop acting like the victim. I snarked at her. *Coward.*

For once, she remained silent, and it bothered me that this was the moment the witch had decided to shy away from. I finally managed to regain my composure, and when I did, I noticed the state of Serena's house—or, more accurately, Serena's mother's house.

"You've been busy." I assumed the change was her doing, anyway. Once a dingy tan, the walls looked ten times brighter in a muted gray that made the room seem warmer and set off the deep burgundy of the sofa and matching chair. "New furniture?"

"What?" Confused, she glanced around the room. "Yeah. Sorry, I wasn't expecting to talk about the decor. Daddy moved into his building downtown, so it's just me and my mom. But that's not the point. You see what I'm going through, right? It's becoming a problem and I don't know what to do about it. You have to help me."

I followed Serena to the kitchen, which had also had a bit of a spruce, and took a seat at the table while she pulled a bottle of fizzy water from the fridge. A year before, it would have taken a herd of wild unicorns or a bulldozer to drag me into my archenemy's house. Now, here we were, calmly sitting together and not spitting insults at each other. It boggled the mind.

As did her plea for help.

"What?" I said, failing to see the problem. "You have an adorable child. I'm not seeing that as a crisis."

She plunked her glass down hard enough for some of the contents to splash out. "Not a crisis?" Her voice went up an octave. "Not a crisis?"

With Kaine out of the room, his effect on me had begun to fade from memory. "Isn't it normal for people to go gaga over a cute baby? At least they're not looking for a polite way to avoid saying he has a face only a mother could love."

Serena burned me with a look.

"I can't take him anywhere without it turning into a mob scene. I was craving those amazing garlic knots from Pastabilities the other night. Easy in, easy out. I mean, the place is a ghost town on Tuesday nights. I even called ahead. But no. We were in there for an hour and a half while every person in the place oohed and aahed over him. I got all the way home before I realized I'd never even made it to the counter, and I really wanted those garlic knots."

Still, there were worse problems to have, and I ran a finger through the condensation drops forming on the outside of my glass while I tried to find a way to frame a statement that wouldn't send us back to our former relationship.

"Is it a Fate Weaver thing?" she asked before anything came to me.

My mouth popped open to answer with an automatic no. Surely, if there'd been a similar disturbance, the faeries would have turned the story into one of the family legends. But then again, if they thought all babies rated an entourage, there would have been no reason to point out how my childhood had been different. "I'll have to check with the godmothers and get back to you on that, but I don't think so."

Plus, I didn't want to check with the faeries. Not after I'd finally managed to create some much-needed boundaries.

"Lexi," her voice dropped to a hush, and I didn't correct her on the name, "I think he's going to be a lot like you—spreading love, softening hearts, and I think he's more powerful than he should be. Do you think it's because of what happened when he was born?"

Why was she whispering? We were alone in the house

except for the baby, and what was wrong with him being like me, anyway? Spreading love and softening hearts didn't seem like bad things to do. Then again, the first rule of witchiness is that intentions matter. Kaine was too young to direct his, and if Serena was right about his level of power, I could see why it might be a problem.

But I didn't have an answer for her. "My Gran and Aunt Mag said there might be repercussions from mixing our blood talismans, so it's possible. I got the impression they weren't sure what would happen, but it had been the only way to ensure a safe birth. Look, he's a darling child and you're a strong witch. You're not alone; we'll handle whatever happens." Kaine rated my best efforts no matter which half of me was running the body.

My assurances smoothed some of the worry lines around her mouth, but not all of them.

On my way back to the car, a case of the creeps stole over my body, starting with a tingling ripple of hair rising on the back of my neck. Someone was watching me. Or Serena's house. But probably me.

One thing that came along with the Bow of Destiny was the enhanced vision that allowed me to zero in on targets from a distance. Until now, there'd been no occasion to use the sight unless I was framing a shot, but that didn't mean I couldn't, and so I tried.

There's nothing dignified about marching along with one eye squeezed shut. What's more, when it kicked in, the sight in my right eye zoomed in and out fast enough to bring on a bout of nausea. If there was an enemy lurking, tossing my lunch at their feet probably wasn't the scariest thing I could do.

Instead, I reached under my coat to scratch at my shoulder blade, focused on staying casual, and hoped I looked less wobbly than I felt.

Stirred by the light wind, bare branches clacked together like the finger bones of the long dead, the noise chilling in the waning light of winter day. Daylight saving time. What a lousy idea for full dark to set in before most people ended their working day.

Snow banked on either side amplified the crunching of my booted feet over the sidewalk, but not enough that I missed the muffled sound to my right. Maybe the low growl of a dog, or the nicker of a horse. My feet froze and the dream came back to me in all its adrenaline-infused glory.

Do you feel that?

Lexi, alert again, funneled magic through me—or us, depending on how you looked at it—and my power, while not strictly magical, fed the flame she called into our palm. The itch on my shoulder blade increased maddeningly and I felt like the cork on a champagne bottle with the bubbling pressure building, and I was about to pop.

Reflex was the only thing that saved the harried mother and son from being scorched as they rushed out their front door and hurried toward the sedan parked behind my car.

"Do you have your skates?"

"Mo-om, I'm going to hockey practice. I'd be pretty dumb to show up without them."

The car doors thunked shut and hockey mom, sliding a little on the icy slickness, took off as the sense of danger dissipated. When her taillights rounded the corner, I was, once again, alone in the street.

CHAPTER
SIX

I don't know why Cupid chose to imbue the bow of destiny with the ability to play music. Maybe, in the days before everyone carried a cell phone equipped with streaming radio in their pockets, he just wanted something to listen to while he prowled around lofting arrows toward the hearts of lonely humans. Maybe he used the weapon's tunes to help clue himself in to the emotions of each target, though why he would need to do so is a mystery, since the little blinking symbols above their heads indicates a heart open to new love. Or maybe, he figured the cacophony would drive mad any other poor soul who attempted to steal and wield the weapon.

I'm betting on some combination of the latter two, because if I had to listen to the lilting notes of another sappy love song, I might hurl myself off the tallest building in Port Harbor. It's more than half the reason why I waste little time drawing the bow and loosing an arrow whenever a twinkling heart catches my eye.

No hesitation, no remorse, and no hanging around in the visions of sugar plums and happily ever afters that flood my consciousness whenever two hearts become inextricably linked.

That's because you're a cold-hearted—

Shut up. I cut Lexi off before she could finish the observation. I'm not saying it wasn't partially true, but no one likes being called names. Especially not by someone who whines.

I can hear what you're thinking, you know, and I was not whining, I was merely pointing out that you're an idiot for not appreciating the uplifting parts of the job.

Suddenly I wasn't cursing the bowsong anymore. Anything would be better than this.

As if you have any room to talk. I was referring to her mocking retreat from the effects of Kaine's magic, and received only a grunt in response before Lexi fell quiet again.

On the weekends, when all the bars are open and the downtown district is filled with hopeful singles, my job is a lot easier. Weeknights are when said hopefuls go on dates with the people they met over the weekend, and that means they're tucked away inside dimly-lit restaurants where I can't blend into the crowd as easily.

Half my job involves being a glorified stalker.

Fortunately, the thrill of the hunt is part of the fun. Knowing it would lead me where I needed to go, I followed the pull in my belly and hit the jackpot outside a small tavern with a folding sign out front that advertised the night's event: speed dating.

Some trends simply refuse to die.

Two blinking hearts flashed in my peripheral vision as I entered and casually sauntered toward the restroom.

When a timer buzzed loudly, the men stood and moved in a clockwise pattern, sitting back down across from the next eager woman. If my calculations were correct, the blond man with the thick eyelashes had already spoken to his intended, a shy-looking woman dressed in basic black. I didn't stop to wonder whether their conversation had gone well enough for them to choose one another at the end of the session, and pulled out my bow to ensure their connection would stick.

See, that's what I'm talking about. There's more to this gig than point and shoot.

The arrows squarely hit their marks while I ignored my inner Lexi voice, and then I got the heck out of there with a smile on my face. One match down, and I was just warming up for the night.

Exiting the tavern, I circled around the corner and into an older section of Port Harbor. Blocks of attached town-houses marched down the edges of the road, like soldiers in a line, gabled hats perched atop their heads. Between every third of fourth unit, wrought iron gates in various states of repair restricted access to an expanse of fenced-in lawn that stretched across the block to meet up with an identical backyard on the opposite side.

My LPS—or Love Positioning System, a fluttery feeling in my gut—instructed me to veer north toward another lonely heart. I took a quick glance around before touching a finger to one of the gate locks and easing quickly through the opening. Keeping to the shadows, I made it halfway across the lawn before I felt a whoosh and a tingle that made the hairs on my neck feel like they were marching in circles.

From somewhere nearby, the stench of dark magic and Chanel No. 5 made me want to gag. I broke into a full-on run and exited the other side of the courtyard a few yards behind the man whose heart had called me to this place.

I scanned the area for a matching symbol. Shooting the guy by himself could have serious repercussions. Or I assumed they did because the only times I'd ever tried it, the bow blasted me with *You Give Love a Bad Name,* and I had to give the bow credit for nailing the song. Still, the message was clear. Don't shoot. Just don't.

The man continued walking toward the spot where, at the far edge of my vision, I saw a glimmer of a matching symbol. I whipped out the bow in an attempt to gain the upper hand, knowing Diana Diamond was bearing down on me and that I had mere seconds to spare our unsuspecting quarry from the sting of one of her cards.

Engaging my targeting sight, I double-checked the symbols, calculated the odds, and decided the shooting order. Man first, long shot after.

"You're out of your league, Balefire." As opening lines went, that one was uninspired. I let my arrows fly and swallowed the giggle that had been bubbling into my throat when I realized Diana's weapon had made contact a split second ahead of mine. The split second I'd taken to decide cost me. Or rather, the man.

The target stopped walking, and I held my breath as

the symbol above his head changed from a pink heart to a red diamond that shuddered and morphed into the black heart that marked him as one of Diana's conquests.

Enraged, I sheathed the bow as I whipped around and came face-to-face with her. Lexi lit up my thoughts with a stream of words unbecoming of a good witch and I fought the urge to lunge at Diana and scratch her eyes out with my bare hands.

"See, I warned you." I wanted to scrape the smug smile off her face with something sharp and pointy, but the damage had already been done, and getting into a hair-pulling fight with a psycho half-goddess didn't seem like the best plan.

My stomach knotted and turned over on itself when Diana approached the section of sidewalk where the man had been standing, picked up the card she'd used on him, and slurped up the blackness left behind by his poor, darkened soul. There was nothing I could do for him now, at least not until I figured out how to reverse her magic. Suddenly I felt no closer to that goal than I had been months before. I needed to find a way to either fully defeat her or banish her back to the Nexus, and even if the act tarnished my own soul, it would be well worth the price.

"You're fighting a losing battle, Diana." I retorted, as calmly as I possibly could. "Don't you understand that the gods don't want you counted among their numbers? You're not welcome in Olympus, so why don't you just give up now and find someone else to harass?"

She shot me a look of contempt. "What would be the

fun in that? You're not fooling anyone with this tough girl act. I know deep down you're still feeling the loss of your precious lover boy." Diana licked her lips slowly, sensuously, "I can taste your pain, and it's the most potent, purest kind. The kind that knows all hope is lost."

Her words stung with truth, and I felt Lexi recoil, heard the hiss of her reaction, and this time anticipated the swell of witchfire in our palm.

"Don't you dare say his name!" Lexi swam to the surface and it was her words that echoed into the night. Together, we hurled the ball of witchfire in Diana's direction, unsurprised when she lithely sidestepped the flame as though we were playing a friendly game of dodgeball.

"Kin Clark is still mine. There's no hope for you, Balefire." Diana's words and her evil laugh trilled through the air even after she'd disappeared back to whatever hole she'd climbed out of in the first place.

Lexi's emotion threatened to pull me into its undertow, so I slammed shut the barrier between us, heard it whoosh into place complete with sci-fi sound effect, and used the silence left behind to gather myself together while Lexi fumed and sputtered. Feelings don't win battles, strategy does. Emotions only get in the way. Since I was the one with the mad logic skills, maybe I should be the one in charge of things. The only one.

Fat chance. Wretched witch put the taste of pickles in my mouth. Sour pickles. It was a sign.

My spirits lower than low, I trudged back toward the city proper, all the way imagining what tearing Diana limb-from-limb would look like. Two blocks from where I'd parked, I felt a tingle of magic and braced myself for another encounter with my nemesis. But when I looked around, it wasn't Diana Diamond leaning up against a frost-covered lamppost—it was Delta the Fiach, and she had her right eyebrow raised as she appraised my outfit.

"I came here to talk to Lexi Balefire, but it looks like I found Catwoman instead." Delta let out a husky chuckle.

"It's cold, and the leather keeps me warm." I staunchly defended my fashion choice. What did a super-natural bounty hunter from Olympus know about current styles, anyway? Delta's six-foot rapier peeked out from behind the fur-lined cloak fastened around her neck. "And darling, who are you to talk? You look like an escapee from Narnia."

Delta grimaced in surprise, looked at her own outfit, looked back at me, and nodded with resignation. "Fair point." We traded smiles that turned into a fit of laughter. I'd forgotten how much fun it could be to trade insults with a good friend, especially since everyone else in my life was either annoyed by my strength or unwilling to accept I wasn't as fragile as their precious Lexi.

"I go by Alexis now, by the way." I explained once we'd sobered up a bit. Delta nodded once and didn't reply, but I squirmed under the heat of her searching gaze. A woman of few words, she saw more than she let on, but allowed the awkward moment to pass.

"So, *Alexis*, you want to tell me what's going on?" she asked. "The stench of dark magic drew me here, though right now, all I'm getting is the distinct scent of recently-flung arrows. What kind of trouble are you in this time?"

She pushed off the lamppost to circle me like a sleek jungle cat stalking prey. We'd been in this position before, and I didn't like it any better now than I did the first time. I don't know if Cupid meant for his bow to be used as a weapon against enemies, and Delta certainly qualified as friend, but I pulled it without thinking.

"Put that away. I'm not here to fight." From behind me, Delta's voice sounded amused. "And then tell me why you smell like brimstone."

"Forgot to put on my deodorant before I left the house."

Deadpanning, Delta replied. "Ha ha."

"I just had a run in with Diana Diamond."

"No, it's not her. She carries a different scent. A cross between dirty motor oil and rotten cheese." Instead, she leaned sideways and sniffed at me again.

Even though it seemed the mark on my shoulder had summoned Delta, I paused for a moment to decide how much to tell her, and then realized it was a moot point since whatever I held back she'd wrangle out of me some-how. "You're right. Come on, I'll show you." I led Delta down a darkened alley, shrugged out of my coat, and moved to strip off my top.

"Honey, if you're that hard up, go back to one of those clubs and find a man who will do for an evening." She planted her tongue firmly in her cheek.

"Get your head out of the gutter, and don't act like you

can't sense the magic rolling off my back. Literally." I replied impatiently.

Delta did as she was told while I told her about the dream. She let out a whistle when she saw the symbol marring my shoulder. "How much trouble are you in?"

"If I knew, you probably wouldn't be here. Do you recognize it?" She touched a finger to the mark, and I felt a sharp pinprick, then the usual itch and burn.

"No, not exactly. The symbolism isn't from this time, that I can tell you. Old. Ancient even. A mixture of some kind." Delta muttered as she poked and prodded. "There aren't many beings powerful enough to penetrate the veil and make contact through a dream."

"Well, it definitely wasn't Freddie Kruger, so what are the other options?"

She sighed, "Look, don't freak out, okay? Just stand still." I heard the whisper of her sword being pulled, and when she laid the cold steel against my already chilled flesh, I flinched.

"I said stay still." A hand came up to clamp on my other shoulder like a vise.

Between gritted teeth, I said, "Just get it over with if you're going to cut me."

The sting hurt less than a paper cut.

Maybe you should ask her for a lollipop, said the sarcastic witch.

"Put your shirt back on before you freeze to death." I'd have preferred sarcasm from Delta rather than gruff resignation. "I don't like this."

She hesitated and I prodded, "What?"

"It's essential blood magic." Emphasis on essential.

Blood magic is almost always dark magic, and that the mark carried darkness was not new information. "Okay, what do you mean by essential?"

"Whatever you saw in your dream marked the essential components that make up your blood."

Still not clear. "You mean like the red and white blood cells and platelets?"

Delta huffed out a breath. "No, those are the elements, I'm talking about the essentials, the essences that make up your heritage. Witch and god. Whoever, or whatever did this, they marked you for being a Fate Weaver."

"Then that's one more reason I need to talk to one of my kind, and you're just the person to locate one for me." I launched into yet another explanation, this one regarding Kaine, and noticed that Delta's eyes didn't quite meet mine. "What?" I asked with a raised eyebrow.

"It won't be as easy as you think."

"For crying out loud, Delta. It's your job to find people. Weren't you the one who told me there were more of us out there? Was that a lie?"

"Let's call it speculation based on a small amount of information."

"I'm calling it bull, thank you very much." I shot back.

Delta sighed again and pulled her cloak tighter around her body. "Look, I've heard rumors here and there of Fate Weavers who went into hiding. It's not like I sit around all day keeping tabs. Take it up with the gods if you're ticked off. What I *can* do is promise to tap my sources and see if I can run down a solid lead, and you know my word is my bond."

She stuck out her hand, and I shook it. She might have glossed over a detail or two, but Delta had never told me a flat-out lie, and I knew she wouldn't let me down.

CHAPTER

SEVEN

Sylvana

I'll admit to shameless eavesdropping. Hell, it's not even close to the worst thing I've ever done. And it's not as though I was around during Lexi's teen years when invading her privacy would have been acceptable and expected. Making up for lost time, that's what I decided to call it.

The first time I spoke to my adult daughter, she was clad in a flowered sundress, looking at the business end of Delta's rapier, and the look on her innocent face was pure fear. Now, she looked like a comic-book hero. Oh, how times had changed, and once again I'd been absent during a transformative period in Lexi's life.

My heart almost stopped when I heard her ask Delta to try to locate another Fate Weaver, then hope kick-started it again, and set it racing as the implications sank in. When the search effort failed, as I suspected it would, Lexi would be left with no other option, and that's when I'd swoop in.

The conversation ended with the Fiach shooting straight into the sky like a rocket. While I stood hidden in the recess of a cobbled stone building covered in what I thought was an impenetrable cloaking spell, trying to decide how to proceed, my daughter took a few steps in my direction and popped her hands on her hips.

"You're aware I can see you, right?" She asked, her voice hard and cold and entirely impassive. My shoulders dropped with my sigh, and I flicked the spell away while vowing to ream the elf I'd purchased it from next time I was in the Fringe.

"I wasn't, no, but I'm not surprised. Your skills have improved since the last time I saw you. I'm impressed."

Lexi's mouth set into a thin line. "Yes, well, it seems I've had cause to hone them, thanks to you."

Maybe my goal wasn't as close as I thought it was. My daughter was still angry, and there's nothing scarier than a ticked off Balefire witch.

"I'm sorry—" I began, but Lexi cut me off.

"I don't care what you are, though sorry does seem a fitting description. What reaction did you think you'd get? I believe I told you to stay away, and I'm betting you're back because you need something. No wait, I forgot who I was talking to. You want something."

"To see my daughter safe," I said, taking hold of the irritation rising in me at her animosity. "And if what I overheard you talking to Delta about is any indication of your status, clearly, you are not. What's going on? Maybe I can help."

The look she gave me would have flash-frozen the balefire.

"If you think I'm stupid enough to believe you care

about me, you haven't been paying attention. I can handle myself just fine." Lexi spat. "And my conversation with Delta is none of your business."

I swallowed a fair amount of frustration and repeated myself, hoping Lexi would hear the sincerity in my voice, "I want to see you safe." And then I made the mistake of telling a half-truth. "And I have no ulterior motive." I really should have left that last part off, and immediately cursed my big mouth to hades and back.

I shivered under Lexi's unbelieving stare, and even though she was right, backing down wasn't my style. "Fine. You know there's another reason. Look, you need a Fate Weaver, and I need to find your father. Two birds, one stone. I watch your back, you watch mine. We both win, and everyone's happy."

My daughter lifted one eyebrow and despite the difference in hair color, it was like looking into a mirror. She didn't say anything for a long moment, and I could see the internal struggle playing out behind her eyes. "Well, at least you're consistent even if your motives are decidedly one-sided. It's not Cupid I need specifically, any Fate Weaver will do. And to be quite honest, I've had enough family reunions to last me a lifetime. Besides, the last time I tried to help you, you betrayed me and left me to my own devices. It's high time I returned the favor."

Great, I thought to myself, *of course my daughter would have inherited my ability to hold a grudge for all eternity.* It wasn't as though I could blame her, but the Lexi I knew was softer and far more pliable than the creature now standing before me.

"We could be a family again. Cupid would want that. He loves us." I insisted.

Lexi smirked. "Is that what you think? Because I saw what happened the day he left and you got banished to the Nexus. Your mother might have shot him with one of his own arrows, but he chose to walk away. Maybe he didn't love us as much as you think he did. In fact, I'm quite certain he didn't."

She certainly didn't pull any punches, and the pain of her words hit me like a sledgehammer. "You don't understand," I protested.

"I understand what I saw, and that you have no loyalty to anyone but yourself, which makes you untrustworthy as an ally. That's all I need to know."

Some people take hard truths and turn them into signposts for change. Others just get pissed off when their foibles are dragged into the light of day. Guess which category I fell into?

"You got the bow didn't you? That's what you wanted." It came out a little more harshly than I'd intended, as did what came next. "And Kin survived, didn't he? No harm, no foul."

Pain flashed across Lexi's face before it turned to stone. "You've been following me all over town. Don't deny it. I've felt you spying on me. Tell me, Mother, how many times in the past week have you seen me with Kin?"

Actually, come to think of it, the answer was none. I'd

just assumed that since Lexi was holding her own against Diana, the spell had been broken. If that wasn't the case, it explained the change in Lexi since the last time I'd been in town.

She'd begun to pace, another family trait we Balefire women employ when trying to work out a particularly frustrating problem—and sometimes when we're just plain furious. I took a step back since it was clearly the latter situation.

"No," I admitted, "I haven't. But I thought—"

"Well, you thought wrong," Lexi snapped. "Your little message from the Faelands didn't help me any, and in case you haven't noticed, Diana the Snake is still slithering around trying to unmake my matches."

"You seemed to have her under control." It was all the response I could manage.

My daughter's eyes narrowed to slits, and once again I noticed how forbidding she could look. "You've been following me?" she asked, her words razor sharp.

Damn, I really should learn to be more careful with my words. "Yes, I have. I told you, I wanted to make sure you were okay, and just for the record, I was impressed with the way you handled yourself."

Lexi ignored my compliment entirely. "I've managed to keep Diana at bay, yes. She has her cards, I have my arrows. Tit for tat has become the status quo, and I can hold out as long as she can."

"Then what happened with Kin?" I dared to ask.

Lexi's face drained of color, and again a more fragile

version of herself showed through her hardened exterior. "I have no intention of sharing my pain with you. Or anything else, for that matter. Goodbye, Mother." With that, my daughter spun on her heel and stalked away.

L EXI

My legs were shaking as the distance between my mother and me widened, and the goddess chose that particular moment to step back long enough to leave me to face the pain of the encounter alone. Just like her to bail when things got too emotional. The one occasion where her strength would be an asset to me rather than a crushing force that rendered me silent but mercifully numb, and she was nowhere to be found.

Though, to be fair, lately the numbness had started to wear off, and I wasn't sure if that was Alexis's doing or through some fault of my own. Seeing Kin, hearing Mona describe him as lonely—it was a kick in the solar plexus. Or in the butt. No, it was both.

Add in the boost of pure love coming from Kaine—those experiences had roused me from my near catatonic state, and I had a feeling it wasn't going to be so simple to crawl back inside this time.

And now my mother had arrived, once again at a most inopportune moment of my life. Part of me identified with her single-minded need to set her disaster of a love life to rights. Part of me even understood what she was going through. I'd been without Kin for such a short time in comparison to the twenty-five years she'd been separated from her lover, and I wondered if that would be enough time for me to get over my devastation.

But an even bigger part of me was happy she was hurting. At least I wasn't alone in my pain.

She's obviously desperate if she's willing to ask for help after everything she's done. You have to at least admire her for having a cast-iron resolve, Alexis unhelpfully pointed out.

I thought the peanut gallery was closed, I fired back, letting irritation and impatience replace the heartache I'd been wallowing in. I felt the control over my mind and body expand a little before Alexis snapped it back into place like a brand-new rubber band.

Don't underestimate me, she purred. *If you were strong enough to handle things, you wouldn't have needed to call me forth. It's* you *who needs* me, *not the other way around.* Her words came out sickly sweet, but with an edge that left no question I was dealing with a lioness, not a kitty cat.

A LEXIS
When I walked through my front door a short while later, I had prepared myself for a full-on assault from Terra for forgetting to call and let her know I was going to be late. But, to my surprise, the house was quiet. I heard a shuffle of feet and a few whispered words coming from the kitchen, and when I chanced a peek, Terra, Evian, and Soleil were huddled near the

sliding patio door. My entrance elicited three equally guilty half-smiles.

Beyond them, through the frosted glass, I could see Vaeta standing in the middle of the backyard, her arms waving fast enough to create a snowy funnel of air. Across from her stood a disheveled Rhys, his goatee coated in a thick layer of ice, and a concerned expression on his handsome face.

That explained the guilt—the faeries had been caught spying, which, even though I'd seen them do far worse, contrasted with their recent holier-than-though attitudes. I merely raised an eyebrow and marched upstairs, grateful for the reprieve.

Normally, letting a demon into my house wasn't something I'd allow, but Rhys had proved himself trustworthy enough to make an exception. He cared about Vaeta, and since I was the last person who ought to be engaging in species prejudice, I'd decided to stay out of it. Whatever lover's quarrel he and Vaeta were having was their own business, but that didn't stop me from taking a look out the dormer window on my way down the hall to my bedroom.

What I saw reminded me again of exactly why I was glad I didn't have to worry about relationship issues. Ever again.

EIGHT

My forkful of impeccably grilled salmon hovered uneaten while I watched Mona Katz and her new husband being seated not three tables away. I thanked my lucky stars her back was to me and she hadn't noticed me sitting alone in the corner. She was the only person who hadn't taken my resting witch face to heart. It was like she looked at me and saw Lexi, not Alexis, no matter what I did.

If I kept my head down, I could probably finish my lunch undisturbed.

Except, now I was trapped here until they left because there was no other way to leave but to walk right past them. Well, that was fine. I didn't have an appointment for the afternoon, and I could catch up on my email right here.

The fork and contents landed back on the plate with a clatter when my ex walked in and took the seat across from Mark.

Great. Now I could sit here and pretend the sight of Kin hadn't set off the witch who lived in my skin. And that she wasn't currently repeating his name in my head.

Shut up, I warned her, but she didn't listen and I had

to work to muffle the sounds of her pain—a distraction I didn't need while avoiding attracting Mona's attention.

I should have been watching Mark.

"Hey, isn't that Lexi over there?"

At about the same time Mona swiveled, it occurred to me that I could have used a glamour to hide my face instead of burying it in my notepad computer. I was a day late and a dollar short on that one.

Mona could have held a grudge against me for my somewhat rude behavior at my office the previous day, but she greeted me with the same level of warmth she always had. I almost felt a little bad for shutting such a good person out of my life, but Mona's ties to the LexiKin history made her a powerful reminder of things best left in the past.

She launched into a flurry of motion that nothing could stop and ended with me ensconced next to Kin at their table. A situation that went from bad to worse in about a nanosecond.

"Kin, you remember Lexi."

"Nice to see you again." I also ignored his outstretched hand. Touching him might send my inner witch into a frenzy and I wasn't sure if I could control her if that happened. This was the moment she needed me most, and I would stand strong. I could do this.

I could carry on a conversation with three people who had an altered perception of our shared history because I was a being of logic, not emotion. Mackintosh Clark meant nothing to me.

What a load of utter—

Hush up in there.

At least she wasn't sniveling anymore.

My appetite flown, I nudged bits of salmon around my plate while trying to keep my eyes away from Kin and concentrate on listening to Mona and Mark—mostly Mona—describe their elopement and subsequent honeymoon.

"It wasn't technically an elopement since our families were all there, more like a small wedding that happened too suddenly to invite everyone." Her tone carried an apology, but a look passed between the newlyweds that made me think another announcement might be forthcoming.

Their order arrived by way of a pretty server who paid extra attention to placing Kin's plate just so. I heard Lexi growl in my head, but he barely gave the woman a second glance.

After taking a bite of pasta that made her hum in appreciation, Mona picked up the story again. "Mark's grandfather couldn't travel, so we all packed up and went to Wisconsin. It was a small, outdoor ceremony. We were married in the gazebo at night with a thousand fairy lights shining on the snow. Magical."

"It sounds lovely," I said. And it did. I wasn't a total robot, you know. I knew how to make small talk, too. "You didn't get those tans in Wisconsin. Must have been some honeymoon."

Mona blushed and Mark explained. "Our families

pitched in and sent us to Cancun for two weeks. The kayaking was incredible." Mona blushed again.

"Did you get to see Chichen Itza?" Kin and Mark launched into a detailed discussion of the Mayan ruins that made me wish I was free to travel for more than two or three days at a time. Only half of my job involves matching soul mates, and I could do that anywhere. The other half keeps me tied to hearth and home. Or hearth, anyway.

As Keeper of the Balefire—the magical flame from which I take my name and my power—my presence was crucial to the process. Witch feeds the flame and flame feeds the witch—it was the Balefire way. A circular issue, I know, but one that meant I could not leave for long periods of time without jeopardizing the health of the fire. I'd nearly let it go out when my magic came in late, and the fallout risked magic for all of witchkind.

Lost in contemplation, I missed the beginning of Mark's next story. "—entourage wherever we went. It was like traveling with the Pied Piper."

"Oh stop." Mona flashed Mark the side-eye. "Well, we did get the VIP tour of the ruins, and I spent a day learning from the most incredibly talented artist. I will never forget the sweet abuelita who taught me how to make exquisite sugar skull designs. Her philosophy about color and style changed my life. I mean that literally."

"No, I mean it in the best way." He reached over and gave her hand a squeeze. "You make friends without even trying. It's one of the things I love most about you."

The praise made her blush and spurred a comment from Kin. "You're one of the lucky ones, man. True love doesn't come around that often, so hold on to her, and never let her go."

Leaning over to interrupt my thoughts, Mona whispered in my ear, "See what I mean? You have to do your thing and help him. He's such a nice man, but look how sad he is. He deserves to be happy."

Of course, that made me look, and once I did, I could see the lines around his mouth and the tension across his shoulders, but mostly it was the hint of flatness in his eyes that gave Kin away. He wasn't happy, not like I'd seen him, anyway.

He misses me. Even if he doesn't know why, he's lost without me.

I didn't disagree with the voice in my head, but the flare of hope tightened my jaw until my teeth clacked together.

Mona lowered her voice even further, "Maybe you *both* could find happiness. Two birds, one stone. He seems like your type."

How did she know I had a type?

"I can try." I heard the words come out of my mouth and still didn't believe I'd said them. Because I hadn't. It was Lexi sneaking past my blocks and taking control when I wasn't paying attention.

If you think for one moment I believe that you have no ulterior motive, such as, I don't know, trying to get him back for yourself, think again. You're not fooling me.

It's not about that, and it never will be. The witch lied.

Mona squeaked and bounced in her chair. To cover, she looked at Mark and said, "Honey, we have to go. I'm sorry, I forgot an appointment."

The poor man let himself be dragged away from his half-eaten meal while Mona pressed a hand to Kin's shoulder. "You stay and talk to Lexi. No reason to ruin everyone's lunch." And just like that, Kin and I were alone together for the first time since the moment in the hospital when true love went down in a blaze of Diana's dark intent.

Another surge of hope pulled me, Lexi, out of the depths, and nearly up to the surface where Alexis still held sway. She tried to shove me back down, which started an internal struggle for control, and I think I surprised her with my determination. Enough so that I stayed closer to the surface than I had in a long while.

Not for the first time, I regretted letting the goddess out to play. Maybe we were supposed to be one and the same person, but *supposed to be* meant nothing to me now. I'd needed time to lick my wounds, but the world—or at least the greater Port Harbor section of it—needed a Fate Weaver. And so, I'd summoned my inner goddess, and now was paying the price. At least, that's how it seemed to me at the time.

Kin smiled, and memories of him instantly crowded

my head. Us meeting, him singing, the kiss that should have sealed our fates, him teetering on the edge of a deathly drop into a chasm. The good, the bad, the sublime. We'd been through so much in such a short time, and I still wasn't certain I was the best choice for him. He'd been in danger more often than not during our months together. Diana Diamond's spell was probably the best thing that ever happened to him.

Alexis was wrong about me wanting to pursue Kin now. It wouldn't change the past, and I wasn't in the market for more pain. Still, I loved him and because I did, I pushed hard against her for control.

Head tilted to one side, Kin studied my face for a moment, and even knowing I should look away, I studied his in turn. Was there a flicker of recognition to pin my hopes on?

"I didn't have a chance to say this yesterday, but you look familiar. Have I seen you around? I play at Driven on Wednesdays and most weekends. Maybe you've caught a show?"

Was he flirting with me? To be honest, it had always bothered me that our relationship had gone from zero to sixty in about two weeks flat. Don't get me wrong—we'd been all kinds of happy and in love, but we had also missed out on those moments of breathlessness that mark the beginning of a courtship.

Driven was on the short list of places to avoid, and while I contemplated, Alexis took over and confirmed that our paths had not crossed. Technically a lie, but one with an edge of truth.

He grinned again and my heart fluttered. Or at least the part of it that Lexi currently controlled, which wasn't much, but enough to warm up the cold tones I tried to use on him.

"So did you just get railroaded by Mona, or are you actually interested in having me find your match?"

Absently, I nipped the garlic pickle off his plate and popped it in my mouth. Then I noted his raised eyebrow. It was one of our things and I'd fallen into an old habit without thinking. Almost every seafood restaurant in town used the pickles for garnish and Kin hated the taste of them.

My face flamed red—not something that happened to me often—as I shoveled a forkful of cold salmon into my mouth and tried to cover the faux pas. "Sorry. I don't know what I was thinking. Here, you can have mine."

His husky laugh sent shivers down my body and he gave a manly shudder, if there is such a thing. "It's okay. I'd rather eat dirt. It's just that I had this compulsion to offer it to you, and I'm not sure why. Then you took it. You know, I'm beginning to think Mona was right about you."

My hands shook a little—partly, I assumed, from trying to keep my disparate bits together, but also from his effect on both parts of me—so I clasped them together in my lap. Anything to help me get through the next few minutes.

"Oh, and what exactly did Mona say?" I couldn't begin to hazard a guess.

"Just that you have a knack for quickly getting to know people, understanding their needs, and giving them what they want. Basically, a glowing recommendation." Kin replied with a grin.

"Yes, well," I said, "Mona has a tendency to get excited, and a propensity for exaggeration."

"Her instincts seem on target to me. It's uncanny how comfortable I feel around you. It's like we knew each other in a past life." Kin winked. "Or maybe it was just fate that brought us here. But what about you, Lexi Balefire? Do you believe in fate?" The husky way he said my name, and his eyes searching mine brought a twinge of familiarity and regret to both pieces of psyche. I shook my head, but didn't speak because Lexi slammed my throat closed too tight to let words pass.

"Are you so busy helping other people you can't take time to find love yourself? Your eyes are sad. I don't like seeing them that way."

Under his gaze, Alexis faded into the background. How could he still see me so clearly?

I tried to deflect and repeated my earlier question.

"Tell me a little bit about yourself and what you're looking for in a relationship." *Quickly, before I can't hold it together anymore,* I added silently.

Glutton for punishment. I guessed she wasn't totally gone.

Maybe I was, but I had to know. Back and forth, my desire to help Kin and my need to quickly exit the situation swung like a pendulum.

He leaned forward, rested his elbows on the table, and tilted his head toward me. "You won't find her. I know you mean well, and so does Mona, but it's a fool's errand because the woman of my dreams only lives in fairy tales."

The admission left me temporarily speechless. Did he remember something about me? Or had he harbored princess fantasies all along? Distracted by wondering, I barely noticed when Alexis took over and I became a spectator in my own life again.

"Snow White or Sleeping Beauty?" If that was his type, then I thought Lexi was well shot of him. Despite my low opinion of the way she handled heartbreak, neither one of us was the *princess in need of rescue* type.

The man was adorable when he blushed.

"Don't laugh, but neither."

"Cinderella? That's even worse."

Kin's brow furrowed. "How is it worse?"

"Snow White and Sleeping Beauty at least had real

enemies—evil queens. Cinderella was a wimp who refused to stand up for herself and had to be rescued." I shuddered a little and then added, to my way of thinking, the cherry on top of the weenie sundae. "By fashion."

He held back a snort, but a smile played around his lips. The server chose that moment to pop up and ask if we needed anything. I shook my head and asked for the bill.

Leaning back to let her clear the empty plates, Kin insisted, "Put hers on mine, please. I'm feeling like a prince today."

This time, I wasn't the one who put up a wall between us. Lexi slammed a door in my head so hard my eyes jittered. For form, I took up the argument for paying my own way, but Kin gave his most charming smile to the waitress and, tossing me an envious glance, she scurried off to do his bidding.

When we were alone again, he turned serious. "I'm not interested in a Cinderella, either. You misunderstand. It's not the princesses who intrigue me. It's the wicked witch I can't get out of my head."

I didn't know what to do with that, so I shut my mouth.

"Come to Driven and listen to me play. We'll tell Mona you're working your magic on my love life and no one has to know that I'm a hopeless case with a fantasy fetish. Tomorrow night, I go on at eight."

"I'll have to check my schedule, but I think I'm

booked." I rose to leave. "I'll...uh, look through my files and be in touch."

"Don't you want my number?" He called after me.

Back to him, I shot a wave over my shoulder and lied, "I'll get it from Mona."

Collar up to protect me from the frigid wind that blasted in from the harbor side of the city, I let my feet carry me on autopilot the two blocks back to my office while I argued with myself the entire way. By the time I stepped into the vestibule, Lexi was no longer speaking to me, and while that suited me just fine, she'd decided to take out her frustrations by giving us heartburn.

You're a child and a jerk.

When silence met the taunt, I called myself an idiot for talking to myself, and shrugged off my winter coat. Winter-dried air, a knit sweater, and the shiny lining material combined in the perfect storm of static annoyance. Pinprick shocks blanketed my back, my hair lifted for a few seconds, then both hair and sweater plastered themselves flat against my body.

Somehow, during the personality split or whatever you want to call it, Lexi and I managed to separate our powers to the degree that I'd have to ask for her help with the static, and I'd rather set my hair on fire than do that. So, I scratched at my shoulder where even the softness of my knit sweater made the dream brand itch, and walked back into my office.

Angela was busy playing telephone deejay, and I barely acknowledged her as I passed through.

"Got any new victims lined up for me?" I was still trying to do something with my hair while simultaneously scratching at my shoulder when I stepped into the inner workings of FootSwept and heard Flix tapping on his keyboard.

"Victim seems like a harsh word." Carl, the man Flix had cut his hair for, leaned against the corner of the desk. "Aren't you supposed to be rescuing people from the big bad stealer of love? You should call them...what's the word for it? Rescuees?"

An ornate mirror with a gilded frame, the one remnant from before the salon remodel, confirmed my hair looked like crap and when I twisted to see the back, there was a spot of blood on my sweater where I'd apparently scratched harder than I thought.

"Thanks for the grammar lesson, Teach, but that's not even a word."

Carl's a nice enough guy, but not one I wanted to flash my boobs at, so with a wince, I stretched the cashmere neckline of my sweater down far enough to bare the mark on my shoulder. From what I could see, it looked normal —as normal as a nightmare brand could look—and there was no trace of blood on my skin.

"Woo-hoo," Flix whistled in a friendly, teasing manner. He must have forgotten we no longer shared an intimate friendship. I looked down and realized I'd miscalculated and most of my bra was hanging out. "Wait a second," Flix's eyes narrowed, "Did you get a tattoo?"

I sighed and turned to face him while setting my outfit back to rights. "Maybe. No. I don't think so."

Carl's eyebrow lifted and Flix looked at me like I'd gone crazy, "You don't know if you got a tattoo? How much of that Twinkleberry wine have you been drinking, anyway?"

"Very funny." I almost kept my lips zipped, but reason won out over stubbornness. Flix was, after all, a faerie, and therefore possessed certain knowledge about super-natural creatures. It was possible he could have the answers I was looking for. "Look at this."

I explained about my nightmare while I showed Flix and Carl the mark. "I feel like I'm stuck in a bad '80s horror movie. It just keeps replaying in my head, and every once in a while this spot itches so bad I want to scratch it off."

The more I talked about it, of course, the more the thing demanded I rake my nails over it. "Whoever these riders are, they've got a death wish, because when I find them I'm going to rip their heads off." Fury-born magic rolled over my skin, and Carl flinched and moved closer to Flix.

He looked so frightened you'd have thought he was the one being chased by a lantern-wielding psychopath instead of me. When he wouldn't look in my eyes, I checked the mirror to see if I looked scary or something, but I just looked like me. Maybe my cheeks were a little pinker than normal, but that was probably due to my blood pressure rising to match my power.

"I know we're—" Flix paused to search for the right way to word his thoughts. "In a different friend space these days, and I'm sorry if this crosses a line, but I'm going to tune back in until the threat has passed." The Fae side of his heritage gave Flix a strong empathic ability which he'd only recently managed to control. I'd suspected part of his process included pulling back from me at roughly the same time I'd needed to pull back from him. His statement confirmed my suspicions.

Between the itching, the uncomfortable direction the conversation had taken, and knowing if I stuck around, I might spill the whole story of my lunch with Kin, it was time to get out of there.

After a quick look at my watch, and a hasty excuse that didn't actually need to set my pants on fire for Flix to see the lie buried within, I bailed.

The next morning I—or rather, the other version of me who enjoyed torturing herself to no end —was blissfully ensconced in a dream involving Kin and very few articles of clothing when a loud banging noise broke through my consciousness. I pushed the purple satin sleep mask onto my forehead and looked around, bleary-eyed, intending to chuck my phone across the room to silence the alarm.

When I realized the sound was coming from downstairs, and that it was actually someone thumping on the door, I sprang out of bed to investigate. I found Salem in the kitchen, his eyes the size of saucers, watching Serena unload enough baby gear to outfit a daycare.

"What are you doing?" I asked, smoothing my rumpled hair. We might be practically related and no longer at one another's throats, but that didn't mean I wanted Serena taking a mental picture of me looking like Swamp Thing.

She glared at me as though I had something to do with her current predicament, and snapped, "I'm going to get my hair done because it looks even worse than yours does, and then I'm going to indulge in a nice mani-pedi.

After that, I'm going shopping for something pretty, and then to Pastabilities where I will have a quiet lunch. Alone. Breadsticks. I am getting breadsticks."

I missed half of what she said due to the bundle of baby cuteness that peeked out at me from underneath the fuzzy hood of a one-piece snowsuit in winter blue. Kaine giggled in what I construed as a conspiratorial manner, and raised one hand as if beckoning me to him. Of course, I complied, and after lifting him out of his stroller, found myself goggling at him while he squeezed my index finger with all his little might.

"Have fun, Auntie," Serena threw over her shoulder as she marched out my front door.

"When will you be back?" I asked, but she'd already slammed it shut behind her. "It doesn't matter, does it, sweet pea?" I cooed, having been completely taken in by the charismatic little beast. I looked around for the faeries, but they were nowhere to be found. Lately, they'd taken to spending more and more time outside the house, and that was just fine with me.

Salem looked like he couldn't decide whether to take his kitty form and risk an inadvertent tail pull or run for the hills, so I gave him an easy out and asked that before he flee he heat up a bottle of the milk Serena had packed into one of Kaine's bags. While he banged around in the kitchen, I took a seat in Gran's old rocking chair next to the flickering Balefire and continued to make ridiculous noises and faces in an attempt to lure a grin from Kaine's cheeks.

Instead, just as I was wondering what was so difficult about this that had Serena's panties in a wad, he scrunched up his formerly adorable face and let out a wail that shook the whole house.

For the next hour, I bounced, jiggled, and sang the only lullaby I could remember, changed a disgustingly dirty diaper, tried unsuccessfully to get Kaine to eat (apparently rubber nipples aren't as appetizing as the real thing)—and vowed to use birth control for the rest of my life. I also took back every bad thing I'd ever said about Serena, even while cursing her for leaving me with her satanic spawn.

Finally, I laid him in the portable playpen that was part of his luggage, and went to get a cup of tea to calm my nerves. I resisted the urge to add a little bourbon to it, and once the kettle had stopped whistling, I realized Kaine had also gone silent. With trepidation, I tiptoed back into the parlor, hoping he'd finally conked out, only to experience a mini heart attack and possibly a stroke at the same time.

In Kaine's hands was a ball of swirling Balefire. I breathed a sigh of relief when I realized he was smiling, and that the same properties that kept the flame from burning my skin were protecting his as well. That was unexpected considering he wasn't an actual Balefire witch. When a miniature fireworks show erupted above his playpen, Kaine let forth a giggle that had me rethinking my recent plans to remain childless.

A burst of love broke through my hard exterior, and it

wasn't just coming from the witch inside me; it was a shared feeling of protectiveness and the knowledge that I —Alexis—would do anything to ensure that Kaine grew up happy and healthy. Honestly, it was a bit much to handle, and made *me* want to run for the hills. Love equals pain; Lexi's experience had shown me enough of that to last a lifetime.

But Kaine wasn't Kin; loving him was as easy as a slow falling rain. Pure, without strings, and fulfilling in an unexpected way, the depth of feeling I had for him gave me a few new insights about the witch and some about myself, too. My capacity for love was as deep as hers; I simply chose not to dive into the deep end.

Since I couldn't just hightail it out of there and never look back, I returned Kaine to his plush cocoon and fastened him into his car seat. It took me twenty minutes to maneuver the contraption into the back of my car, and by the time I'd settled into the driver's side, he was sound asleep despite having been jostled to and fro.

Serena had dropped Kaine off before I'd even had time for a cup of coffee, and I used the need for caffeine as an excuse to leave the house. Really, I couldn't resist the temptation to see for myself how people responded to Kaine, and I figured the coffeehouse was as safe a place as any to sate my curiosity. Turns out, I couldn't have been more wrong.

I was accosted mere seconds after walking through the door, and was thankful for my status as a regular when the barista bustled out from behind the counter to unburden me of the large diaper bag slung across my shoulder. At least, that's what I thought she was doing, until she nearly snatched Kaine out of my arms. My auntie bear instincts kicked in, and for a millisecond, I thought about blasting her across the room.

"Aren't you just the sweetest thing I've ever seen?" She cooed. "You don't mind, do you?" Wide hazel eyes turned on me with such longing I didn't have the heart to tell her *no, you presumptuous cow, give me back my baby.*

By the time I made it through the line, my eyes on Kaine the entire time, a crowd had gathered around him and I had to fight my way back through to retrieve him. Little stinker looked happy as a clam, holding court while his loyal subjects fawned all over him. I sighed with relief as I took him back into my arms.

"He's ready for a nap." I slid into the booth in the corner and faced away from the dissipating throng. *Out of sight, out of mind* didn't quite cut it, and I could still feel hungry eyes following our every move. The implications raced through my head while I sipped my coffee and rubbed soothing circles on Kaine's little back.

This isn't good, Lexi murmured. *We have to do something.*

I ignored her, even though she was right, and tried to figure out why I was feeling the tug in my belly that meant I'd zeroed in on a potential match. The sensation had come up suddenly, without my touching anyone directly prior, and was strong.

When the caffeine finally kicked in, I realized the love

alert wasn't coming from inside me at all. Kaine's concentration was focused on the next table over. His mile-wide grin had captured the attention of a woman seated to our right, and there was magic welling up inside him.

"I'm sorry. My name is Katie, and I just have to touch him." Eyes slightly glazed, the woman turned from the man she'd arrived with to reach over, almost as if she were compelled to do so, and her hand brushed Kaine's fingers.

A shot of electric energy ran through Kaine and into me with a rush that made whooshing sounds in my head. This wasn't my first experience with being drawn into a vision of someone's fate, but it was the first time I wasn't alone. Kaine joined me as the woman's possible futures played out in full, living color.

This wasn't the same as the visions I usually experienced when mating two souls, and it was a good thing Katie was too entranced by Kaine to notice my slack-jawed expression as I let the sensation roll over me.

I could see what Kaine saw, and much more. Just a babe, he couldn't process the practical implications of Katie's future, but I could. He tuned in to her emotions, letting the colors of her aura and the feelings her touch transferred to him guide him in the act of weaving her a fate that would satisfy both her head and her heart. It was so much simpler than Lexi's method of using her own experience to weight the options and hopefully choose the best of them. Except the method of weaving was somehow close enough to my point-and-shoot one that I felt a sense of superiority.

Kaine's intentions were pure; he was a happy baby who wanted to make other people happy too. He didn't take the time to weigh options or consider which future would be best from his own point of view. It came naturally to him, and he acted out of instinct rather than a sense of obligation.

Katie was at a turning point in her life. A talented writer, she'd been offered two positions that would both help her meet her goals. One, right here in Port Harbor, would provide financial stability and lead her directly to her soul mate—who was not the man she'd arrived at the coffeehouse with. If she accepted, there would be no muss and no fuss—and no sense of accomplishment. If she chose the other option, Katie would relocate to the west coast and work her butt off in low-level positions before finding her professional footing. She would experience a long period of misery filled with self-doubt, and ultimately wind up right back in Port Harbor with her intended. Either way, the romantic outcome was the same.

It seemed a simple choice. Why go through heartache and strife to end up in exactly the same place?

When Kaine gently nudged Katie's subconscious toward the more difficult option, I wanted to protest—wanted to wave my arms in the air and shout *No! Take the easy way!* But he had used his innate skills to see through the obvious and focus on what would be the best option *for Katie*. This tiny baby knew, instinctively, that she'd appreciate her happy ending if she'd had to work for it instead of having it handed over on a silver platter.

Moreover, by living that life, she'd gain valuable experience she would eventually use in her work.

My sense of superiority landed back into the pit of my stomach with a sickening plop. And what's worse, I didn't have time to think about any of it before all hell broke loose.

"Paul, I have to go." Katie said to the man sitting beside her. I could feel desire to have her oozing out of his pores, but knew it didn't matter. Desire does not equal love, and certainly not true love. True love is based off more than just hormones and physical attraction, though people often confuse the two. That's why so many of them miss out on their soul mate.

"What do you mean, you have to go?" The poor guy looked bewildered, but I noticed an edge to his voice that smacked of desperation.

Katie began to gather her things, stood and faced Paul, and announced, "I'm taking that job in L.A. Unfortunately, that effectively ends our relationship. I'm sorry, I'll see you around." Despite the seemingly breezy message, her expression was grim when she turned to exit, and he grabbed her arm with more force than I'd expected.

"You're what now? I don't think so, Katie. We agreed. You can't just change your mind now." His raised voice had caught the attention of the other patrons, who were now staring at Paul with expressions ranging from disdain to outright disgust.

"Like hell I can't, Paul. You don't own me. Now let go." From grim to furious, Katie shook her arm free and I'm almost positive I felt a rush of magic flowing from Kaine because she didn't have the strength to slam the guy into the plate glass window so hard it vibrated at the impact. And yet, that's exactly what happened. Paul landed on his rear end, his eyes bulging out of their sockets, and stormed after Katie, slamming the door behind him.

Kaine looked me square in the eyes and let out a giggle that let me know he was quite proud of himself.

TEN

The front door slammed open, and the blast of frigid air it let in didn't just come from the icy weather when Serena's faerie godmother stalked into the house. Cold fury carried her right into the parlor where the Balefire reacted by shooting up green sparks. Kaine's giggle sounded loud in the sudden silence.

"You," she pointed at Evian, who cradled the baby in her arms, "are a stain on the name of faerie godmother. Look at you, cavorting with your charge. It's unnatural and it sets a bad example for others. If you had any dignity, you'd step aside and let someone else take over."

Was that even possible?

Deliberately, Evian handed me the baby and turned to face her accuser. Ocean-blue eyes turned stormy, and I backed away because for one thing, this wasn't my first time around a furious faerie of the elemental variety, and for another, I'm not an idiot.

The same could not be said of Fawn.

Not good. This is not good. Do something. Lexi repeated what I already knew when the air in the room turned heavy and the floor rumbled. What on earth was Fawn thinking to come here and use her industrial-sized opener on a can of faerie worms?

Despite Kaine's obvious effect on people, the faeries could override his magic if not his adorable face, and not even he could stop this fight from starting. Fawn had it coming, anyway. She'd tossed down the gauntlet, and now she'd pay the price.

The chill in the room intensified by another few degrees. "How dare you suggest I'm unfit for my duties? Did someone die and make you queen?" Where most voices might go up an octave, Evian's dropped and her tone reminded me of whale song. Appropriate, I supposed, given her affinity for water.

Droplets of moisture formed around her, but it was the force of Vaeta's anger that lowered the temperature and let them freeze. Evian's blue hair went ice white, literally, but Fawn lacked the sense to shut up and leave. A pity.

She puffed out her chest, lifted her chin, and sneered. "Good thing for you the answer is no. If I were queen, you'd be getting a demotion to junior tooth faerie for the next thousand years until you proved yourself capable of handling sensitive situations."

And then she capped it by extending the slur to the rest of the family. "Not that I should have expected more from an elemental. Unfocused, the lot of you."

"Exactly how sensitive is the situation?" Evian demanded. "We've shown ourselves to Lexi for her entire life and the world hasn't rained down sulfur. With the queen's blessing, I might add."

The queen they were referring to happened to be a Balefire witch, though one I'd never have the good fortune to meet. She lived in the Faelands, wife of the Faerie King, and was incapable of returning to the human realm. It's a long story, but the point is that Fawn had no better idea of the queen's opinion on godmother-witch charge relationships than any of the rest of us.

"Blessing? Ha. Is that why you're not allowed in the Faelands anymore?" Fawn pressed. She was partially right, but there was no way any of the faeries were going to kowtow to Serena's crotchety old godmother. Technically, Vaeta could come and go as she pleased; it was only her sisters who'd chosen the path keeping them from their home.

Snaking tendrils burst out of the floor around Fawn's feet, a gust of wind whipped at her clothes, and lightning slashed from the ceiling to flash-fry her beehive hairdo. Ashes drifted down around her face, which went from surprised to angry with beetled eyebrows and grimly twisted lips.

She looked a little bit like a burned-out match—if matches were chubby in their middles. At that point, Fawn could have made any one of a dozen choices designed to diffuse the situation. Instead, she fixed a sneer on her face and called Evian a nasty name.

It was on.

Do something to put a stop to it before things get out of hand.

Why? I asked the witch. *They're grownups, aren't they? Let them handle their own problems for a change.* Besides, I wanted to see what Fawn brought to the table. Color me curious.

I suppose, given her name, I should have known what form her magic would take. Fawn and fauna aren't too far apart. She must have called every mouse in a block-wide radius because they teemed up through the floorboards. Not the wisest thing to do in a witch's house.

Eyes bugging out of his head, Salem skidded into the room, his body quivering in ecstasy while he chose his first target. He geared up to pounce on the nearest of Fawn's minions. Seeing she'd put the poor thing in mortal danger, Fawn clapped her hands and the mouse went poof. To his great disappointment, Salem came up empty-pawed.

Fawn looked a little concerned when Vaeta called the wind to her service and sent the rest of the mice skidding across the floor and out the open door. I sidestepped the onslaught nimbly, hopping into the kitchen with Kaine securely tucked into the crook of my elbow. His eyes followed the four-legged rodents with interest even though the pressure in the house made my ears pop and must have bothered his as well. He probably thought the whole fracas had been created for his entertainment; he was that kind of baby.

Vaeta's wind blew the last of the ashes from Fawn's

head, leaving her virtually bald. A perfect canvas for Terra, who flicked her fingers and spread a layer of soil from which a tangle of moss erupted in the bad seventies perm version of a woodland hairstyle.

I had to press my lips under and bite them to keep from laughing.

Frankly, as faerie fights went, this one seemed almost tame. Even if Fawn had no idea, I could tell the godmothers were holding back. Sensible, really, from a warrior's standpoint. Never showing your full strength to your enemies was just good battle sense.

If all Fawn had to offer was a slew of woodland animals, she was in way over her head. Terra's affinity for earth gave her an unfair advantage since it extended to include both flora and fauna. Serena's godmother was outclassed in every way, even if, logically, I could see the point she'd been trying to make.

Terra, and the two sisters who'd joined her to care for me when I was left a virtual orphan hadn't been the most orthodox of parents, but I'd never been in any doubt they loved me, or Lexi anyway. Enough to put emotion ahead of logic and cast their judgment into doubt. What Fawn said did hold a kernel of truth. None of my godmothers had access to the Faelands save for Vaeta, who hadn't been part of my adoption and the subsequent slide into blatant flouting of the rules.

They didn't seem to mind being shunned, and I gathered that the banishment was only temporary, so I'd never given it much thought. What I also hadn't given much thought to was how the godmothers of other witches might feel about Terra's decision. She'd bucked tradition, shown herself to her charge, and then taken it one step further with her choice to raise a witch baby as her own. Such scandal.

I could see more clearly now that I wasn't hampered by an excess of emotion. Well, except for when it came to Kaine. He'd wormed his way past my defenses, and that he'd done it so easily was something I should probably examine. But not at the moment.

Instead, leaving them to it, I bundled the baby back into his snowsuit and popped him into his stroller. As I hustled down the walk, I saw Mrs. Chatterly peeking through her curtains and gave her a jaunty wave and a big wink. The old biddy thought her picture window was a one-way mirror and no one could see her when she spied.

"Ready, little man?" Kaine's eyes lit up, and he turned his head and looked right at the old busybody. Her face softened, and surprisingly, didn't crack in half when she smiled. "Better get going before she decides to come out here." We set off down the sidewalk at a brisk pace.

Every bump made the baby giggle, and every time he giggled I bit down on the urge to babble at him, but it wasn't easy. He was just so darned cute. In that manner, we made a circuit around the neighborhood. Only once did we meet someone else out walking in the cold, and I managed to dodge to the other side of the street and avoid a Kaine love-fest incident.

A half hour had passed by the time I stood on the sidewalk in front of the house and assessed whether it was calm enough to go back inside. Concentrating on the flash of light and the soft, booming echoes, I didn't hear footsteps coming up beside me until a voice startled.

"Who's this cute little guy? Yours?" Kin stroked a finger down Kaine's cheek and grinned when his touch elicited a sparkling laugh, but seemed otherwise untouched by the strength of the baby's magic.

"My nephew. I'm babysitting while my, uh, roommates are testing out some new lighting effects." Nothing like a little deja vu in the afternoon. The first time I'd met Kin I'd been standing in the same spot and staring at the windows of the house wondering when it would be safe to go inside. "They're designers." I used the same lame excuse as the last time, too. But he bought it.

"Looks cool. Do you have a card on you? I might be able to throw them some work."

"Not at the moment."

"Then bring it with you when you come to my show tonight."

Had I agreed to that? In my head, the conversation from the restaurant replayed. No, I hadn't given him a firm commitment. "I'm—" There wasn't time to say I wasn't going because he already had.

ELEVEN

By the time Serena returned, Kaine was fast asleep with a cherubic smile on his face, and the last vestiges of the mess the faeries had made were scuttled back into place thanks to a convenient cleaning spell I'd recently perfected. I handed her a small glass of Twinkleberry wine and surveyed her as she sunk into the recesses of the parlor sofa.

"You look much less stressed than you did earlier." I noted that her hair shined and was, for once, its natural color. Her skin looked soft, and the dark circles under her eyes had nearly disappeared.

Serena took a long sip from her glass and glanced over at Kaine with that look you only see on the faces of mothers: half adoration and half scared to make any loud noises lest the little monster awaken prematurely. "I missed him," she stated simply. "I know I sounded like I was about to leave him on a fire station door mat, but I love him with all my heart and I'd do anything for him. It's just..." Serena trailed off.

"You didn't realize you'd be doing this alone." I finished her sentence.

"I didn't expect to be doing this at all. You've met my

parents; goddess knows why they stayed together so long when there was nothing left but contempt. Still, somehow, I expected to escape that life and wind up with a happy little family one day. Never mind that half the kids we grew up with came from a broken home—I clung to the belief that my family was the anomaly. Now, I watch television or read the paper, and I realize there's no such thing as normal, and these picture-perfect households with a mother and a father and two-and-a-half kids just don't exist." Serena finally got to her point, her matter-of-fact tone laced with sadness.

I nodded in understanding, "That ought to make you feel better, but I'm guessing it doesn't."

"Not really. Then throw in the fact that my son is a descendant of Cupid's and a Fate Weaver...well, I'm in over my head."

"You're not alone, Serena," I promised, hoping my words rang true to her ears, "though I do think it's time to call in reinforcements." I explained to Serena what had happened at the coffeehouse, how I'd watched Katie's fate play out, and the resulting aftermath of Kaine's fate weaving on the unsuspecting couple.

Serena's brow darkened, "It scares the hell out of me, Lexi. He's just a baby, with no way to defend himself other than a type of magic I can never fully understand how to help him use. I mean, does he have latent powers from his father? I was never sure with Jett because he bragged a lot, but I still ended up doing all the spells and such. I have no idea how Kaine would handle himself in a tough situation, but I suspect some latent talent might pop up, and then I'd be dealing with a whole other can of worms. It's a good thing the coven are all besotted with him. At least I know they'd pool together and perform a memory charm on anyone who happened to see anything weird."

"That's a worst-case scenario situation. We'll figure out a solution, I promise." When Serena's expression didn't lighten, I decided maybe she needed a laugh. "Speaking of cans of worms, you should have come back an hour ago. You'd have seen your faerie godmother wearing a weave made out of moss. She and Evian got into a little disagreement, and it escalated."

The mental image worked, and Serena couldn't help but let a giggle escape her lips. "Tell me you have pictures."

"Naturally."

While Serena swiped her way through the photo gallery on my cell phone, I heard the front door slam and looked down the hallway to see Vaeta surreptitiously peeking through the curtains at something outside. Salem was crouched, in his cat form, at her feet, sniffing the doorway like there might be a crab cake stuffed in the crack.

"What are you doing?" I asked, and I swear she flinched even though taking a faerie by surprise is about as difficult as wrangling a wild eaflock.

Vaeta took one more look and closed the curtain. "Nothing, I guess. I thought I saw something outside. Probably just a stray dog."

A shiver ran up my spine. It wasn't often that Vaeta was wrong, and it wasn't the first time a feeling of being watched had made the hairs on the back of my neck stand up. Just as I was thinking it might be Sylvana lurking around and keeping tabs on me, the doorbell rang. I nearly jumped out of my skin.

"It's Delta, open up," floated through the closed door before I swung it open to find the Fiach more disheveled than I'd ever seen her. She all but jumped over the threshold. "Close it, quickly."

"Are you being followed?" I scratched at my shoulder blade while scanning the yard and street for anything that would freak out a bad-ass supernatural bounty hunter like Delta.

Delta hung her coat on the already overburdened rack in the hall and sidestepped some of Kaine's accoutrements as she made her way into the parlor. "I'm not sure, I might just be paranoid."

"Seems to be going around." I replied, and offered her a seat by the flickering Balefire. "Besides, you're only paranoid if they're not actually following you."

Ignoring my joke, Delta got to the point. "I've got news and you're not going to like it. No, Serena, stay here. This concerns you, too," she said when Serena initiated a spell to gather the baby's things.

Serena stopped what she was doing, and the diaper bag settled back onto the floor with a plop. Her mouth firmed into a thin line, and she leaned forward with her elbows on her knees in anticipation.

"You're in danger, and Kaine might be in danger as well." Delta dropped the bomb and didn't bother waiting around for our reaction before she plodded on. "I had to use some pretty unorthodox information retrieval methods, and I now owe a favor to a demon from the Fringe, but it turned out to be a solid lead so I'll worry about that later. You're being hunted, Alexis, and by something I've never seen the likes of before. Something that likes to feast on the souls of Fate Weavers. Have you ever heard of a Balmorrigan?"

I looked from Vaeta to Serena to Salem, who had shimmered into his human form prior to Delta's explanation, and received three simultaneous head shakes in return.

"What is a Balmorrigan?" Serena asked, her voice shaking.

"That's the thing—they've been off the bad guy map for as long as I've been doing this job. I managed to gather up the gossip, and while most accounts are wildly varying, the one thing that seems to be a consensus is they're the product of an ill-fated match between a demon and a witch." She slumped back into the cushions as if imparting the knowledge took something out of her.

"So they're like what...the opposite of a Fate Weaver? Like the anti-Lexi?" Serena turned to me for validation, but I had none to give, so I shrugged and asked Delta to continue.

"It's almost as if all the information pertaining to them has been erased from the history records. The mark they left on your shoulder..." Delta pointed to me and a hiss escaped Vaeta's lips. I'd have to pay for not having mentioned the dream and the mark to the faeries, and it probably wasn't going to be pleasant, but Vaeta knew better than to interrupt such an important conversation just to yell at me. "It's an amalgamation of two archaic symbols, and roughly translates into *soul stealer of love bringer.*"

Fear rippled through me while Lexi shouted in my head, *We have to do something. We have to protect Kaine!* I shared the sentiment.

"Vaeta," I said, my voice brooking no refusal, "you can reprimand me for withholding information later. Right now, we need your sisters—" I stopped short as Evian, Terra, and Soleil flitted into the room in their tiny faerie forms and grew to regular size like something out of a Disney movie. She must have tapped Evian's communication shell woven into the hair above her left ear so the rest of the faeries had heard enough of the conversation to know they were needed.

When everyone was filled in, Evian sprang into action. "We're on it, Serena, don't you worry." She fastened a necklace around Serena's neck, a tiny shell dangling from the chain. "We all wear these in our hair, and if you tap it once, then talk normally, I'll hear you. As his official godmother, I'll immediately detect any distress on Kaine's part and will, of course, come running. The shell is in case *you* need me."

We worked out a plan for round-the-clock monitoring, setting aside the tension that had been hovering in the air ever since I'd committed what the faeries considered a punishable crime and stopped treating them to every detail of my personal life. Vaeta fluttered out of the room muttering about increasing security, and after a few minutes, the floorboards began to rattle with the strength of her efforts.

"Alexis," Delta said in a quiet yet still strong voice before Evian and Serena prepared to skim home with Kaine, "what about me? I have no intention of leaving you all to your own devices. I have skills, and I'm prepared to put them to use. For you. You all are the closest thing to friends I have, and I don't care what my orders state. I am at your service." She performed a little dip that wasn't quite a curtsy, her fingers grasping the handle of her formidable rapier.

I'd tried very hard to eradicate anything close to weakness from my emotional repertoire, but Delta's pledge of allegiance made my feelings tingle. Just a little.

"Thank you, Delta."

"No problem," She snapped her spine straight and looked somewhat embarrassed at her show of devotion. "But we do have *a* problem. The only person who would be able to tell us what we're up against would be a Fate Weaver who was at least a few hundred years old. The problem is that outside of wildly varying rumor, I have no idea where to look. It would be a lot easier if I had some help tracking one down."

It wasn't like Delta to admit a weakness of any kind.

"What exactly do you need?" I couldn't go haring off on a grand adventure with her, but I could probably draft one of the godmothers. "I bet Soleil would be happy to—"

She cut me off. "Not that kind of help. I need something touched or owned by a Fate Weaver."

"You mean the bow?" Could I give it to her even if I wanted to? Or would it drive her mad inside of an hour?

The look she tossed me was pure Delta. "Don't be foolish. The bow looks only to you now. Even if another besides your father had touched it, I'd never be able to get enough trace for tracking." She sighed. "I'm talking about a personal item."

"Sure, let me just go pull something out my supply of Fate Weaver-owned objects." I swear, I wasn't trying to be snippy, it just came out that way.

"It was just a suggestion," she said, scowling at me. "I'll keep searching."

I caught my reflection in the rear view mirror as I circled two blocks out looking for a decent parking space near Driven, and didn't know how to feel about the fact I looked more like myself than I had in months. The goddess had quieted, giving me an unprecedented amount of control, though I imagined it was part of her game to see whether I could handle an evening involving Kin without having a complete and total meltdown.

Good luck with that, she piped up. *I try to protect you from making stupid decisions, and this is the thanks I get?*

Well, who asked you to be the life police anyway?

You did.

Did I? You keep saying that, but I remember it quite differently. I was hurt and wanted a chance to lick my wounds, and you jumped in and took over. You chopped off my hair, you redecorated my bedroom. You cut Salem out of my life. Did I really ask you to do all of that? Because I don't think I did.

Oh please, this was nothing more than the typical behavior of the tragically dumped. I gave you a makeover, streamlined your office, bought you some privacy in that madhouse of yours, and don't tell me you—

The internal argument fizzled when a familiar sense of dread washed over me. I was really beginning to wonder if I'd been three kinds of a fool to wish for my magic all those years it was late to the party. Trouble followed me like a plague once it kicked in, and while no one could call my life boring before, I almost longed for the simpler days when the worst that could happen was a disco swampfest of faerie fight in the living room.

What was worse, I'd put myself in danger by going to Driven alone, knowing there was a new enemy circling. I knew I should have stayed home, but Kin's siren song was too loud to ignore.

I'll handle this. My inner goddess jockeyed for control, but I gave her a taste of her own medicine and shut her down. Witchfire playing along my fingers, my power went questing out in a circle.

In my peripheral vision, greasy light oozed along the brick wall while I played the unwitting sheep. With my nerves already on edge, I reckoned my stalker might be in for a nasty shock. Waking Lexi and dreaming Lexi? Not the same. Especially not with the double shot of Alexis added in.

Spell rhymes chased through my mind, fiery intention built in my hands, and I started a countdown in my head. *Get ready to jump in if this goes bad,* I told the goddess because I'm not so big a fool as to use only half my resources in a fight. *In five...four...three—.*

"Are you sure we're going the right way?"

"Nothing looks familiar, but I could have sworn this is

where we parked the car." Bright voices interrupted my preparations to fight.

"Says the person who reported her car stolen because she forgot which mall entrance she used."

"Hey, parking lot A and parking lot B look exactly the same in the dark."

As I passed the two twenty-something women searching for their ride, my entire body prickled like a foot that has fallen asleep in the night and I heard one of them mutter to the other, "Well hello, Hottie." Was she talking about me?

No, her eyes slid by me like I didn't exist and fixed on someone behind me. Turning, I saw him. Tall was my first impression. At least six feet five—maybe more. A chiseled chin, piercing eyes. Linebacker shoulders stretched the black, hooded sweatshirt across his chest, and I could see why the young woman's mouth was hanging open.

But it was more than just his looks—the man had a supernatural bad boy vibe that both attracted and powerfully repelled. When his gaze lasered my way, his eyes flared green. Probably a reflection from the streetlight, yet still unnerving, though not half as much as the shivery feeling I got from having his full attention on me or from the adrenaline still coursing through my system.

It's coming from him, right? The freaky stalker energy? Alexis might not have overt magic, and I still wasn't sure she could pull out the bow for self-defense, but we got our ability to parse truth from our father, and it was strong.

Feels like it.

"Hey, have you seen my car? It's a Honda, sort of a dark red four-door." As opening lines went, I'd call it a three, but at least she batted her eyes nicely. Not that it did the young woman any good.

"No." His voice rumbled.

Miss Lost Car pouted, but the man barely focused any attention on her at all.

"Is that it over there?" Figuring there was something to the idea of safety in numbers, I'd slowed my steps to join the two women, and we'd managed to cover enough ground during the distraction they'd provided that I could see the side door of Driven.

She pointed her key fob in the general direction I'd indicated, and hit a button. When the lights flashed on, a laugh trilled out of her companion, and in a flurry of motion, the two women made their way down the street.

By the time I turned to look, my stalker was gone, and before I took another ten steps, I'd half convinced myself there'd never been any danger at all. Stress, panic, and nerves can play hell with the imagination.

My stomach still jumping, I walked toward the club and prepared to face the man I'd spent the last few months avoiding like the plague. What level of idiocy made me show up here, anyway?

Because you're a glutton for punishment. I wasn't sure if it was Alexis's voice or my own echoing in my ear. I pretended not to hear her, and did what any woman would do: prepared for battle. I was already dressed for it in one of Kin's favorite outfits—a short skirt over thick black tights with spangled threads that made my legs look amazing—even though I knew trying to entice him was a bad idea for a hundred different reasons.

Wasn't it you who branded me a coward just a few hours ago? Which is it—am I supposed to feel or not feel? Make up your mind, I shot back at Alexis.

There is no good end to this, and we both know it. But if coming face-to-face with that fact is what you need, please, proceed.

I sucked in a breath and squared my shoulders, then headed for the side door where a hulking man stood with his arms crossed in front of him. When he recognized me, his face lit up and revealed the teddy bear hiding beneath his forbidding exterior.

"Lexi Balefire. Hello, stranger." The man closed the distance between us to envelop me in an overwhelming hug. "I haven't seen you in ages. Where have you been?" He demanded.

I couldn't help but soften. As half of one of the first matches made when I was just starting out, and prior to opening FootSwept, Tim held a special place in my heart.

"Oh, here and there." I said, noncommittally, my tone light. "How's Sandy?"

An indulgent grin spread across Tim's face, "Good and ready to be done being pregnant, and spending all my money on Hot Fries and ice cream."

"Interesting combination." I grimaced, and then smiled, suddenly grateful I hadn't given in to my second thoughts and circled around to the front entrance. The mundane conversation with Tim brought me back to earth, and when I took my leave and strode into Driven, it was with the confidence of the old Lexi, who had been on a first name basis with everyone who worked and frequented there.

Even in the darkened atmosphere, my eyes were drawn to Kin as he stood near the sound equipment next to the stage and talked animatedly with one of the crew. A gust of wind that came either from the back door or the force of my attention, I wasn't sure which, blew a golden ringlet from his forehead and caused him to rake his hand through his hair in a gesture so familiar my stomach dropped into my shoes. When he looked up and caught my eye, I waved hello and indicated a seat at the bar where I'd be until he was finished with his set.

It struck me, absently, that I'd been out of the loop at Driven for longer than I'd realized when an unfamiliar bartender leaned over and asked for my order. The request for a cranberry and ginger ale died on my lips when Alexis piped up with a wry, *You're going to need a real drink for this, and you know it.*

"Vodka cranberry, please, and make it a double." I took her warning for truth but vowed to nurse it and avoid saying something either stupid or too familiar to Kin. I was wading into dangerous territory, but continued plodding down the path as though it were lined with roses and daisies.

Kin did his thing on stage, bringing back a flood of memories that were both horrific and sublime. When he got to the point in his set where he was slated to sing the song he'd written for me, I closed my eyes and sent a spell his way even though I knew changing his will might garner me an unpleasant cosmic kickback.

We witches live by the rule of reciprocity; whatever you put out into the world comes back to you threefold. Gods, however, are a bit more flexible on that particular guideline, and I figured whatever might happen couldn't be worse than the effect of hearing Kin sing the words he no longer remembered were meant for me. Okay, it could, but I'd just have to suck it up if my punishment was to hear the same annoying bow song on repeat for a week or something. He played another song instead, and I breathed a sigh of relief.

Somewhere during the last half of Kin's set, the air in the club suddenly changed, turned cold as ice, and I had to check the exits to make sure someone wasn't holding the doors wide open. They hadn't, and as my eyes swept back across the dance floor I noticed a woman dancing. Actually, noticed isn't the right word. This woman was born to stand out, and she demanded to be stared at.

Jet-black hair hung in wild curls, framing a face that could easily have graced a magazine cover or a Paris runway. Piercing eyes beneath a dark brow presided over chiseled cheekbones that slashed toward full, blood-red lips. Strips of some sort of spandex material clung to her curvy figure, leaving little to the imagination. Lethal was the word that came to mind, and it referred not only to her ability to render a man tongue-tied with lust but the fact that she also appeared fully capable of kicking physical ass if the necessity arose.

Her cold beauty reminded me of the man I'd seen outside, and my supernatural senses went on full alert. As if she felt my gaze, the striking woman's eyes met mine and the chill intensified for a fleeting moment before she turned on her heel and retreated into the crowd. Once she was gone, the effect dissipated and I shook my head as if to dislodge an uncomfortable thought, then returned my attention to Kin.

When the set ended, he slowly wended his way through the throng to where I was waiting.

"Hey, you came." Kin said when he approached.

"I'm a woman of my word." I replied, "Want to find a place to sit?" Without waiting for an answer, I headed around the corner of the curved bar to the one booth insulated enough to hold a conversation even with the loud music.

Kin shot me a funny look. "Tell me, Lexi Balefire, are you some kind of mind reader?"

"No," I said, shaking my head, "though that would be an excellent super power to have." I almost mentioned that I'd been here before, but remembered in the nick of time that I had already lied to Kin about that fact. Suddenly, I was pleased that very few of the people who would recognize me were present tonight.

"Want to know what I'm thinking right now?" The husky timber of his voice made my head spin.

I felt like a planet caught in his orbit. Unable to break

free, but knowing if I got too close, I'd burn up in the fire and heat of him. Part of me didn't care about the pain of flaming out of control as long as he was the sun that consumed my soul. The rest of me thought this was just the worst kind of torture, and when his hand rose, a gentle finger poised to stroke my cheek, I knew exactly what was on his mind. Dimpled smiles, a low pitch to his voice, the tilted head. All signs I'd seen before.

Quickly, I pulled away before his hand could make contact. This time, I was certain Kin was flirting with me, and that wasn't even the thing that freaked me out the most.

You're probably wondering why, when the man I loved more than life itself was standing right in front of me practically holding a sign that said *Yours for the taking*, I couldn't just sit back and enjoy myself. It stood to reason that, since he had loved me before, it was possible that Kin could love me again. I could have everything I ever wanted, if I was willing to reach out and take it.

And he wanted me to do that very thing.

Except I wasn't. I wasn't willing to spend the rest of my life living a lie, and pretending that the months we'd shared as a couple had never happened definitely fell into that category. Yes, I probably could find the right time to tell him everything, and we probably could move past our past. Everything would *probably* work out just fine. Or, he wouldn't believe me, freak out, and dump me again. Nope.

Besides, somewhere in the deepest recesses of my heart, I could hear a little voice telling me that if I walked away now, Kin could *never* be hurt by me and my crazy life ever again.

He'd been cursed, nearly killed, battered, and broken more than once, and for me, once was too many times. I'd rather see him find someone who wouldn't put him in mortal danger on a regular basis than drag him back into my insane supernatural world. And no, it didn't occur to me to consider what Kin might want, because as far as I was concerned, the Kin I knew was already gone.

This was his second chance, and it was mine to give him even if he would never know. Even if my heart shattered, there was no other way.

Are you nuts? Alexis broke her silence. *He's your ex and you want to help him find someone else to love?*

I love him and I want him to be happy. He deserves a good life and none of what happened was his fault. We have *to help him.* Lexi insisted.

No. We're not doing this. Alexis tried to put her mental foot down before I let a pipe dream shatter me to pieces too small for her to pick up. See a symbol, point and shoot. With Kin it had to be that simple. He carried no symbol, so helping him would mean more contact than I could handle. *We are absolutely not doing this.* She tried to protect me, I'll give her that.

I chose to ignore her completely, but I could hear her thinking that if I wanted to play with fire, maybe I deserved to get burned.

Fine, if that's the way you want it, but this is going to go bad, and don't say I didn't warn you. You're on your own.

It might kill me to learn he had another fated match, but I had to try.

Loving him meant putting his happiness above my own, but there was no symbol hovering over his head, so this meant going old school.

Before the Bow of Destiny and learning about my goddess heritage turned my life upside down, I used my gut and heightened sense of intuition to successfully match couples. The problem for me now was that I needed to touch Kin to activate my internal LPS and I didn't know if I could handle casual contact without freaking out.

Rather than focus on my worries, I scanned the area around Kin's head in case his floating heart symbol was hiding somewhere. No such luck.

In some part of my brain, I managed to keep a level of conversation going while experiencing my internal freak-out. Kin said something amusing and I used my laugh as a cover to steel myself and then lay a hand on his arm.

Only because Alexis hadn't forsaken me did I manage the brief touch at all. She tightened my gut, straightened my spine, and did the dirty deed.

Nothing.

No intuitive pull in the belly toward a match. Not even a tingle. Okay, maybe a jolt of electricity, but not the kind that would help me find his match. What was I supposed to do with this?

If Kin truly believed his soul mate had passed him by —and I knew that to be true, since, well, she was me—I'd have to find a way to divest him of that notion before his heart would open for another. True love of the fairytale variety was forever, but the real world didn't always work that way. People die or life happens, and sometimes soul mates part. The Bow of Destiny and its heart-shaped arrows made ironclad matches. Otherwise, things happen.

We are the product of our experiences. Sounds glib, but it's true. No one is limited to a single soul mate except by choice. That was why I would engage in this madness even if it would kill something inside me to know there was another choice for him. It didn't matter that there would never be one for me.

You're going to get hurt, she fired back at me. *And then what? Crawl back into your cave and leave the mess for me? Can you handle losing him a second time?*

I ignored her and plodded on, though it would have made more sense to listen to her this time. The road to hell, and all that, but now that my feet were pointed down the path of good intentions, I couldn't go back. Finding him a mate was the last thing I wanted to do, and the only gift I had left to give him. Alexis couldn't stop me; I wasn't sure anyone or anything could, not even me.

Addicts know they shouldn't indulge in what they crave. I was no different when I rested my elbow on the table, my chin in my palm, and stared my fill at the one man I could never resist.

"Tell me about you, Lexi Balefire," he said, looking at me like I was the only woman in the club. "You make me feel like I'm in a fantasy world whenever you're in the room. Like magic exists and I'm under your spell."

Kin picked the exact phrase to throw metaphoric water in my face.

The undertow of pain sucked me down again. It burned a path through me, leaving nothing but the aching thunder of devastation, and suddenly I realized what a colossal idiot I'd been to have come here in the first place. And so, I did something I knew I might regret later but was my only way out of an unbearable situation: I dove back down into my subconscious and left the problem for Alexis to solve.

I *hate you.*

That was a lie. I didn't hate the witch, just the way she ignored all my advice, got herself into trouble, then bailed. Kin was staring at me like he knew something had changed and she'd gone so deep I couldn't even hear her thoughts.

But I could read her feelings and the cherry that sat atop the sundae of my life was that I'd begun to feel something for Kin, too. Not love, mind you. More like a little flutter of softness in the region of my heart. An emotional cancer that needed to be sliced ruthlessly from the whole and destroyed before it spread.

"Well, this has been fun," I lied, "but I have other clients to see tonight." Also a lie. There still wasn't the faintest glimmer of a symbol in the place. Even if I wanted to make a match, there were none to be made by my preferred method. At that moment, I longed to send a shining arrow into the heart of an unsuspecting target just to feel the rush and release of living gold carving a painless, bloodless path into flesh.

Better yet to sink my weapon into Kin's heart and be rid of the one thing Lexi clung to above all else. Hope.

"Stay. I'd like to dance with you, Lexi Balefire."

"Not tonight." Or any other. "I'll line up some dates and give you a call." In uncharted territory, I had no other choice. Kin sported no symbol and my LPS wasn't working. All that was left was to fling date spaghetti against the wall and hope something stuck.

I felt his eyes on my back as I dodged my way through the crowd, and it took every ounce of willpower not to look back.

CHAPTER

THIRTEEN

S YLVANA

As I sat in the shadows, Kin's singing slid under my defenses and tried to pull my most bittersweet memories out into the light where I'd have no choice but to look at them. His fingers slid over the guitar strings, tweaking them into notes of both sadness and mourning. This was a man who had known loss.

I knew plenty about loss. First, my father went out for the proverbial pack of smokes and never came back. Then my mother, well, that was a complicated story, but I hadn't lost her so much as thrown her away, and Lexi along with her. All for the love of a god among men. Literally.

Oh, and did I mention he left me, too?

Only now was I coming to understand the price might not have been worth it, but even so, my heart craved him, and here I was, with no idea my daughter was experiencing similar pain, staring at her with an ulterior motive for getting my man back. Could I be any more pathetic?

"What are you doing here, Sylvana?"

I nearly jumped out of my seat when a mini tornado deposited one of Lexi's faeries in the second seat of my shadowed—magically enhanced shadows no less—booth at Driven.

"Vaeta, right?" Made sense, given the flair of her entrance. "Aren't you worried someone might have seen you popping in like that?"

She waved a hand and cocked an elegantly shaped gray eyebrow at me. "Please. With the glamour you're casting over this table, I could have ridden in on a rainbow-farting unicorn and no one would have batted an eye."

I'd always considered my glamours impenetrable, so her seeing right through one was disconcerting. "Well, I had to do something. Back in my day, bars were darker, smoke-filled places. Easier to go unnoticed." My twenty-five years in a cage had seen a lot of changes ushered into the world.

"You didn't answer my question. I know you've been following Lexi around, and I'd like to hear your intentions." Her magic raised the tiny hairs on my arms, tickled across the back of my neck, and tingled across my tongue.

Well, two could play that game, so I pulled up a little power, channeled it into the palm of my hand, and let the witchfire flicker into a marble-sized ball. Deliberately, I held Vaeta's gaze and played the ball across my knuckles, letting it grow larger as it rippled back and forth.

"And what exactly did you see? Nothing nefarious, because all I've been doing is keeping an eye on my daughter. Making sure she's safe."

Vaeta shot me a skeptical look, nipped a stale peanut from the bowl on the table, and said, "Your intentions haven't been honorable thus far, so you'll excuse me if I seem skeptical. We've been the ones looking out for her, and we'll continue to do so even if it means removing you from the equation."

The threat chafed. Lexi was my daughter, but these faeries seemed to think they had the bigger claim. The worst part was I couldn't even be pissed off about it. They'd taken her in and protected her when I couldn't. Owing debts to faeries is tricky enough business when there's time to hammer out ironclad terms. Even then, a person could end up needing to pay the proverbial arm and a leg in actual arms and legs if a deal went wrong.

So far, the godmothers had asked for nothing in return, but that didn't mean I had to like them. "Cool your jets. I'm trying to help Lexi. No ulterior motives, I swear." Mostly truth. My motives were a little more complicated, but that was none of Vaeta's concern.

Still, telling an air faerie to cool it down was a bad idea. She did, and I shivered in the frosty results of her magic.

Crooking her finger, Vaeta called an empty glass from behind the bar and poured a beer from the pitcher I'd ordered but barely touched. "And how did that work out for you last time?" Had to give her credit for the level of snark in her tone. Really top notch. I could probably like her if I didn't hate her.

She sipped, grimaced, and blew on the beer as if it

were hot and she wanted to cool it down. An icy ring formed around the rim of the glass. A handy talent.

"Okay, I made some bad choices." An understatement. Bad choices seemed to be my default. "But I'm trying to make up for my mistakes, so cut me some slack."

The chill eased along with the set of Vaeta's shoulders and I let my gaze travel back to where Lexi sat across from the man I didn't think was good enough for her. But what did I know? My love life ranked right up there on the top ten list of tragic failures.

"Was he good to her?" Needing to ask was a bitter pill, but I had to know. I might not have been there for my daughter when she needed me most, but I could feel the pain of his loss inside her now. Whether because I'd lost my own love, or because she was my flesh and blood, I couldn't say and I didn't care. Under the collected exterior, Lexi's cries echoed in my heart. "Tell me what happened. I know Diana Diamond was to blame, but I'd like to hear the rest of the story."

I knew some of the details, but what I'd heard had come from an unreliable source, so I wanted to hear what happened from another perspective.

Before she answered, Vaeta downed her glass and poured another. "He broke her heart, but it was none of his doing. The man lived for her and would have died for her, I've no doubt. Nearly did, thanks to you."

Because there was no defense for choosing the Bow of Destiny over saving Lexi's man, I shrugged. Would I never live that mistake down? Would I make it again if I could go back and relive that moment of choice was the bigger question.

"That viper used one of her cards to turn Kin's heart away from Lexi and focus his attention toward another woman. There was more to it, but the upshot is there was a curse attached, and even though Lexi broke the spell, she was too late and he doesn't remember being in love with her."

No wonder Lexi seemed so different. Not only was she nursing a broken heart, but she'd taken an ego bashing, too. I picked up my glass Vaeta's chill had left dripping with condensation and stamped out a few rings on the paper napkin.

"This quasi date they're on is how she's trying to get him back?"

Vaeta sighed and the breeze from it smelled of meadow and gusted my hair back. "You don't know your daughter at all, do you? Deep down that's what she wants, but it's not a date, it's a matchmaking consultation. She's going to try to find him someone else to love because she values his happiness above her own. Unlike you, there's not a selfish bone in that girl's body. Don't you think it's time you stepped up?"

I doused the ball of flame I'd been turning over and over in my hands, but before I could form an appropriately nasty response, Vaeta dropped a bomb on me.

"How much danger is Lexi in because of your history with Diana Diamond?"

A heated retort jumped to my lips, but I bit down on it

because the question deserved honesty, and for once, I wanted to tell the truth. "Some. Maybe more than some, though from what I've seen, Lexi can hold her own there. How did you know?"

The faerie looked at me like she was considering how much information to reveal, and even though I wanted to be ticked off about not being trusted, I really didn't have a leg to stand on. She finally shook her head and answered, "In Port Harbor, there's a portal to a Nexus. I believe you're familiar with it."

"You know about the Nexus?" My mother had imprisoned me in the space between worlds for twenty-five years, and if I ever found the person who'd managed to let me out, I owed them a debt of gratitude along with a slap upside the head. As much as I appreciated my freedom, the act of gaining it had also released the Darkest Heart back into the world. A woman otherwise known as Diana Diamond.

In clipped tones, Vaeta answered, "I do. It leads to the underworld—my unwilling home for the past hundred years, and when I finally escaped, it was through that portal."

"Are you saying you're responsible for freeing me?"

She drained the rest of the pitcher of beer and signaled for another. "Not directly, but in a sense. I didn't provide the ammunition, but I was the one who pointed the weapon. That's a story for another day. Right now, I'm more concerned with how we're going to work together to atone for our sins."

"We? We're a *we*, now?" No one who knew me would ever call me a joiner. I'd been an *I*, mostly by choice, for my entire life. Too stubborn to ask for or accept help. Yet, being considered part of a team, even a team of two, might not be so terrible.

In answer, Vaeta leaned across the table and let her glamour slip enough to show the faerie underneath. Terrible beauty is the best way to describe her face. Eyes blazing like the golden rim of sunlight around a storm cloud, her features refined down to a series of points, she bared her teeth at me.

"You're a selfish piece of trash and I don't like you. Let's just get that clear right now, but I love your daughter, and I'm willing to work with you to help her. So if you're feeling all warm and fuzzy, get over it, and when we're done, we're done. Clear?"

"Crystal." I spat the word at her. "While we're on the subject of who's at fault for what, maybe you could tell me why you all let her close herself off the way she has. Look at her." I pointed toward the woman who barely even looked like my daughter anymore, and certainly wasn't acting like her. "I've spent enough time with her to know this persona she's adopted isn't healthy or normal."

Vaeta had put her everyday face back on and now it registered pain. "I know. She's compartmentalizing. Maybe helping Kin move on will let her do the same. We can't fix it for her no matter how much we wish we could. The heart heals in its own time and fashion. All we can do is support her until it does."

"So basically, you're doing nothing." Outwardly, I sneered while inwardly knowing they were probably right to let her work through it in her own way. But if anyone knew how she was feeling, it was me, and passive acceptance had never been the strongest Balefire trait.

"What exactly have you been doing besides skulking around and watching her?" Vaeta shot back while I watched my daughter chase after a broken heart. Again.

Feeling powerless makes me cranky. "Trying to figure out what's going on with her, and how to get through to her. Believe me or not, helping Lexi is my priority."

I cocked my head under Vaeta's scrutiny and pretended I had no other motive than love for my daughter. I did love Lexi, so it wasn't a stretch, and I must have passed her scrutiny because she frowned and brought me up to speed with what Delta had learned of the beings who hunted Fate Weavers like Lexi.

"There are rumors that a Fate Weaver or two survived, but no verifiable sightings in at least two hundred years. For all we know, Lexi is the last besides young Kaine, and no one is left to provide answers about the Balmorrigan."

She'd been sitting here all this time, judging me, and for once, I had information to share. Leaning back, I rested my wrists on the table, took a deep breath, and said, "What if I told you a Fate Weaver still lived a hundred years ago? And I can prove it."

Vaeta pursed her lips and raised an eyebrow in disbelief.

"How could you possibly be able to prove something

that happened long before you were born?" Vaeta tilted her head and waited for me say something stupid. I did not oblige. "This is too important for you to get her hopes up over nothing. Lexi has questions that need answers. About herself, but also about little Kaine." A smile flitted across her lips as she said the baby's name and her gaze went unfocused.

What was it about that baby?

She circled a hand to get me talking again.

"Twenty-five years is a long time to be holed up in silence, so Diana and I...well, we talked some." Truth be told, I talked more than she did, but in my defense, I hadn't known she was evil incarnate at the time. Still, she'd let some things slip, including the information I was about to tell Vaeta.

"A hundred years ago, at least one Fate Weaver helped build the portal to the underworld Nexus in Port Harbor." If I expected a smile or at least some indication the news I had was good, I didn't get it. Vaeta only frowned, so I continued. "And I have proof because he dropped his wand near the prison bars. It's probably still there."

Not near enough for Diana or me to reach it, but close enough for her to know it for what it was and rant about it on multiple occasions. If what Vaeta said was true, the Balmorrigan and Diana had one thing in common: hating Fate Weavers.

As if I hadn't said anything and a new thought just now occurred, Vaeta said, "I don't suppose Cupid ever talked about his other children."

"He had plans for Lexi, but he didn't share them with me or talk about his family much, and I never really pushed it. I figured we had more time and there were other things to do."

Eyes rolling, Vaeta said, "There's more to life than sex."

If I have one downfall, it's letting my emotions get the better of my magic, so Vaeta's snark got under my skin and set free the beast. Her eyes flickered when she felt the sting of my power, but she continued as if nothing was happening.

"Delta's most reliable sources all agree the Balmorrigan were out for Fate Weaver blood. If they're back—and Delta's convinced they are—we need to find a Fate Weaver with direct knowledge of what's fact or fiction. It's the only way to keep Lexi safe."

Vaeta looked at me like she thought I might have one of Cupid's other children locked up in my basement or something. Well, the joke was on her. I didn't even have a basement.

"I've never heard of these Balmorrigan, but the solution is simple. If Lexi needs a Fate Weaver, why not go to the source: Cupid? Her father will have all the answers."

Smirking, Vaeta raised an eyebrow. "Does your mind have any other track?"

I huffed and drew my brows down in irritation. "I can't just pull a Fate Weaver out of my ass, Vaeta, as much as I'd like to help. It's not like he ever took me to his family reunion."

Vaeta leaned forward in her seat, a forbidding expression on her face. "Come on, Sylvana, he must have told you something."

Not nearly enough, I was coming to learn. "He said Lexi was the child of his heart, and that her heart would be her greatest gift."

"That's still pertinent information, Sylvana. You should have told Lexi about it." Vaeta scolded.

I snickered. "Yes, well, when would you have liked me to tell her that? Before she reamed me a new one and took off with fire and brimstone in her eyes, or after?"

Maybe I was stupid to get involved with an elemental faerie—even one that had Lexi's best interests at heart. We might scratch each other's eyes out before we managed to help my daughter. But, what other choice did I have?

FOURTEEN

I dug through the kitchen cabinets in search of some of Terra's Twinkleberry wine, and let out a rare grunt of frustration. Well, rare for me at least. Lexi almost always let her emotions get the best of her, but it wasn't a habit I had any intention of indulging, regardless of how many of her feelings were leaking out and threatening to pull me under.

Just as I let out a slew of curse words that died on my lips thanks to Terra's no swearing charm, I heard a noise behind me and whirled around in surprise. I thought I'd been alone, but there was Vaeta, watching me from the doorway with the hint of a smile on her face.

"Do you find me amusing?" I asked wryly, abandoning my search.

"Not any more than usual, *Alexis.*" She put enough emphasis on my name that I swallowed hard and wondered just how much the sister dubbed Airy Faerie actually knew. It wasn't the first time her seeming lack of wits proved to be a falsehood, and once again it occurred to me that her sisters didn't give her nearly enough credit.

Vaeta pulled a bottle wrapped in twine from behind

her back and handed it to me while calling two stemmed glasses toward us on the wind. "Let's drink."

I knew when she said *drink* she actually meant *talk*, and even though it was the last thing I wanted to do, the thought of losing myself in a faerie wine inebriation was too much temptation to pass up. Especially after having spent an uncomfortable evening arguing with myself while trying to find my ex-boyfriend a new girlfriend. It sounded like something out of a bad soap opera, and so I poured myself a nice big glass.

A generous gulp of the liquid went down my throat on a sigh, and suddenly my head felt clearer than it had in days. Potent stuff, faerie wine, and poor Lexi could only ever handle one glass before becoming plastered enough to engage in scandalous acts like dancing naked around the ritual fire. I'd already discovered I could retain more of my senses than she, and tucked into the drink as though I'd been dying of thirst.

Vaeta merely raised an eyebrow and used the situation to her advantage. "Why don't you tell me the thought process behind the extreme dye job."

"Oh come on, really? I'm all liquored up, you can ask me anything, and that's the burning question on your mind?" Frankly, I found it refreshing. "I like pink, and it looks better against white than any other color."

What was it with people getting so keyed up about the color of my hair? Wasn't it, like, standard operating procedure to get a makeover when your love life went belly-up?

"Okay, my turn. Did you meet anyone in the underworld that would surprise me? I mean, like Elvis, or Houdini?" Why I pulled those two names out of my brain, I couldn't say.

"Pshaw." Vaeta scoffed. "Elvis went back to the Faelands."

Made sense to me. I poured another glass of wine and downed it in three gulps while Vaeta watched enigmatically. The buzz hit me harder this time, and I welcomed the feeling of not giving a tiny tater tot about anything for a little while. Until Vaeta went and ruined the moment.

"Tell me what you're holding back. I promise not to judge." Since faeries are incapable of lying, I believed her, and if I were going to spill my guts to any of them, Vaeta would have been my first choice by a mile. She'd been on the receiving end of her sisters' bad graces due to her own decision making plenty of times.

"Ah, Vaeta. No matter what I do, I find myself split in two."

She kept her mouth shut, sipped her wine, and sat back in her chair while I got up from mine and began to pace and rant.

"Up until last year, I was stuck using only the most passive parts of my power. I plodded along, trying to find fulfillment by spreading love in the world. The whole time, I knew I had a higher purpose but lacked the tools to realize it. Then, I finally got my powers, retrieved and fixed the Bow of Destiny, only to have to circumnavigate some asinine system constructed by the gods to confuse me with symbols and visions. Oh, and let's not forget having to combat some whacked-out demi-goddess who's hell-bent on breaking into Olympus for an unknown but most definitely nefarious purpose. I haven't beaten Diana Diamond, not really, and Kin might as well still be under her spell. To top it all off, I've got to try to make sure a fate-weaving toddler doesn't wind up either exposing magic to the human population of Port Harbor or driving his mother batshit crazy. All while battling waves of complicated feelings that I'm not equipped to handle. I'm supposed to be a goddess, not a sniveling pile of emotional goo."

I let it all out, pacing and ranting while Vaeta listened. Spewing my guts felt good, but fell just short of supplying a full sense of release. When I'd exhausted myself and fallen back onto the parlor sofa with a huff and a sigh, she refilled my glass and then threw me for a loop, "What you need is a little distraction, and to let off some steam. Follow me."

Vaeta led me to the sliding glass doors that opened out to the backyard where she and her sisters spent most of their time. I'd seen more weird things happen in the magically-enlarged space than I could count. Some of them were beautiful and some of them were downright hair-raising—like the Dragolian bullfrogs that could take the head off a house cat with one snap.

With a whirl of Vaeta's hand, she called to the wind and summoned what looked like two large poppets made of sticks and leaves and who knows what other elements of nature. Each one had a red circle painted on the front, and when I looked in her direction, Vaeta was holding two hunting bows, a collection of arrows strewn at her feet.

"You know I have one of those in my actual bones, don't you?" I said, referring to the Bow of Destiny's resting place.

"Of course, but that's not what this is about. Here," She handed me one of the weapons and an arrow. "This is about stress release. No magic allowed." With that, she nocked her own arrow and took aim, but missed the bullseye. Her arrow bobbled back and forth, its tip embedded in the dummy's crotch area.

"Was that intentional? Do you want to talk about it?" I mocked.

Vaeta indicated for me to take my turn. "No, it wasn't intentional, but it was fitting. You're not the only one having man trouble."

"This isn't about *man trouble*," I insisted, my tone derisive.

"Okay, whatever you say," she said lightly, shooting again and hitting the outer edge of the target.

"Fine, maybe it is a little bit about man trouble. For one stupid second I thought maybe Kin and I could reconcile. But then I realized it's a moot point. He's never going to remember our time together, and I'd be living a lie." The fact that I'd ceased referring to Kin as belonging to *Lexi's* past, and now considered him part of my own marked a change that I'd completely missed. Talk about having your head buried in the sand.

"What difference does a measly few months make,

anyway?" Vaeta asked, her brow furrowed as she frowned at me like I was the stupidest person to have ever lived.

I struggled to formulate a response, but came up with no good reason. "It just does." I insisted, and then turned the tables on her, "Enough about me. I spilled my guts, so now it's your turn. What's up with you and Rhys?"

"If you think dating a human is tough, try dating a demon who has more secrets than you and I combined. He's dodgy and distant one minute, and then overprotective and smothering the next. I don't want to be kept in a cage. I need to fly free on the air, that's my jelly."

I'm pretty sure Vaeta meant that it was her jam, but she still hadn't gotten a handle on modern vernacular after being stuck in the underworld for a hundred years.

"What kind of secrets do you think he's keeping?" It was one of the more prying questions I'd ever asked Vaeta, and part of me doubted she'd even deign to answer, but the other part—the one who'd had enough Twinkleberry wine not to give a damn—well, didn't give a damn.

I was surprised with her candidness when she replied, "That's the problem. He's involved with the Inter-Magical Alliance, so it could be anything from a rogue vampire clan to a rabid manticore loose in the streets. Or maybe he's found a water nymph to cavort with. Who knows?"

I raised an eyebrow. "I hope he's not that stupid. Your sisters are just waiting for a reason to tear him limb from limb."

"And that's why I'm out here target practicing and yammering on to you about it instead of them. Besides, all they'd give me is a big, fat *We told you so*, and frankly, I'm even less in the mood for one of those than I usually am. At least they don't blame Kin for your current debacle, otherwise you might have found him flayed and on display in the front yard."

"You're probably right." I said, lobbing an arrow straight through my poppet's heart.

Vaeta put her bow back down on the ground and surveyed me thoughtfully. "So, explain about the problem with Kaine. I've rather begun to like that slippery little Snodgrass witch, and her son is pretty adorable as well. What's going on, exactly?"

"I have no idea, to be honest." I sighed. "Serena thinks because I'm a Fate Weaver I must have all the answers, when in reality I don't even know the secret knock to get in the clubhouse. Hell, I'm not even sure there *is* a club-house. Kaine's already matching couples, and everywhere he goes, an entourage of adoring fans pops out of the woodwork. If you could bottle charisma, it would have that kid's face on the label. If we're not careful, he could grow up to be some shady huckster bilking people out of their money, and they'd be happy to give it to him."

Picking up three arrows, I fired them in rapid succession to form a downward pointing triangle on the target. With my eyes closed, no less.

"What's the plan," Vaeta asked. "I know you have one, or at least an idea of one brewing in that little head of yours." I wasn't sure if *little head* was a euphemism for *tiny brain*, but I let it go and tried not to smile when she picked up her bow and tried to emulate my performance with less-than-stellar results.

"The only option I can think of is to find a Fate Weaver with more experience and see if they can fill in the gaps. I'd like to get Serena the answers to all of her questions. Mine too, while I'm at it. Delta says she's heard there are still some out there, but she needs something to use to track one down. Like a personal item that belonged to the Fate Weaver. As if I know where to find something that belonged to someone I don't know and have never met."

Vaeta's eyes widened, and she opened her mouth to respond, but was cut off by a sharp clap of what sounded like thunder and a cloud of smoke. When it cleared, Flix and his boyfriend Carl were standing in the middle of the backyard, right in front of the dummies Vaeta and I had been shooting at.

"If you'd popped in five minutes ago, you might have lost a very important appendage." Vaeta said dryly, pointing to the arrow she still hadn't removed from its target.

FIFTEEN

"What are you two doing here?" I asked, a little snarkier than I'd intended, but men—any men—were on my unwanted list. "Is everything all right at FootSwept?"

I expected Flix to whip a quick retort at me, but he wouldn't meet my gaze and answered quietly, "Yes, everything is fine there. But Carl has something he needs to tell you."

Carl looked as though he'd walked into the den of a lioness, and cast a nervous glance between me, Vaeta, and the dummy while shifting uncomfortably. My hackles went up, since the whole gesture smacked of dishonesty. I could tell Vaeta was thinking along the same lines, because her smoky eyes narrowed to slits. A rush of anticipation washed the effects of the Twinkleberry wine from my veins and suddenly I was completely sober.

"Should I sit for this?" I asked, keeping my voice calm even though I wasn't sure if I wanted to hear the answer.

"Let's go inside." Flix said quietly.

I led everyone into the parlor, where the Balefire flickered cheerfully and warmed my toes, and looked expectantly at Carl. "Am I dying or something?" I asked dryly.

"Lexi," It was Flix who spoke next, though he sidestepped my sarcastic question, "I know you've always had a suspicion that there was more to Carl than meets the eye. You were right, but he wasn't trying to deceive you. Please listen to him with an open mind and remember that he's important to me."

The Academy should have given me an award for keeping my composure, because it took a fair amount of effort not to snap at Carl. If Flix felt the need to preface whatever I was about to hear with a plea like that, it meant nothing good. "I'll do my best," was what I offered in reply, "but if someone doesn't tell me what is going on here, I'm not making any promises." Even though I liked Carl well enough, and Lexi and Flix had a history, they'd picked the wrong night to show up and try my patience.

Carl sighed, "Flix, love, it's okay, it's my story to tell and it's not as bad as you're making it out to be. At least I hope you'll see it that way, Lexi." Leaning forward, he made eye contact and cleared his throat before launching into his story.

"I wasn't surprised to learn that Flix had Fae blood, and even if he hadn't filled me in, I would have pegged you for a witch from the moment I laid eyes on you. I'm human," he hastened to add when my eyes narrowed, "but there's something inside me—maybe it's in my DNA —that recognizes supernatural beings. Some kind of radar, I don't know."

If I hadn't been on the edge of my figurative seat—my actual butt remained firmly planted—the analogy would have made me giggle. At least, for a moment, before he said what he said next.

"My ancestors were witch hunters." Carl nearly whispered. His face flushed a dull red. "I know I should have told you before now, but I'm not like them."

Vaeta began to swirl at the edges, the wind she commanded whipping into a howl that could have stripped the flesh from a mortal's bones if she'd infused it with the intention.

"Relax, Vaeta." I implored, but added for good measure, "Give him a chance to speak." She sat back down, but revealed her true face for a split second to snarl menacingly at Carl.

Carl nibbled at his lip before continuing, "I swear to you, Lexi. The Jagers have been out of that world for generations. I'm deeply ashamed at having to admit to it at all, and I promise I mean you no harm. I want to help, and that's why I realized I had to come and talk to you."

"He speaks the truth." Vaeta said simply, letting the mini tornado she'd summoned die down into nothing, but she needn't have bothered. I could feel Carl's misery from across the room.

"When you showed me the mark on your shoulder, I recognized it right away. I should have told you then, and I'm sorry I didn't. I was afraid. You see, I've spent my entire adult life trying to figure out the hows and whys of my heritage. That's why I became an anthropologist—to get answers."

Hands balling into fists, I worked to keep my tone

level. "I could do with a few of those myself, but it's nice of you to show up now, at least."

Carl ignored the hint of sarcasm and continued. "The Balmorrigan, the riders from your dream—they're a whole different level of evil. They cut a path across England, Scotland, and France, and then came here to continue their reign of terror. Until, at least, sometime in the late 18th century, around the 1770s to be exact. They fell off the map for almost a hundred years, popped up again in the late 19th century, and then disappeared. Again. Unfortunately, my ancestors, save for one die-hard historian, stopped keeping records. The last recorded sighting was about a hundred years ago."

I tried to put the pieces together, but they didn't make any sense. Something niggled at the back of my subconscious, but was interrupted by Lexi's thoughts. *Cut him some slack. Please.*

We might not always see eye-to-eye, and I might consider her a sniveling pile of emotional baggage, but I'd come out of my closet in order to, ultimately, protect Lexi. I wouldn't do anything she wouldn't be able to forgive me for later. I raised an eyebrow but kept my mouth shut until he was finished.

Carl squirmed a little under the silence. "There's more. The Balmorrigan aren't working alone. There was a third presence. I could feel it...in the dreams."

"What dreams?" For Lexi I could keep my temper in check, but I had to force the question out from between clenched teeth.

"Our dreams. I've been there, too. Seen them chase you. Or not really. I was chasing you. Inside the rider. So much hate, it was hard to think. And the fear coming off the lanterns," he shuddered. "So many lost souls. The lanterns capture the soul of a Fate Weaver. And, the Balmorrigan, I think someone's controlling them. They have orders. They won't be free until those orders have been carried out."

Carl stopped talking, looked at me as if he were deciding whether to stick around and hear my response or run for the hills before I did to him what I'd done to the archery dummy.

"Who? Who is controlling them?" Only one person came to mind, and if my instincts were on point, it would answer several of the questions I'd been asking myself since this whole thing began.

"I don't know for sure, but I heard a woman cackling in the nightmare. Her voice was like nails on a chalkboard, and it scared me to the bone."

"Diana Diamond. The Darkest Heart. She's the only one with a motive, and the laughing you heard was definitely her. I should have known." I grew quiet while the implications set in, and Carl looked like he was about to make a run for the front door.

I sighed, "It's all right, Carl. If anyone understands being ashamed of where they come from, it's me. It's not your fault, and I know how hard it must have been for you to come here and explain yourself. But, I expect complete honesty from here on out. Understood?" He'd shown up with valuable information, so how mad could I be?

"Of course." Carl was more than happy to oblige.

"Now," I clapped my hands together, ready to get down to business. "Have you, during the process of your research, come across anything that might lead us to another Fate Weaver?"

Flix answered my question. "What do you think we've been doing with all that equipment at the office, Lexi? I know you didn't ask for my help, but I've been paying attention to the subtext. Those Fate Weavers of yours are either exceptional at hiding their tracks, or there are very few left to find. I'm guessing it's a combination of both."

"That's what I figured." I said, my frustration showing through as I began to pace the room.

"What about your friend Delta?" Carl asked. "Isn't she a supernatural bounty hunter?"

"I've already asked her, and she's doing her best. But so far, she's come up empty. The last time we spoke, she said she needed an object belonging to a Fate Weaver in order to track one down, but all I have is the bow, and I'm certainly not going to hand it over after everything I went through to get it. Not to mention, that would only lead to my father, and it's a stone I'm not willing to turn over."

Vaeta's eyes widened and the look that crossed her face could only be described as sketchy.

"What?" I demanded.

"Well, I have a lead on the type of object you're referring to. But you're not going to like it. It involves your mother."

SYLVANA

All hope of getting a private moment with my daughter collapsed when she strode out of the house ahead of Delta and the air faerie. Apparently, someone subscribed to the notion there was safety in numbers.

"We'd probably draw less attention if it was just the two of us." My helpful suggestion earned me a scornful glance and nothing more. "I'm just saying, portals to the underworld can be dangerous."

Lexi spared me a dirty look, but I could tell it took an effort. "Delta's packing heat and Vaeta has an in with a demon; we're not in any danger on that front. We'd probably be safer if you'd tell me what to look for and stayed behind." She waited for me to make the offer and when I didn't, she turned her back on me and climbed into the driver's seat with Vaeta taking shotgun. That left me in the back with Delta, and I didn't trust the Fiach much past the end of the blade she carried on her back.

I paused a few seconds. Unless I rolled over, they couldn't do this without me since I was the only one who knew where the wand had fallen or what it looked like. I could probably throw my weight around and refuse to go unless it was on my terms, but doing that wouldn't gain me any goodwill with my daughter. I did, however, drop my backpack full of supplies into the space between me and Delta. Just for insurance.

The drive was tense with silence that I felt compelled to break. "Once you get to the city, I'll give you directions to the portal."

Lexi didn't even bother to turn around. "Unnecessary, I know where it is."

I gave Vaeta's seat a kick, and when she turned her head, I mouthed the word *how*. All I got in return was a head shake, so I shut my mouth, focused my attention out the window, and wondered what else I didn't know about my daughter.

Not that anyone cared, but I'd rather have eaten a scabby Band-Aid than return to the place where I'd spent a quarter of a century hating my mother and railing at my fate. Vaeta had asked how much danger I'd put Lexi in with my loose lips, and the truth was that I had no idea. I'd ranted and raved even before I'd known there was another presence nearby.

A sympathetic listener, Diana encouraged me to spill my guts while keeping fairly quiet about herself. I'd been too caught up in my own drama to realize how skillfully she'd drawn details out of me. She knew things about my relationships with my mother, and with Cupid. Oh, I'd complained plenty about both of them.

Still, I hadn't told her much about Lexi, other than to

describe my daughter as a beautiful baby. I mean, what more could I say? She'd been barely out of the *rolling over on her own* stage when I made the worst decision of my life. I'd been trying to exert my independence when I picked the fight with my mother, not blow all our lives to smithereens.

Lexi turned down a street in the formerly-abandoned industrial section of town that once fell under the pall of the Darkest Heart's influence. At least someone had benefited from Diana Diamond's release back into the world.

Delta let out a whistling breath. "Busy spot for a Nexus portal. Don't you think people will notice four women disappearing off the sidewalk in broad daylight?"

The grin Lexi exchanged with Vaeta softened her features enough to show me a shadow of her former self, and it gave me hope. The softer side of Lexi was what I needed.

"It won't be a problem." Vaeta assured her. "Just find a secluded spot to park."

Easier said than done, or so I thought, but Lexi made two turns, spun the car into reverse, and whipped into an alley between a pair of long, many-windowed factory buildings.

"Perfect. Now just let me—" Concentrating, Vaeta made a pulling motion with her fingers, then flipped her hand over and completed the spell by rotating both hands as if stirring the air. Which, I realized when a whirl of wind settled over the car, had been an accurate assessment.

A cone of circling air gently enveloped us, car and all, and the world around us turned to a watery shimmer. "There," Vaeta dusted off her hands with satisfaction.

"I don't get it." There went my intention to remain silent.

Lexi rolled her eyes, but didn't explain. Taking their cues from her, the others ignored me as well. Fine. If they wanted to play it that way, I could do the silent treatment, too. It wasn't like I was just tagging along for the ride. We wouldn't be here if I didn't have something to offer, but if they wanted to act like children, so be it.

Vaeta's cone of air gently lifted my hair, but didn't carry any extra chill, which I appreciated given the near-zero temperature of the day. When I turned to look back at the car, I saw nothing but a brick wall.

"Nice magic." My mouth and my mind are not always connected, and so it ignored my decision to just shut up. But, since Delta echoed the sentiment, I didn't feel quite so left out.

With Vaeta's efforts filling in our tracks and keeping us from view, we stomped through pristine, calf-deep snow to the center of a clearing between buildings. Snow-covered park benches clustered around a mermaid fountain marked the edge of the portal. A good look at her face made me think the faeries had had something to do with this bit of urban beautification since she looked an awful lot like Evian.

Power slithered up from where it lay curled inside of me, tendrils of it snaking out from my fingertips to test the portal. The last time I'd passed by here, I was in such a hurry to escape, I hadn't bothered to check the barrier for origin. It had been open and I was free. That had been enough for me. Now, I sensed witch, faerie, and my beloved Cupid. Essence of demon provided the dark element to seal the portal since the Nexus it contained led to the underworld.

"We're wasting our time. We need a demon to get through unless the Fiach has a dark history."

Delta rounded on me and drew her sword so quickly I saw nothing but a blur. "What did you just imply about me?"

Crap. I hadn't meant to piss her off, but I'd managed it quite handily. The woman had a hair trigger and an itchy sword hand. Dark fire crackled between my fingers like sparks of lightning flickering between the clouds during a summer storm. Shadows filled my vision as the desire to feed the flame built inside me. Along with great power comes great temptation. I felt the weight of Lexi's gaze and let the magic trickle into the snow even as I enjoyed the mental image of the Fiach racing away with her hair on fire.

Sucking in a breath to wash the satisfying but inappropriate image out of my head, I held up empty hands in surrender and tried to look sincere enough to be believed. "I'm sorry, I didn't mean that the way it sounded." It was the truth anyway.

The tip of the sword, so close I went cross-eyed looking at it, wavered and then disappeared as quickly as it had come. I heard the snicking sound it made against the hidden scabbard as Delta sheathed it. Her eyes burned into me the whole time.

Lexi sighed and rolled her eyes at me in utter scorn. I recognized the look, one I'd used on my own mother when I was a teenager. Seeing it on an adult Lexi made me wish I'd not missed those years with her.

"We're fine," Lexi said. "Vaeta will handle the demon element. She has a special"—the two exchanged a look I couldn't interpret— "dispensation."

The way Lexi seemed to unbend around the air faerie simply annoyed me. I'll admit to that base emotion, but not to being jealous. Much.

With a slight smile on her face, Vaeta twisted the ring she wore on her right hand until the flawless, blood-hued ruby faced inward, then rested it next to her left hand against the portal. Dark light flared red against the wavering curtain, and when Lexi rested her palm nearby, a doorway opened to show a concrete wasteland that looked familiar.

"What was in that ring? Demon essence?" It felt powerful, and I almost envied Vaeta the owning of it. I'd always craved power more than I probably should.

"Something like that," was all she allowed.

A shock of electricity rippled along my nerve endings as I mustered up every shred of will and stepped through to my former prison and something of an anti-climax.

Gone was the pervading mist that had isolated me from my surroundings and my former cellmate. Sitting on a square plinth, the cage lay empty, missing its door, and from this perspective seemed less bleak than I remembered.

"If you're through with the stroll down memory lane, could we get on with the matter at hand?" Lexi's voice cut right through me.

I rounded on her. "Have a care how you talk to me, young lady." Ugh, I sounded just like my mother and had the urge to bite my own tongue in half because that was the last thing I wanted.

She hit me with the eyeball-rolling sneer again, which sent my blood pressure into the red and I heard myself say, "We can turn right around and go home if that's the way you want to be." Cliche mother speeches must be passed down through the blood or something. Mine boiled and stirred and if I hadn't clenched my teeth and forced it back down, tried to shoot my magic into the destructive zone.

Of all people, Delta stepped in to chide Lexi. "Cut her a break—she's trying to help. This is the first real chance we've had of finding anything that would lead to one of the Fate Weavers. First rule of a successful mission: hauling baggage around can get you killed, so leave it at home."

A band of tension squeezed my temples until my pulse throbbed painfully, and I tried to breathe through the moment without lashing out. I'd earned a level of mistrust, so I might as well own it because I needed this mission to go well. Otherwise, Lexi might never trust me enough.

To that end, I projected confidence and circled around the far side of the cage. "It's right over here near this pile of stones." Except it wasn't, and my heart sank as I scrambled around to search the area where I remembered seeing the wand, nearly hidden between two rocks and just out of arm's reach from the cage.

Without needing to turn and see it, I could feel Lexi's withering stare on my back and had to fight to keep my shoulders squared.

"Are you absolutely sure you weren't hallucinating? How did you even know it belonged to a Fate Weaver? We're probably running a fool's errand." Lexi snapped.

I counted to five, slowly, before responding, in an attempt to keep my temper under control. "Because once Diana pointed it out, I could sense the magic signature that went into the making of it. It's a talent I developed at a young age. Same way I know Delta's sword is dwarf-made. A witch fashioned that wand, but it was carried by a son of Cupid." There was more to it, but I make it a point to never tell everything I know.

I did, however, give Lexi a poke because she pissed me off. "Same way I know the difference between Alexis and Lexi."

Lexi blanched, and it wasn't hard to see why. I'd hit the nail on the head, and now she knew that I knew she'd become a fragmented version of herself. I'd like to say I understood the extent of it, but my daughter was still holding her cards as close as she possibly could. It might have been fun to let her squirm, but I didn't have the heart to do it, so I explained as much as I could.

"Blood magic, but no darkness, went into the making of that wand, and the stone tip was bound with a piece of bowstring. I'm sure you can figure out the origin of that element on your own."

"And why am I just learning about this now?" Lexi demanded. "Didn't it occur to you that a wand like that might be helpful to me? I mean, I'm only fighting for my life here, no big deal," she spat.

I sighed, "You have the bow. I figured that was a better substitute, and you seemed to be getting along just fine with it. Besides, I don't know the exact formula for crafting your wand, so it's a moot point. If we could find your father, he could tell us how."

"Everything circles back to that, doesn't it?"

"You're just being stubborn. It doesn't take a genius to see that he's our greatest asset, if nothing else. And there's plenty else." I shouldn't have had to explain to my daughter why it was important to put our family back together, but she wasn't having any of it.

"Did it ever occur to you that he doesn't *want* to be found? If he did, he'd be here. I saw him. He walked away. On. His. Own."

I reared up for a snappy retort but Delta stomped her foot with such force the Nexus itself shuddered, dust raining down around us like snow. "Enough," she roared, forcing us all to refocus. I knew she was right, and we were acting like children, but there was no way I'd let her know that.

"Maybe you're looking on the wrong side." Vaeta's gentle suggestion was meant to be encouraging, I was sure, but didn't quite come off that way. "Would it help to step back inside and get your bearings?"

Heat flared up from my belly and colored my face darkly. "Why? So you can slam the door behind me and leave me here? Not going to happen, sister." I wouldn't put it past her, and so I readied my defenses, which made the faerie do the same.

She stepped closer and we squared off.

When she felt the wild magic creeping over her skin, Lexi looked at me and said, "Oh, go put your panties in the freezer and chill down a notch." It was the first time she'd sounded like herself since my return.

Delta's snort diffused the tension with Vaeta.

"Getting back in there won't help," I said, cutting the cage a wide swathe. "I know this is the spot. See the markings on that stone?" I pointed out a chunk of blue-gray stone with web-like veins of quartz running over its oblong surface. "That rock was the prettiest thing I had to look at the whole time I was here. Trust me, I would recognize it anywhere."

Just for form, though, I did another circuit of the cage with the other three women on my heels.

The search turned out to be as big a waste of time as I'd expected. "I should have known she'd come back for it, or maybe she grabbed the wand on her way out. If I hadn't been in such a hurry to escape, I might have thought of that myself."

I slumped down on the corner of the concrete base and leaned my back against the bars of my former prison. This wasn't the time to indulge in a pity party, but it did seem like the universe would never let me catch a break. So much for making a good impression.

Lexi drove the nail home. "Yes, well, that would have required you thinking of something other than yourself, and we both know that's not your strong suit is it, Mother? You'll always choose to save your own skin."

She stood before me, eyes fired with fury, shoulders wide, and back ramrod straight, and I felt an obscene sense of pride in my daughter. Right before her words cut me, anyway.

"I didn't have to bring you here, did I? But I did because I thought I could help." I tried to stay calm. "It's not easy for me, you get that, right? Ending up in here wasn't exactly my biggest triumph. It cost me you and everything else I loved."

One flawlessly shaped eyebrow arched toward the ruthlessly straight fall of bangs over Lexi's forehead. "Nice to know you are capable of feeling something for anyone besides yourself, but you sure have a funny way of showing motherly love."

Maybe this wasn't the best place for a fight, but it seemed like Lexi was spoiling for one, and who was I to deny her what she wanted? I launched to my feet and got all up in her personal space. "What do you want from me?

An apron and a tray of cookies? If that's the kind of mother you had in mind, I'd have been a disappointment from the word go."

Lexi glared at me like I'd just insulted her and curled her lip. "Clearly, you have no idea what I wanted or needed. You don't honestly think my godmothers dropped the ball, do you? They met every stereotypical motherly standard in the book. But, they weren't witches, and they didn't even know I was a Fate Weaver. What I needed was motherly guidance, and you were the only one who could have provided the brand I required. Now, you want to swoop in and be my bestie. Well, I can tell you right now, that's not going to happen."

"Yeah, I can see that," I retorted, raising my voice another couple of notches until we were just plain shouting at one another. "A *friend* would have told me about the Balmorrigan, and wouldn't have refused my assistance. Instead, I had to hear that you're in mortal danger from Vaeta."

Lexi scowled in Vaeta's direction, but the airy faerie simply avoided eye contact and allowed us to continue the argument.

"Show me the mark." I demanded, stalking toward my daughter and grabbing her by the shoulders. I spun her around and lifted her shirt, even though I could tell my encroachment on her personal space made her want to punch me in the throat. Thankfully, she resisted the impulse and deigned to let me see what all the fuss was about.

A little bigger than a quarter, the ringed symbol meant absolutely nothing to me, but I could have at least offered Lexi a balm for the red, irritated skin that surrounded it.

"And, do you have anything helpful to contribute, now that you've seen it?" Lexi's voice was cold and dispassionate.

"No," I admitted, utterly deflated, "I'm sorry. For that, and for a lot of things."

"So I've heard." For a moment, I thought she might soften, but I should have known better. Lexi was, after all, a spitting image of me in more ways than one, and I wasn't kidding when I said I could hold a grudge for all eternity. I also had a tendency toward vindictiveness, and apparently so did my daughter.

She pulled back and delivered the knock-out punch. "Since we're baring our souls, here's something you didn't know. On the day you were sprung from your prison, I was here with the guardian angel and the godmothers. I fell and hit my head right over there," she pointed to the corner of my former cell and then to a small scar on her forehead. "My blood was what set you free."

Leaving me open-mouthed and stunned, Lexi turned on her heel and exited the portal. At least she had the decency to leave it open, but when I made my way back out, it was to find she'd driven away and left me there.

SEVENTEEN

I should have known better than to get involved with Sylvana. The woman was duplicitous, and even if she was telling the truth, it always held a fraction of a lie. Not for the first time, the feeling that maybe I'd been better off not having been raised by her crossed my mind. It always made me a bit sad to think of my own mother like that, but I hadn't been the one to set the status quo, and it wasn't up to me to repair the relationship.

Combined with the fact that we hadn't found what we were looking for, I felt the overwhelming urge to blow off some steam. And for me, that meant doing a little after-hours fate weaving. The air had turned from chilly to downright frigid, though, and the normally busy streets were eerily silent, with not a single shimmering heart symbol in sight.

Without a target, I let the anger and confusion over Sylvana deflate like a balloon and instead turned my thoughts to Kin and the dates I'd arranged for him after our last disastrous meeting. He had sent several text messages over the course of the week, each one more bemused than the last. I reread them for about the hundredth time.

Blind date #1 didn't show. Or, she came into the restaurant, saw me, and left. My ego has been damaged, and I may never recover.

Most women seemed to swoon over Kin, so I highly doubted he'd been stood up for any other reason than some kind of personal emergency. I had replied with a time and place for his next setup and left it at that.

Blind date #2 had an allergic reaction to my cologne, couldn't breathe, and had to be rushed to the hospital via ambulance. I'm 0-for-2 and feeling even more like a pariah.

The image had brought a wry smile to my face, but it came with a burst of frustration. Getting Kin matched would close the book on that chapter of Lexi's life, and maybe then we could both find some peace. I hoped the woman slated for tonight's meeting would work out better than the first two, and decided that if I couldn't find anyone else to help, I could at least check on Kin's progress with my own two eyes.

Setting him up without benefit of the bow or my LPS hadn't been easy, and meant I'd had to resort to some kindergarten-level matchmaking. I'm ashamed to say I redirected a few leftovers from bow-made matches. You know, the woman left behind when a symbol-carrier met his match. I was not proud of the method, but it was all I had to offer.

I knew he'd chosen The Coffer as a meeting place, and since I wasn't far from there anyway, I looped around Tidewater Park and headed for the historic district. An old bank, The Coffer used to be one of my and Kin's favorite hangouts, and it stung a little to know he might be having a good time there with someone else. Why I had come to care about that, I couldn't say. I'd been perfectly content to leave Kin to his own devices, but it felt like Lexi's feelings were leaking out of the box she'd stashed them in, and now I couldn't seem to get the man off my mind.

When I was only a few blocks away, another message dinged into my inbox.

Okay, I'm starting to doubt your skills, Ms. Balefire. Date #3 thought I reminded her too much of her brother, mumbled something about being sick, and never came back from the restroom. If you're not busy right now, want to come help me drown my sorrows at The Coffer? You can't miss me. I'm the one crying into my bourbon and coke.

I let Kin down quickly, *Sorry, I'm in the middle of something. Maybe some other time.*

Please. His simple reply tugged at my resolve.

I felt my heart flutter, watched my fingers type back a simple *OK*, and cursed Lexi for her rubbery spine. *He's not yours anymore, and all you're going to do is get yourself hurt.*

That was all you, sweetheart. She echoed back. *And now you can deal with it.* The connection between us slammed shut so hard it made my eyelids flutter, and then she was gone.

. . .

"It doesn't look like you're drowning in your sorrows to me." The words came out sounding like an accusation, but Kin just tossed me one of his knee-buckling grins and threw his third dart without bothering to watch its progress. When it pinged into the bullseye and the electronic display jingled like a slot machine, he glanced back in surprise and did a little victory dance that brought an involuntary grin to my face.

Kin merely smiled like he was a cat who'd just finished a delectable serving of canary. "It's karaoke night, and I can't handle all the bad singing by myself."

"Flimsy excuse."

He shrugged and led me to a waist-high table in the corner, waving the waitress over on our way, "One bourbon and coke, one vodka cranberry, and you can put it on that guy's tab," Kin pointed toward the dart game loser, who gave the thumbs up along with a slight grimace. "That's what you wanted, right?" He asked after the girl had returned to the bar. "I don't know why I just assumed."

"Vodka cranberry works just fine." I replied lightly. "I'm easy." I felt a blush creeping up to my cheeks because that had come out entirely wrong, but Kin didn't seem to notice. "So, what am I doing here if not comforting you?"

It was Kin's turn to turn a little pink. "I wanted to see you. Is that so terrible?"

I wanted to reply in the affirmative, but felt myself being pulled in by his husky voice and the glint in his eye that I suddenly remembered with alarming clarity.

Without Lexi's constant presence in the back of my mind, I couldn't brush those memories off as remnants of her infatuation.

"No, of course not." I heard the murmured words come out of my mouth and wondered if I had gone temporarily insane. And then it hit me; he'd ordered my drink of choice without needing to ask what I wanted.

"Okay, so dance with me." He said when one of the other patrons began to sing a halfway decent version of Make You Feel My Love. Kin's eyes searched my face, and when the waitress dropped our drinks off at the table and gave me a moment of reprieve, I was grateful.

I tossed back the contents of the glass, and stood to place my hand in Kin's outstretched one. "All right."

He led me to the dance floor and wrapped his arms around me to pull me close. The scent of him went straight to my head and I felt myself sighing into a comfortable position. Memories dredged from the past and pulled me into a little montage where I, and not Lexi, took center stage. Kin had loved all the parts of me, even the ones that scared him, and I couldn't keep pretending that wasn't true.

When I had been frightened, he'd held me. When I felt fractured, he'd helped make me feel whole. There had been moments where he'd been afraid for me, and he'd been strong enough to stand up, even to the goddess part of me, and insist that I should be more careful. Had I underestimated his ability to deal with all that my being a Fate Weaver entailed? Had I been worried about his safety, or had I been worried about the state of my own heart if something bad happened to him?

All the thoughts crowding my brain really belonged to the Lexi half of me, and I tried to shove them off, but the heat of Kin's skin on mine made it difficult to do anything besides revel in the way it felt to be held close after months of pushing everyone away.

The song ended, and the spell was broken, though I still faltered getting back to the table, my legs like jelly. I wished I could blame it on the alcohol, but that had nothing to do with it.

"Want to play a game?" Kin asked on the way across the floor.

"I'm not good at darts." Actually, that wasn't true at all. I had impeccable aim, after all, but I knew from experience that playing with him would turn into foreplay, and I couldn't go any further down that road. He'd watch me walk back and forth to retrieve my darts, I'd put a little sashay in my step, and when I beat him handily, he'd tell me it was sexy as hell to get shown up by a woman.

Kin sized me up and raised an eyebrow, "I highly doubt that, but I was thinking more along the lines of some people-watching fun. See that couple over there? He's clearly done something to tick her off—look at the way she's got her body turned away from his, and of course there's the face she's making. What do you think their story is?"

"This one's a piece of cake," I breathed a sigh of relief; keen observation was part of my job, and getting into the zone kept the more confusing aspects of the evening at bay. "She's upset because the blond at the bar won't keep her eyes to herself. Duh."

"Okay, I admit, I saw that a mile away, too."

We'd never played this game before, and I'd had no idea Kin was so astute at reading people. "Corner table, looks like a double date of some kind. What's your take?"

He took his time, appraised the situation. I liked that about him. It showed an analytical mind under the charisma and charm. "Whoa. Not going to end well. Dude on the right has eyes for his buddy's girl and she's giving it right back. I feel bad for their dates."

While Kin watched the group, I watched him. Not just because he was easy on the eyes, though that was part of it, but I wanted to see his reactions. This whole situation felt like cheating. Not the kind of cheating that might happen between the couple at the far table. But because I already knew Kin's soul, his goodness, and decency, I had an unfair advantage. And though I'd tried not to, maybe I had, without knowing, used that advantage to get him to start falling for me. Love at first sight. Sigh.

"What about this one?" Kin pointed in the opposite direction.

I burst out laughing when I spun around to where a woman in her late 30s, clearly plastered, danced on stage while belting out an off-pitch rendition of "Walking on Sunshine".

"Recent divorcee. No question." I fired back.

With every verse, the poor drunk woman danced closer and closer to the back end of the platform, and it appeared she had no clue there was a gap between the edge of the stage and the wall behind it. The scene from "It's A Wonderful Life" where Jimmy Stewart and Donna Reed are dancing on top of the pool, oblivious to the fact that the cover is opening up right behind them, flashed through my mind.

Kin's eyes widened as he watched, but there was no way either of us would have made it across the room in time to warn her, even if we could have stopped giggling long enough to try. When she toppled off toward the floor, I sent a burst of magic to lessen her impact on the ground, which made me feel a little better about having laughed myself silly at her expense. She still went down in a heap, and the look on her face when she popped back up was priceless. To her credit, she finished the song, albeit a little less exuberantly.

"You've got to admire that kind of grit and determination."

"Tell me something, Lexi Balefire, do you believe in love at first sight?" Kin asked, out of the blue during the lull between songs. His eyes smoldered into mine, and I was caught completely off-guard. Not a usual occurrence for me, but the idea that I should be concerned about that quieted to a whisper in the deafening roar of Kin's question and its implications.

"I wouldn't be a very good matchmaker if I didn't, now would I?" I tried to keep my tone light. "But I've also seen a fair amount of infatuation at first sight, and they look pretty similar."

"Is that what this is, then? Did you put some kind of spell on me? Because I can't get you out of my head."

It felt like I'd been dipped in ice water and then tossed in a scalding shower, the way my body went from cold to hot.

"I'm sorry you feel that way, but you'll have to try. My life is complicated and I'm not in the market for a relationship. You know how it is, always the bridesmaid, never the bride." Totally the wrong analogy, but it was the only one that came to mind.

But I might as well have spewed gibberish for all he listened.

By the time he was walking me to my front door, I'd given in to the inevitable. There was heat between us, but there was more.

No, I know what you're doing, and you can't. You're supposed to be the strong one. Where's that iron will? What if we end up together again and something else happens?

I ignored Lexi, and the fact that we'd changed roles somewhere along the way. Kin's hand in mine felt all kinds of right. Didn't we deserve a chance to see if it could all work out?

EIGHTEEN

The world spiraled in tight until there was nothing but the smell of Kin's aftershave and my heart thundering in my ears like a dozen galloping horses. He slid his arms around me and pulled me in close enough that I could feel his pulse racing every bit as fast as mine.

One hand came up to rest against my cheek, then slid through my hair to cup the back of my head, and he whispered my name. My knees turned to water.

His head dipped, his breath teased across my lips and sent a wave of electric energy shivering over me. In that moment, I felt weightless, poised to fall in a gentle arc like a feather on the wind.

Our last first kiss hadn't affected me nearly this much, but at the time, I hadn't known we were fated for true love's kiss.

Twice.

At least I hoped so. To find out, all I had to do was lean closer, bridge that inch of distance, mingle my breath with his, and let his lips take mine. I wouldn't—couldn't —wait another second.

And then the lights went out.

. . .

SYLVANA

Standing in the shadows at the far end of the porch, I watched my daughter share an intimate moment and knew she wouldn't thank me for playing the voyeur. But there was a lot riding on this kiss and if it didn't go well, I wanted to be there to pick up the pieces.

The look of sheer bliss on Lexi's face as she leaned in made my heart both sing and weep. I missed the love of my own life so much it caused me physical pain, and I would have taken it double if it meant my daughter would never have to feel the same way again. So tenderly did Kin handle her it made me rethink my opinion of the man. He held her like she was precious, and fine, and he couldn't count his good fortune for being in this place and time. It was a beautiful moment.

But it wasn't about him. Lexi had reached the point in her life when, in many ways, partner replaces parent. I'd missed the time when I would have been the center of her universe, and now that honor would defer to another regardless of my feelings. At least, it would if this kiss went well.

I heard the sigh of his breath, the sharp intake of hers, and then the thundering of hooves. That's when things went from whoop to poop.

For all the noise they made, the horse's hooves barely touched the earth as they swept across the front yard. Booted feet thumped on the ground as the pair of riders practically rolled off their mounts. In the sickly lantern light, I saw one black figure seize Lexi by the shoulders and spin her aside while the other had its sights set on Kin.

They moved so quickly it was as if time sped up for them, but slowed for everyone else except me, and I was stuck in the place between a nanosecond and eternity.

Magic burst from me, but unlike the Sylvana who had damned her mother to twenty-five years as a statue and landed herself in a Nexus, I didn't just throw it around willy-nilly. I would not be doomed to make the same mistakes I'd already suffered for—this time, I focused all of my intention toward my goal with love in my heart instead of anger. I would protect my daughter or die trying.

The spell snaked from my fingers, and it took everything I had to hold it steady. A forcefield of magic enveloped the riders, its intended effect to turn back the ravages of time and allow Lexi a few moments to skim her and Kin away to safety. Unfortunately, I underestimated just how powerful the two beings were, and all my spell did was make it appear as if someone had pressed the *slow* button on a remote control.

Before I could end the spell and toss another, one of the Balmorrigan had Lexi in his grasp. Kin glanced at me with terror in his eyes and clutched for the woman I still wasn't sure he understood to be his soul mate. His fingers grazed her shoulder blade, and it looked as though a shock rang through his entire body. I watched as he pulled his hand away and stared incredulously at a gold-tipped arrow with a shaft of what looked like bone.

Do something with it! I thought, but didn't have time to shout, and it didn't matter anyway because Kin was already in motion. With no other option, he brandished the arrow toward the first rider, who let out a howl as the barb slashed into his skin and drew a swath of blood.

Kin's actions bought me a second or two. Just enough to toss a ball of witchfire at the second lantern-carrying figure, see the shimmer of faeries coming to help, and to make a decision. Trusting the Fae to protect my daughter as they had been doing for most of her life, I made a grab for Kin and skimmed us both through space to safety.

"What just hap—"

"I do not have time to explain it to you. You're just going to have to trust that I'll take care of it, and stay put." I pierced him with a warning glare and spun on my heel.

"Lexi." Her name on his lips echoed in my ears as I left him standing in his own kitchen. If there'd been time, I'd have wiped his memory, but my daughter needed me, so he'd have to figure out a way to deal. And if he couldn't, well, then Lexi would have to get over him once and for all.

The trip to Kin's and back took only a matter of seconds—being a witch comes with some pretty impressive perks—and I landed on the walkway just in time to dodge the flying hooves of the mare and stud carrying their riders away.

"Sylvana!" Terra stopped me before I made more than

a few running steps down the sidewalk alone. Furious, I turned on them.

"What is wrong with you? They're getting away." But all thought of retribution popped like a balloon when I saw Lexi sprawled across the porch floor. In fact, all thought drained out of me entirely. Dark lashes rested against paper-pale skin, and from this distance, I couldn't see if her chest rose and fell.

I needed but ten steps to get from where I stood to where my daughter lay, and each one felt as if hundred-pound weights were tied to my ankles and dragging behind me. "Is she—" I had to know, but didn't want to hear the answer.

Footsteps pounded up the sidewalk and I turned with magic at the ready, but it was Kin who sprinted past with only a glance spared for me.

"She lives."

The combination of Terra's assurance and Kin's appearance broke through the bubble of terror stasis and I vaulted the steps to lay trembling fingers against her neck. The steady thrum of her pulse did little to slow the thunder and hammer of mine.

Kin slapped at his pockets. "My phone, I don't...we need to call 9-1-1. Does anyone have a phone? She needs an ambulance, the police. We need to file a report. They're going to ask questions and I'm not sure what happened. And what am I supposed to do with this?" He pulled the bloody arrow from his back pocket and stared at it like—well, like he'd pulled it out of his girlfriend's body, which I'm sure was more than a little disconcerting.

Trying to chafe some warmth into Lexi's cold fingers, I met his questioning look with as blank a face as I could manage. "Leave it here and just go home." Even though I tried for calm, it came out more like a bark. "We'll take care of everything." Any more magic in front of him seemed like a bad idea.

"Please, Kin. Everything will be all right." Terra, in her motherly fashion, sounded certain, but when he heard her voice, his face changed.

"Have we met? I feel like I know you." Each of the faeries got a searching look. "All of you. Why is that?"

My daughter had just been attacked, and we were having this conversation on the front porch, out in the open and over her injured body. "This is not the time or the place. We need to get her inside and safe. Now." That last I directed toward Vaeta, who could use her power over air to carry Lexi gently.

"I'm not leaving her. I can't." Before Vaeta had a chance to do anything, Kin scooped Lexi up and nodded to Soleil, who was closest. "Open the door." The man had no idea what he was walking into, and short of hexing him or physical combat—neither of which would happen while he was holding my daughter in his arms—he had us over a cauldron. Witches and faeries have no need for barrels.

Soleil hesitated, so Terra reached past her and turned the knob, then turned back to give me a look that spoke volumes. I shrugged it off. He'd sink or swim. Lexi was the priority. Well, that and vengeance.

NINETEEN

"Is someone going to tell me what in the hell is going on around here?" Kin demanded again, once we'd settled Lexi on the parlor sofa with a soft pillow cradling her head. I settled on the edge of the sofa, took her hand in mine, and tried to funnel some of my warmth into her. If Kin hadn't been standing there, I'd have scooped a handful of Balefire and used that instead.

Soleil, Evian, and Vaeta looked to Terra, Lexi's official godmother, for her opinion. "I say we tell him everything," she declared. "I've had just about enough of tiptoeing around the situation. Agreed?"

Vaeta nodded, "I've been thinking the same thing for a while now." Evian and Soleil nodded their agreement, and I watched as Kin's world was flipped upside down for the second time.

"You might want to sit for this." Terra waited for Kin to comply, but he remained on his feet and fixed her with an impatient look. If he'd had any memory of what she could do, he might have been more careful of his face. As it was, she flashed him a raised eyebrow, and he frowned but stood strong.

"I can't remember how or why, but I know I've been

here before." Assured that Lexi was in no imminent danger of dying, Kin paced across the parlor to glance down the hall. "The kitchen is that way, and there's something odd about that fireplace." He turned to point toward the Balefire. "It all feels like a dream, or maybe I'm dreaming now."

For all her fire, Soleil carried a tender heart, and was the one to try to comfort Kin. "It's not a dream, and you're right. You've been here before." She stepped close to put a hand on his arm.

His gaze fell on Lexi again, and his face softened. "Something in me recognized something in her. I thought it was just a powerful attraction, but I have a feeling it was more. Tell me, and don't hold anything back. Whatever it is, I can take it."

Now I was starting to see why Lexi had fallen for him. Kin's willingness to stand for her made me think fate and true love's kiss were fine and epic events, but it was the day-to-day things that really counted. Yeah, I know. Hit me with the maturity stick. I'd be looking at my relationship with her father in a new light once there was time for a moment of contemplation.

Would Lexi be happy if someone dropped the witch bomb on Kin? Probably not, and call me selfish, but that was why I wasn't jumping up and volunteering to be the one lighting the fuse. Let Terra take the heat on this one. After all, they'd offered to cut me out of Lexi's life through whatever means necessary, so if this went in the toilet, I'd come out clean.

She hesitated a moment, then plunged right in. "Lexi is a witch." The bald statement rang true. Even if Kin needed a moment to comprehend the words, he could see the conviction behind them.

"A real one, not the kind from television. And I'm her faerie godmother." She let her everyday glamour slip just enough to give Kin a flash of the pink granite irises she hid from the mortal world. She could have shown him more, but freaking him out probably wasn't her intention.

He blinked twice, stared at Terra, and then shot a glance at the front door, as if he was expecting Ashton Kutcher to show up any second and declare that he'd been Punk'd, but didn't say anything.

Terra plodded on, "She's also part god. Lexi, I mean. A Daughter of Cupid, a Fate Weaver. And on top of all that, she's Keeper of the sacred Balefire flame." She pointed toward the hearth.

"Sacred flame? Is that to keep the Easter Bunny warm?" His voice was filled with sarcasm, but I detected an undercurrent of hesitation. Deep down, somewhere in his subconscious, Kin held memories of all the supernatural components of Lexi's life. Why those memories hadn't surfaced until now was on Diana Diamond's head, but I was grateful that at least one good thing might come from the mess we were all now mired in.

"No, the flame feeds the witch and the witch feeds the flame. It's a symbiotic relationship—there's more, but I'll let Lexi tell you all about it when she wakes up." Terra stopped talking and sized him up. "There's more *if* you have the...guts to stick around." She stopped short of revealing anything about Kin and Lexi's romantic history, which I thought was more to spare herself from Lexi's ire than anything else. "Decide now." It was an order.

Kin hesitated, and for a moment, the loudest sound in the room was the pop and hiss of the Balefire flame. He shook his head as if to dislodge an errant notion and shot Terra the kind of indulgent smile generally used on young children who are convinced the boogie man lives under their bed. Only this one had a little edge of *you're crazy* thrown in for good measure. It was the kind of look that would have earned him a taste of Terra's unique brand of magical discipline had he used it on her with full knowledge of her Fae heritage.

"Enough." Vaeta decided to put an end to the dithering altogether and dropped her glamour. She did a little twirl that set the dust motes around her spinning and sparkling in the light of the Balefire. She transformed into her mini form, complete with tiny faerie wings, and hovered right in front of Kin's face. "Do you believe me now?" Her voice sounded like she'd inhaled a balloon full of helium, and under normal circumstances would have made me laugh out loud.

I thought his eyes were going to bug out of his head, and his Adam's apple bobbled while he tried to swallow several times in a row. "Yep. I definitely do."

"Good," Terra said, as Vaeta reverted to regular size, "because we don't have time to ease you into things. Trust me, you'll get used to it. And faeries can't lie, so you've got no choice but to believe us."

When someone tells you they can't lie, it's generally the first thing you suspect them of doing, but Kin nodded and stepped back to flatten himself against the wall. His eyes flicked back and forth across the room while his brain worked to come to terms with what he'd just been told. When they fell on Lexi, they held both sorrow and joy.

Since he'd apparently decided to stay, Terra dismissed him and turned her attention toward me. "We have to call Clara and Margaret." Her gaze traveled my face for any trace of an argument. I gave none, even though inside I was screaming that the last people I wanted to have to deal with tonight were my mother and my aunt.

The last time I'd spoken to Clara, we'd been locked in a convergence of ill-intended spells, the result of which had cursed me to a magical prison cell and rendered her a stone statue. That was twenty-five years ago, but the joint betrayal still stung, and she hadn't made any attempt to contact me since Lexi had freed her with Cupid's arrow and a ball of flaming Balefire.

Aunt Mag had always hated me, even when I was a child. She'd made no bones about the fact that she considered me a spoiled brat, and predicted I'd use my power for nothing but nefarious purposes. Unfortunately, she was partly right on that score. The last time *we'd* met, Lexi and I had broken into her house looking for clues to the Bow of Destiny's location, and she'd made it clear that forgiveness wasn't on the table.

Nobody had bothered to ask about my intentions, even though witches just love to harp on the importance of them when spellcasting. After a while, I stopped trying to justify my actions and simply did as I pleased. It may not have been the best series of decisions to have made, but I'd had my reasons and they weren't as evil-minded as Mag wanted to believe. Truth be told, we had more in common than either of us would have liked to admit.

Terra strode across the room and pulled two medallions out of a drawer, pressing her fingers against the engravings. My mother and my aunt carried their companions, and once summoned could instantly skim to Port Harbor, giving me mere seconds to prepare myself for their arrival.

There was a murmur of voices as one of the faeries filled in the new arrivals and then, "Where is my granddaughter?"

The voice of my mother echoed through the front hall and down into the parlor, where I refused to move from my daughter's side. The concern in her tone made me shiver and brought out a feeling of jealousy I hadn't been expecting. Nor had I been expecting the sense of anticipation and hope. The dread I felt, though, was right on par. Hunching over, I held my breath.

When Clara reached the parlor and laid eyes on me, my Aunt Mag at her heels, I thought my heart might beat out of my chest or that my head might explode. She glanced between Lexi's prone form and me, as if making a difficult decision. I swallowed hard and tilted my head toward my daughter, indicating to my mother that she should tend to her first.

Clara nodded and rushed to Lexi's side. To be honest, I was grateful for the reprieve, even if she was careful to maintain some physical distance from me.

Salem bolted into the room, saw first Lexi, and then Clara. In a flurry of black fur, he transformed to his human form. "Lexi! Is she okay? What can I do? What do you need?" He turned to Mag and asked in a tone that suggested they shared a close relationship. Maybe they did, for all I knew.

"Start gathering everything with healing properties, and I'll meet you in the sanctum." She leaned down near Lexi, and ran her hands along my daughter's hairline in a supremely loving gesture, then proceeded to take stock of her condition. Mag's fingers probed Lexi's temples, and her eyes ticked back and forth beneath closed lids as though she was looking for something. When she opened them, I couldn't tell if they were filled with hope or defeat.

"She's in stasis, as far as I can tell. If that *thing* had gotten his hands on her for any longer, she'd be dead. Her pulse is strong, but the longer she stays under, the more danger she's in." Part of me preened at the thought that my spell and quick thinking might have saved Lexi's life, but if I thought my Aunt Mag was going to stroke my ego I was sorely mistaken.

"I'll be back with the most potent potion I can brew on the fly. I certainly hope Lexi has kept the sanctum well-stocked. Otherwise, you'll be taking a quick trip to the

Fringe." She shot me a scathing look, which I, with a concerted effort, largely ignored other than to nod in assent.

" I didn't have anything to do with this, I swear," I promised my mother when we were well situated in the rear corner of the backyard and therefore out of hearing range of even the faerie godmothers.

Clara's expression ran through a gamut of emotions, some I recognized—like surprise and anger—and others I couldn't put my finger on but hoped were more benevolent in nature. When she'd asked me to join her away from prying ears, part of me had wanted to run out the door and down the street as fast as my legs could carry me. But, if there's one thing you can't call me, it's a coward. "Of course you didn't," my mother finally sighed.

That threw me for a loop, but I ignored it and spat, "Well, Aunt Mag sure thought so."

"That's your problem, Sylvana," my mother said, sharply. "You are constantly assuming that you know what everyone else is thinking. Unless you've become a telepath during the last twenty-five years, maybe you should make more of an effort not to do that."

And here we went again, arguing as usual. I should have known no good would come from sticking around until Clara showed up, but I wasn't about to abandon my daughter when she needed me. I'd done that too many times. I stood, ready to stalk back into the house and chalk our conversation up to another failed attempt at reconciliation when my mother reached out and touched my arm.

"I'm sorry," she said. "As usual, that came out harsher than I intended. I'm a little nervous, if you want to know the truth. Asking for your forgiveness is something I've thought about for a very long time, and now I'm messing it all up."

My eyes widened in amazement, "What do you mean, asking for my forgiveness? I'm the one—"

"No, you're not. I mean, yes, you are, but just because you made a mistake doesn't mean I didn't make one too. More than one, truth be told. I had a lot of time to stand and think, and I realize that I failed as a mother in many respects. I should have done so many things differently, and now it's too late." A tear trickled down her face, and I could feel them welling up behind my eyes as well.

"I also had a lot of time to think," I said around the lump in my throat, "and I'm aware that I was bratty and self-absorbed. And then—" My breath hitched, "And then I went and turned you to stone! I'm so sorry, Mother." The tears flowed freely now, as memories of that day in the clearing washed over me like a downpour.

Clara wrapped her arms around me and sobbed, "I thought I'd killed you, Sylvana. My own baby girl. I thought I deserved to be turned to stone, and it didn't take me long to accept that I'd spend eternity reliving our last moments. When you came back, well, I can't tell you how much I wanted to jump up and down. And then things got all topsy-turvy. I wanted to find you, but when you didn't come to find me, I thought you must hate me even more than you did before."

"I never hated you, Mother. I love you. And I love Lexi too. We have to fix this. I want a relationship with my daughter. And, with you."

"What about your Aunt Mag?" my mother asked, a twinkle in her still-teary eyes.

"We'll see," I said and pulled her closer still.

CHAPTER

TWENTY

Two full days passed with no change in Lexi's condition, and the tension started to wear on everyone in the house. Faucets spat water or ice every time Evian got within three feet of them, Soleil started cooking and couldn't seem to stop. She baked so many loaves of bread she had to load up the van and make a trip to the homeless shelter to donate the excess.

Houseplants either shriveled or doubled in size if Terra so much as walked within three feet of them, and Vaeta set off a miniature hurricane in the mudroom that ruined the floor and took the walls down to the studs.

They say idle hands are the devil's playthings, and while I've never met the man so I can't say if it's true, I did know myself pretty well by then. Standing around waiting for Lexi to fight her way out of stasis wasn't just wearing the faeries down to the nub, it was tweaking hard on my last nerve, too.

If I didn't find something to occupy my time, I'd get cranky, then I'd make everyone around me cranky, and then there'd be trouble.

I grabbed Vaeta and tracked down Delta, who was

sleeping on the sofa in the workshop behind the Balefire. She'd heard the siren song of Lexi's distress, but had arrived too late to do anything. She'd insisted on berating herself for it even though out of the group of us, she had the least to be sorry for. Even from a close distance, we had been rendered useless, and that didn't sit well with me or the faeries.

"Wakey, wakey." I kicked the leg closest to me and then jumped back in case Delta pulled out that pig-sticker of hers and came after me.

Instead, she slitted one eye open. "You'd better have a good reason for bothering me."

"You, uh, up for a challenge?" The rhetorical question included both women. "Diana Diamond was behind this attack, and she also has something Lexi needs. I think going after it would provide some stress relief. Seems like a little breaking and entering is order. You in?"

The other eye popped open over the delightfully wicked smile spreading across Delta's face. "As long as I can break *her* if she gets in my way, I'm all over it." Graceful as a gymnast, she flipped her body from prone to standing. Privately, I had to admire the way she'd gone from relaxed sleep to full alert in a matter of seconds. "You have a plan?"

I let my eyes go hard. "We go, we find the wand, we take it. Anything comes up, we play it by ear. Diana gets in our way, and we do what we have to do."

"I kind of hope she tries something." Vaeta showed

her scary faerie face and I grinned back at her. What can I say? She was beginning to grow on me.

"Believe me, so do I. Give me ten minutes with Lexi and then meet me out front. I'll drive. I need to stop at my place and grab a few supplies." I kept a heavily warded apartment above a diner in the city.

Apparently my tone aroused Delta's suspicions. "Supplies? What kind of supplies? You're not planning on using dark magics are you? I'm working outside the parameters of my primary mission, so I'm not looking to add fuel to the fire."

Vaeta didn't seem too worked up over the possibility. She shot me a little eyebrow waggle from behind Delta's back and I sighed. "There's a difference between protective or defensive spells and dark magic, and contrary to popular opinion, I am aware of the distinction."

Mostly, though, I was aware that using dark magic would kill any chance of getting Lexi on my side, where I needed her to make my ultimate plan work. Otherwise, Diana Diamond had earned an ass whooping and I didn't much care what color magic it took to put a hurt on her. Karma had to know she was the bad guy in this scenario, so I figured it wouldn't hit me too hard.

To that end, I widened my eyes and vowed my intentions were honorable—and technically I didn't lie.

Twenty minutes later, we were loaded up and sitting outside Diana's lair. Okay, lair might not have been the appropriate word for a penthouse apartment in the arts district that had to cost her close to five figures a month in rent, but it seemed fitting to me.

With Lexi down, Diana was free to bust up soul-mates with abandon. She passed by the cloaked car on her way out to do just that, and the smarmy smile on her face put murderous thoughts in my head. I cursed the gods for my inability to engage. Alerting Diana to the fact that we knew she was the one controlling the Balmorrigan would only incite a head-on battle, and now was not the time for that. Better to keep our ears to the ground and learn as much as possible before taking the first swing—but it took every ounce of self-control I had not to pounce on her and shove a ball of black witchfire down her throat.

"First things first. We need to get past security." Which was tight, and most of the reason for the exorbitant rent in a city that wasn't known for being all that pricey. "It won't be easy since the elevator to the penthouse is only accessible with one of those key-card things."

Vaeta giggled and the sound of her mirth carried more than a hint of her power. "No need for all that, I have a better way. Follow me." She got out of the car and walked confidently around the corner of the building.

Truth be told, I'd been looking forward to the stealthy elements of the heist, but I followed her anyway.

It seemed the mad level of security didn't extend to the business side of the place, and there were plenty of shadowed areas where someone could stay hidden. A single spotlight lit the service exit and barely extended into the small lot designated for employee parking.

"Where are you?" I hissed and slid into the shadows, but Vaeta was nowhere to be seen. Flaky faerie.

A little bit of pale light reflected off the concrete wall and touched half of Delta's face, but it was enough to let me see her annoyed expression. "Amateurs," was all she said.

"Psst. Over here." Vaeta called from someplace off to our right, and we slowly picked our way through the darkness. "Get ready," was all the warning she gave before wind slashed my hair in my eyes and I felt my feet leave the ground.

Now, I've flown before. On a broomstick, and yes, I realize that's considered something of a cliché, but I had control over my flight. This was nothing like that, and it was nothing like skimming either. I'll confess to stifling a scream as I zoomed straight up into the black night. Delta let out a soft eek sound when the upward motion stopped. We shot sideways another few feet before landing behind a large potted shrub on Diana's penthouse terrace.

"Well, okay then." I patted wind-tossed hair back into place and tried to look like my stomach wasn't still down on the ground, and being lifted six floors up the side of a building by essentially nothing but air was an everyday event. The fact that my eyes were still bugged out probably meant I didn't entirely pull it off.

Delta wore her hair slicked back off sharp, predatory

features—probably for the sake of convenience. The rapid trip through the wind tunnel had whipped the normally sleek tail into a frothy, snarling puff that somehow managed to still look model-chic. We Balefires share pretty genes, so I wasn't exactly jealous; I only noted the fact because it seemed to annoy her to the point of distraction.

Flicking a finger toward her, I funneled a whisper of magic in her direction. "Extricus." The knotted mess untangled itself. "Can we please get on with it before she comes back?"

Not quite hiding a smirk, Vaeta stepped from the shadows and ran a hand through the space around the door handle. "Warded," she pronounced. "Nasty one, too."

"And that's why I planned to go in through the front door. She couldn't risk hexing any of the building staff, so the wards wouldn't have been as strong." Only an idiot would try to disarm the tangle of spells laid over this door. "This was a waste of time."

"Not entirely." Delta's sword sang against the sheath as she drew it free. "You witch types think you're the only ones with magic, but I've got a trick or two up my sleeve." Holding the weapon aloft, she said a word in a language I'd never heard before but suspected was Dwarvish. Blue light pulsed through the gleaming metal as she brought the blade down to slash through brick and concrete like the wall was made of paper.

Three quick slices opened a door in the wall to the left

of the patio slider. "Amateur move, warding the door but not the wall." Sheathing her sword, Delta squared her shoulders and stepped into Diana's apartment. Grinning, Vaeta slipped inside, and knowing I'd lost control of this whole mission, I followed suit. Hell, who was I kidding? Faeries do what they want to do, and the Fiach wouldn't pee in my ear if my brain was on fire. I'd never been in control.

But I was the only one who knew what to look for, so in my head, I danced around singing na-na-na-na-boo-boo while on the outside I kept my face serious.

"Posh." Vaeta admired the decor which, not surprisingly, ran heavily to black leather, metal, glass, and sleek, stark lines without so much as a pillow on the sofa to lend softness or a pop of color. A curtainless expanse of glass overlooked the small city of Port Harbor and framed it prettily.

"If you like the idea of living in what amounts to the biker boot of apartments, I suppose." I let her continue her tour of the space while I tried to think like Diana. Where would she hide one of her prized possessions?

"We're looking for a wand. Polished hickory, maybe eight inches long, with a bowstring-wrapped citrine point for added focus." Nodding, Delta crossed the room to scan the selection of objet d'art in a lighted wall of built-in shelving cubes.

It looked like Diana spent little time in the spotless kitchen, but Vaeta opened the nearly empty cabinets anyway. "How does the woman live like this? There's nothing here but wine glasses and paper plates." Appalled, she whipped open the refrigerator. "She doesn't even have condiments."

"She probably orders take-out. Not everyone makes a three-course meal for breakfast." I couldn't help the subtle dig. "We're not here to assess her on the Betty Crocker Scale of Housewifery. Just keep looking for the wand."

Heading deeper into the apartment, I started opening doors. The first led to what was probably meant to be a home office, but was completely devoid of furniture or personal items of any kind. The next was a guest bathroom that looked equally unused. Then I hit pay dirt and found Diana's bedroom.

This was where the woman lived, and it tickled me a little to discover she was something of a slob. Okay, that was an understatement. Expensive clothes mounded over what I assumed was a chair next to the closet, based on the size and shape of the pile. Jewelry spilled across the top of a dresser and dripped down into the open top drawer. All her shoes lay in a pile in one corner beneath a series of dents in the wall. I could picture her walking in and kicking them off without much care for where they landed or what damage the heels did when they hit.

I realized I'd been right about the take-out when I saw the stack of empty containers and the drift of crumbs across the rumpled sheets. Eww. Diana liked to eat in bed and didn't seem too concerned about sleeping on greasy linens in a pile of her own filth.

If anyone had been taking bets about her sex life, I'd put money down on her having none at all. No wonder she was so cranky all the time.

The idea of pawing through the mess sent a shiver up my spine that had more to do with the heebie-jeebifying possibility of finding a nest of maggots than Diana figuring out she'd been burgled and tracing the crime back to me.

"Did you find—" Delta poked her head into the room and abruptly lost the will to speak. "Um," was all she said before she beat a hasty retreat. I heard her tell Vaeta, "Don't go in there. Just keep searching out here. You'll thank me later."

Wimps.

Still, Delta succeeded in distracting my attention away from full-on shudder mode, which was a stroke of luck. When I turned back to survey the mess, I'd lost the sense of revulsion and gained some perspective. This was a puzzle to be solved. A messy, disgusting puzzle, mind you, but I'd always been good at seeing patterns in chaos.

Closing my eyes, I dragged in a few meditative breaths. When I opened them again, I kept them slightly unfocused—partly to keep from getting grossed out a second time, but mostly to let the sheer mountain of detritus render itself into manageable chunks. Then I stepped into her shoes.

Not literally because...yuck!

I was Diana Diamond coming home from a long day— or night—of screwing up people's lives. What did I do?

Well, if it was a good night, I danced around a little as I kicked off my shoes and on a bad one, I just winged them into the corner as hard as I could and put on—. I glanced around and my gaze fell on a pair of well-worn slippers. Bingo.

And the soft robe hanging off the doorknob. Double bingo. Jewelry hits the dresser and I'm shrugging off the day with takeout in bed.

No, that wasn't right. Diana would need to track her progress in some way. Maybe with a calendar or a list— and none of this was helping me figure out where she'd hide the wand and time was running out.

Concentrate, I told myself. *You're only seeing what's there. What's missing in this organized disorder?*

I made another circuit of the bedroom, and as I passed the open doorway leading to the master bath, it hit me. There wasn't a mirror in the place. Out of character for someone like Diana, who wore nothing but designer clothes and thousand-dollar shoes. Vain people liked looking at themselves, didn't they? So where was the mirror?

Now that I knew what I was looking for, the pattern fell into place. Framed artwork danced across the wall behind the bed. Diana's tastes ran to splotchy abstracts and even numbers. Two on the left of the headboard, two on the right. The adjacent wall carried three and three, but with one difference—a large space between the canvases. One that would be about the size of a wall mirror.

Pay dirt.

Except it wasn't quite.

I tried every revealing spell in my arsenal and when all else failed, threw a ball of witchfire. Okay, maybe I was frustrated, but the fire picked out the outline of a rectangle, which proved I was on the right track.

Stupid thing was probably keyed to her finger or voice print.

Fury bubbled up through the well of magic pooled behind my belly. I let it out in a low shriek that brought Delta and Vaeta running.

"What happened?"

Tiny tongues flickered along the wall and I gestured toward them because I didn't trust my voice for more than a short, growled description. "Invisible mirror. Hidden by magic. No key. Dead end."

Shockingly, Delta grinned. Didn't she hear what I said?

Her sword was in her hand almost before I heard the sound of it leaving the scabbard. The metal burned bright and blue and sang as she brought the tip up to slash a path through the air around the edges of the mirror. When she closed the rectangle, the flare dazzled my eyes and the popping sound pulled at my eardrums. How did I not know Delta had that kind of game?

Spots danced through my vision for a solid minute, and when they cleared, I let out a string of language not becoming a lady. Not that I considered myself in that class anyway. Lexi would have recognized the room that had essentially sucked me through the mirror. This was Diana's actual lair, the place where she could be her truest self and count her victories on the wall covered with the darkness-laced cards she'd played.

As I stepped closer for a better look, I heard a tapping sound and looked behind me to see Delta and Vaeta's anxious faces peering at me though the looking glass. Their mouths were moving, but I had no idea what they were saying, so I shook my head, and turned back toward the wall of shame.

More tapping, frantic this time, and Vaeta used her breath to create steam on the glass. Her finger traced out two words. She's coming.

Uh oh. Time to find the wand and get out.

Reluctantly, I focused on the only other two things in the room: a bare table and an old, painted cupboard with one door hanging slightly open. More tapping nudged me into yanking my sleeve down over bare skin to nudge the door open without leaving my prints behind. There wasn't time to do much more than grab the wand and skedaddle back through the mirror, but I couldn't help snagging one of the Tarot cards from the deck sitting on a shelf alone.

The mirror sucked me back through to the bedroom before I had time to worry how it might work, and Delta reversed her mojo to hide it behind me.

"Elevator's on the way up, we have to go. Now." To hurry things along, Vaeta drew a strong breeze to push us back toward the open doorway and Delta twisted around to seal it almost before we were clear. "Hold on." I heard Vaeta's tense order while I felt her hand on my arm. With both me and Delta in tow, she jumped off the roof just as the elevator doors dinged open.

Then we were falling and I forgot how to breathe.

CHAPTER
TWENTY-ONE

L EXI

My head buzzed like a mosquito on steroids.

"Where am I? We? Alexis, are you there?" No answer.

A flaccid, slanting light lit the space around me in a small enough diameter that I couldn't make out anything other than a few shadowy shapes. Nothing moved; there were no sounds other than the rasp of my breathing and the lub-lub of my heartbeat.

"Hello! Is anybody there?" Louder now, I practically screamed into the uncanny silence.

"Shut up." Alexis stepped into the light. "I'm here."

Seeing her outside my body and in solid form, it struck me how tired she looked.

"Where are we? What's the last thing you remember?" she asked.

The first question I had no answer for, but the second made me stop and think. "We were standing on the front porch. I was annoyed because you were the one who said we shouldn't try and get back together with Kin and then, there we were, about to kiss him."

Graceful, Alexis sank down to sit cross-legged on the...

well, it wasn't a floor, exactly, just a nondescript, gray surface. She yanked me down to join her, and I did, though with far less panache.

For half a minute, we simply stared at each other in silence.

"Do you think we're dead? This could be purgatory." I looked around at the dim nothingness.

Alexis took stock. "I don't feel dead, but then I've never had the experience, so I can't be certain. I've never heard of a witch version of purgatory though." She pressed the tips of her fingers to her temple. "Besides, I have a headache. Dead people probably don't get headaches, right?"

"Probably not." Now that she'd brought it up, I realized my head wasn't feeling so hot, either. The power of suggestion, maybe.

As if she heard my thought, Alexis huffed out a sigh. "When are you going to learn we're the same person? If my head hurts, you're going to have a headache. It's not rocket science, Lexi."

I hated the snide, condescending way she talked to me. "You're a jerk, you know that? A cold, heartless robot with no sentiment whatsoever. Logic isn't the answer to everything, you know. Sometimes you have to follow your heart. Let your feelings be your guide."

"Oh really? And where did that get you, Lexi Balefire? Following your heart right down the tubes is where. Nothing about this is normal."

"Pfft. Like I don't know that. Normal took a hike

around the time the Bow of Destiny dragged you into my life." Since then, it had been one strange turn after another. Sure, there had been some good mixed in with the bad, like getting Gran back, and meeting Aunt Mag. Ending a years-long feud with Serena and getting to meet Kaine.

The throbbing in my temple went up a notch when Alexis stared at me for a full minute with her worst version of the *you're an idiot* expression. I'd have slapped it off her if I wasn't nearly certain I'd feel the blow.

Except I didn't really want to hurt Alexis, and I knew she didn't want to hurt me.

"This might not be the best time and place to have an existential crisis." When she raised an eyebrow, I corrected myself. "Okay, it might not be the best place to try and solve an existing existential crisis. Let's see if we can figure out where we are and how to get out of here first." Without waiting to see if she agreed, I rose and strode out of the circle of light and into the darkness.

S YLVANA

"Nothing is working. She's slipping away— can't you feel it?" Just when I'd found my family again, it was being ripped apart. "Come on, baby. Fight. Please, you have to come back. Just come back."

I'd hoped to see a change in her condition when we returned with the wand, but if anything, she'd gone deeper into stasis, and another day passed with no change

"Kin's here." I turned to him and noticed he looked about as miserable as I felt. He had bags under his eyes and they looked hollowed out over a two-day scruff of beard. In fact, none of us looked like we'd slept or eaten in a week. Aunt Mag had her skirt on inside out. Given the garish nature of the print, it almost looked better that way. "He's waiting for you to wake up. We all are."

Not a twitch or even a flicker under her eyelids to show she'd heard me.

"Kiss her." Soleil's command seemed a little too cheery for the somber tone in the room. "Go on, Kin. Kiss her like she's Snow White and you're Prince Charming."

She glanced at the sea of raised eyebrows she'd caused and said, "What? It could work. What have we got to lose?"

"Besides my dignity?" Red-faced, Kin took a step back, then looked at Lexi and shrugged. "I wasn't all that attached to it anyway." Shoulders squared with purpose, he settled down next to her, leaned close, and laid his lips over hers.

Every other person in the room sucked in a breath.

"It's not working." Soleil stated the obvious.

"Then he must be doing it wrong. Go ahead, plant one on her, boy. Make it count. A great big smackeroo, and put some wax on it." Mag rubbed her hands together.

Despite the somber atmosphere, Vaeta let out a little snort, and Mom kicked her sister in the ankle. Glowering, Mag subsided.

Kin looked like his fondest wish would be for the floor

to open up and swallow him whole, but he bent his head and tried again.

ALEXIS

Silent, clinging to each other, eyes straining to see more than a few feet ahead, Lexi and I walked through the dismal twilight for about an hour that felt longer than forever.

"If we ever get out of this, I'm going to start carrying one of those little penlights in my pocket," I said and then I jumped at the sound of Lexi's hand slapping her forehead.

Witchlight dazzled my eyes when it flared to life in her palm. "Don't say it. I already know I'm an idiot, you don't have to tell me," she said when I opened my mouth.

"I was going to say that was good thinking, but we can go with yours if you prefer."

"Maybe you could just shut up and work with me for once." Lexi griped.

I sighed, and turned to face her, "I *have* been working with you, you've just been too angry to notice. You're the one who decided to fracture yourself, and now I've got to listen to you whine about it. And considering I'm just a part of you, all you're doing is irritating yourself."

Lexi narrowed her eyes and I thought, for a moment, that she had finally started to come to terms with the notion that we were one and the same.

"We've been here before. I recognize that shadow.

We're just going around in circles," she wailed, ignoring me completely.

Maybe it really would be better if I took over operating our body. The witch was positively daft. "Of course we've been going in circles. That's what we've been doing for months. Possibly even years."

"That's ridiculous. I didn't even know you existed. I was supposed to be a witch—I didn't ask to be part goddess. I didn't ask for you at all." And there was the rub.

"Suck it up, buttercup." I retorted. "There's nothing you can do about it. You are who you are. And all things considered, I think I've done a pretty good job of keeping you safe while you've been wallowing. What's so wrong with being part goddess anyway? It's more than insulting that you keep acting like I'm some redheaded stepchild."

Lexi's eyes widened. "That's offensive to redheads, and unnecessary. I never said there was anything *wrong* with being a half goddess. But all I wanted was my powers—I never asked to be in charge of people's fates. I don't want that level of responsibility."

I huffed a breath out through my nose. "So you'd rather just act like a spoiled brat and turn the other cheek? Guess what? You can't get out of this, and deep down you don't really want to. Otherwise, you would never have opened the door to me in the first place."

• • •

L EXI

I stomped off into the darkness, hoping I could lose Alexis somewhere along the way. Go back to how things were before. But she followed at my heels like a little yappy dog you just want to kick.

"There's no getting away from me, Lexi. And if you'd stop being so stubborn, maybe we could work together to find our way out of this mess. I do have useful skills, you know," she snapped.

"Oh yeah, such as?" I popped my hands on my hips and stared Alexis down. "Because as far as I can tell, all the magic comes from my side of the family. Without Daddy's little bow and arrow, you've got nothing."

"Is that what you think? You think the ability to bring two hearts together means nothing? That weaving the threads of fate to make the world a better place doesn't count as power? That's all on me, sweetheart. Always has been." Alexis had begun to pace while she ranted. "You wouldn't even *have* FootSwept if it weren't for me. I told you, I've always been there. This has always been your destiny. Maybe I can't shoot witchfire out of my palm all by myself, but don't you dare think for one second you'd enjoy the level of power at your disposal if it weren't for me."

Maybe she was right. Or *I* was right, whatever. But I still wasn't ready to admit it. "Just stop talking. You're making my headache worse."

"Right back at ya."

"Why don't you put some of your special powers to

good use, then, and help us find a way back home?" I demanded.

Alexis crossed her arms and stared at me, "I don't think it's going to work that way. We're going to have to go together or not at all. That's what my gut is telling me. And you know our gut is never wrong."

She had a point. I'd always trusted my intuition, particularly when it came to making matches. The pull in my belly I'd always called my Love Positioning System had never led me astray. I'd just assumed it was part of my witchy powers, but standing there staring at the goddess half of myself, I realized I didn't feel a thing. Alexis was right, I'd become so fractured I'd lost the one thing that had been a constant for as long as I could remember.

Maybe there was something to what she was saying. "Fine. Let's work together then. What did you have in mind?"

"Give me your hand," Alexis said, and grabbed it before I could comply. Our fingers entwined and we both closed our eyes and pooled our power. "Lexi, look." My goddess whispered.

When I opened my eyes, it was to find a ball of swirling witchfire in my hand. Except, this time it wasn't white or blue or even black—it was bright, shining hot pink—the same color of the symbols that floated above the heads of our potential matches.

"Holy Hecate!"

"Yeah, that's new, isn't it?" Alexis grinned like an idiot, and I returned the expression.

Our elation lasted for about thirty seconds, and when nothing happened, my good spirits deflated like a three-day-old party balloon. "Nothing's happening."

"Yes, it is. Look." The pink fire trailed off into the distance, and up ahead I could see a gilded door. It looked like the proverbial gate to Heaven, and quite frankly scared the living daylights out of me.

"I don't want to die yet."

Alexis pulled me forward anyway. "It's not that kind of door." She jiggled the handle, which looked like one of those old-fashioned cut-glass numbers, but I suspected was actually diamond from the way it sparkled and shined. The door swung open, and I could see through to the other side.

Kin was kneeling next to me where I lay on the sofa in my parlor, his lips hovering just above mine. It looked like a scene from a fairytale. I shoved forward, and whacked my already-bruised head against an invisible barrier.

"I don't think we can both go through." Alexis said. "You go. It's your life."

I wanted what was on the other side more than I'd ever wanted anything in my life. "No. I won't leave you. There's another way. It's time for this madness to end. Alexis, I love you. You're part of me and I love you." I repeated the words over and over, squeezing her hands in mine as I did, and the goddess returned the sentiment.

"I love you too, Lexi. Now, let's go home." When I walked through the door, I was finally in one piece.

• • •

SYLVANA

"Are you keeping your lips firm and moist? No one likes rubber-lipped kisses." After the second round failed to wake Lexi from her stupor, Evian jumped in with advice. "And no drooling. Shows a lack of control that could be a detriment in other areas, if you know what I mean."

Kin stood, and despite being mortified, came back with a sharp retort. "I've never had any complaints."

Their comments might have been amusing if my daughter wasn't edging closer to death with every shallow breath. "This isn't working. Now leave the poor man alone." If I had to lose my daughter, she should go out with peace and respectful dignity, not with the faerie version of the three stooges putting on a skit in the background.

We all faced off, and I could feel the level of energy in the room rising to a crescendo. Tensions had been running high for days, and if we weren't careful, we'd take the whole house down with us. Just as I was about to try to put the kibosh on things, a voice piped up from behind me.

"Hey, you guys. Want to take it down a notch?"

I spun around, and when my eyes lit on my daughter, awake and intact, they filled with tears of joy. Kin stared at her with an unfathomable expression on his face, and suddenly it was as though the room wasn't big enough to hold all of us.

There would be time for reunions later. Right now

belonged to Lexi and Kin. I pulled the rest of the entourage out of the room to give them a bit of privacy and prayed to every god and goddess I could name. *Please, give her a happy ending.* And for once, there wasn't an ounce of selfishness in my heart.

CHAPTER

TWENTY-TWO

As I walked toward Kin, I let all the pieces of me fall away. Goddess and witch and Fate Weaver shed like clothing under the hot fire of the sun warming a cold day, leaving only the woman behind. Not because they were parts of a fractured whole, but because I needed this moment to be simple and pure.

Man and woman. Leave your cosmic roles at the door.

My heart raged and my fingers tingled, but not with Balefire magic. The only power I carried in the most essential heart of me was the enormity of my love for him. A love that had nothing to do with fate, or destiny, or the kisses that sealed both.

The Bow of Destiny slipped out of my fingers to land, for the first time since I'd repaired it, solidly on the floor. My hair spilled from a ruthlessly cropped slash of pink-tipped white to curl down my back in a chestnut fall of silken glory.

Kin blinked, shook his eyes, and stared at me. Being told I was a witch, and seeing it were different things, but at the time, I didn't know he knew.

"I'm not the wicked witch, Kin, and I'm no princess, either." I was both and neither and everything in between.

I was Lexi Balefire, and for the first time in...well, ever really, I knew exactly who I was and what I wanted. Damn Diana Diamond and her interfering ways, but I was going to get my man—and then I was going to deal with her black heart.

He shook his head, but I wasn't sure he heard me.

Somewhere underneath the confusion, I saw something else. A spark of recognition, a flare of the heat we'd once shared; even if he didn't quite remember me as I was before. We had something between us now, and that would have to do.

"Lexi, I feel like...something is happening to me. Something big."

"Yes." I breathed the word on a sigh that fluttered gently into the air between us. "It is." And I closed the distance between us.

"How did—"

"Shut up." I ordered as I twined my arms around his neck and offered myself to him. Just me. Just Lexi, the woman who loved him more than life.

Full of hope, I pulled him into a kiss. For a breathless moment, he stood rigid under the assault, and I died a thousand deaths knowing all was truly lost and he didn't want me. Would never want me. Ice shivered through my veins. Not even the Balefire could warm me now.

"Lexi?" I heard him say my name, felt it against my lips like the brush of butterfly wings.

When the dregs of Diana's spell seeped out of him, it had nothing to do with the power bestowed on me by the blood of my ancestors—either side of them. Love conquers all and has its own magic. The kind stronger than anything I could conjure or cook up in a cauldron and stronger than a living gold arrow tip forged by a god.

"It's you. It's always been you." Then he was kissing me back like a man who had stumbled out of the desert to find an oasis of shining blue. He drank me in.

I tasted the unique flavor of Kin salted with the mingling of our tears and it was good.

True love's Kiss: a one time event. Nope. Not always.

Nothing born of magic would touch us again. Diana Diamond could ascend to Olympus and take up with Zeus himself and that still wouldn't give her enough oomph to shove so much as a splinter between Kin and me now.

My head was still spinning when Kin's lips finally pulled away from mine. "You really remember everything?" I asked him, even though I already knew the answer. I wanted to hear the words come out of his mouth, wanted to revel in them before I had to come back down to earth and face everyone I'd treated so abominably over the last few months.

"I remember everything. I remember you, and me, and all that us being together entails. And I'm never going to forget it again." We lost ourselves for another moment before the sounds of sniffling alerted me to the fact that we were being watched by my entire family.

I felt like Dorothy, fresh off her trip to Oz, only instead of recounting my journey, I needed to make amends. Salem and the godmothers topped the apology list, and

I'd virtually ignored Gran and Mag while I worked out my issues.

"I'm so sorry." The sorry came out muffled when I ended up in a group hug that made me feel like a quarterback in the middle of a team huddle. "I've been an absolute mess."

"It's okay." Terra said and I suddenly became angry.

"It's not okay. I appreciate your forgiveness, but it means you're still handling me with kid gloves, and I don't deserve it. Terra, when have you or any of the rest of your sisters ever let me get away with acting like a jerk? You've been holding back, and I appreciate that, but I know it cost you, so say what you need to say. I can take it."

She grimaced and then set her mouth in a determined line, "You're an adult, Lexi. I think the time for lectures has passed."

More fiery than her sister, and with good reason, Soleil might as well have sprouted devil horns on her head when her narrowed eyes zeroed in on me. "You want to hear the truth? You acted like a spoiled brat. You disrespected your godmother, and me, and my sisters, not to mention the rest of your family and friends." She had been walking toward me as she talked, and now with every word the pointed tip of her fingernail dug into my shoulder. "You should have known better, should have handled your problems like an adult if that's the way you wanted to be treated."

I'd been around the block a few times, and I recognized the signs that Soleil was about to pop. We were T-minus five seconds from steam pouring out of her ears, but I didn't have a leg to stand on and merely allowed her to berate me. Then abruptly, her kettle stopped boiling and she placed a gentle hand on my cheek, her eyes boring into mine. "But we still love you, and we understand you were hurting. Just don't shut us out next time."

"Now," she clapped her hands and I heard pans rattling in the kitchen. "You must be starving."

A great howling wind rent the air, and blew some papers off the console table in the foyer. The entire house shook, and a loud knock sounded on the door. When I answered, Delta stood on the stoop, somewhat disheveled. "I hate to break up this happy reunion, but you need to come with me."

I didn't have time to revel in the realization that I'd not only been fused together in all my frayed places, but that I also had Kin back and was surrounded by the people I loved most in the world. There was still work to be done, and I knew my reunion with Kin had resulted in a wave of love that Diana Diamond and her hideous minions must have felt.

In the most savage corners of my psyche, I hoped it burned her proverbial butt.

I glanced toward my mother, who sat near the fireplace and watched me like a hawk. An uncomfortable conversation was coming my way, but that too would have to wait.

"You're not going to drop everything and take off with that Fiach, are you?" Aunt Mag asked with an edge to her voice that let me see her concern. Worry etched a few extra fine lines into her face, and my heartbeat ratcheted up a notch. I leaned into Kin's hand, which seemed to have taken up permanent residence against the small of my back as if he was afraid that if he stopped touching me, the events of the past few hours would reverse and he'd lose me again. Needless to say, it was a sentiment I shared wholeheartedly.

"She's going to have to," Delta insisted. "We're running out of time. We got the wand, Lexi. Your mother and Vaeta and I. And now Diana knows we know she's behind the attacks."

I winged another glance at Sylvana, who held my gaze as though threatening me to blame this on her, but it was Vaeta who jumped in to exonerate her. "It's not her fault, Lexi. Maybe we shouldn't have gone off half-cocked, but you were in danger, and we thought we were doing what we had to do. I still think it was the right choice."

"So do I," Delta agreed. "She was probably going to figure it out anyway, and now we've got the wand. And, she's shown her cards, pardon the pun. She's running scared. Her offices are shut down, and her penthouse is empty. I say we go find this Fate Weaver and figure out how to mount an attack. Diana might have gone back into hiding, but that doesn't mean she's gone."

"The girl just woke up from a three-day coma," Aunt Mag griped. "Can't you see she needs to recharge?"

"Lexi will be safe, Maggie," Gran said, coming to Delta's defense. "Whoever owned that wand has done an excellent job of outsmarting his or her enemies thus far, and if there's a lead, she has to follow it. You know you'd do the same."

Aunt Mag nodded once and declined to respond, but I heard her mumble something about getting her hands on whatever cloaking spell the mysterious Fate Weaver was using. I doubted very much that Mag had any need of it, considering she'd been out of the combat magic game for decades, and that she and Gran were quite safe in the little nearby town of Harmony.

"Evian, please go let Serena know what's going on, and tell her she can bring Kaine here if she wants to. I've got a flutter in my belly, like the one I get when I'm tracking down a match, but it feels like more; like something big. I'd feel more comfortable with everyone together."

"Of course, dear." Evian squeezed me into a tight hug and planted a kiss on my forehead before she flitted out to complete my request.

"Could we?" Delta held out a motorcycle helmet.

I looked at it and then at her. "Are you kidding me? In this weather? We'll freeze to death."

"Suck it up, Balefire." Handing me back the wand and shoving the helmet into my hand, she practically dragged me out the door. I managed a single backward glance at the room full of my loved ones and hoped I'd see them again.

Okay, maybe I was being a little melodramatic.

Seated on the bike, I heard Delta's voice in my ear. "Hold on, we're going to take a shortcut." Before I had a chance to think, she'd stomped one foot down in the snow and used it as a pivot point to whip the bike around and point it in the opposite direction. The motor screamed, and I think I did, too, as the icy wind found its way inside my clothes and tried to burrow into my bones.

There was a crash of thunder, the smell of ozone, and then blessed warmth. I opened eyes I didn't remember closing and found we were speeding through the gray area between worlds.

When Delta took a shortcut, she didn't fool around. This was my second trip to the middle dimension, or whatever it was called because she never said, and the first time hadn't been a piece of cake either, but that was a long story.

Gray area aptly described not only the color, but the feeling of the landscape. Gray light slanted over everything, making trees and houses look flat and featureless. It was as if we were driving through shadows, but without darkness or light to make them stand out. The atmosphere seemed heavy, and turned the roar of the engine and the hum of the tires into buzzing echoes.

We drove for maybe two minutes before she pulled up at a crossroads, cut the motor, and dismounted.

"This is where you earn your keep." She pulled out the

Fate Weaver wand and handed it to me. In the washed out light, the faceted stone tip dulled to a charcoal-colored lump. "What are you waiting for? You're a Fate Weaver, activate the stone."

She might as well have said *dogs do cartwheels in the bathtub*. It would have made the same amount of sense to me.

And, frankly, I was getting tired of people assuming Fate Weaver blood came with some kind of secret handbook. Worse, it seemed like she knew something I didn't. Again. So, I did what any self-respecting witch would do: I tried to fake it.

"Okay." It had been only a couple of hours since I'd come out of a magical coma where I'd spent time getting my emotional poop in a group. The last thing I needed was a test of how well I'd done.

Letting my eyelids flutter closed, I concentrated on drawing magic up from where it pooled behind my belly button, and funneling it into the wand. The wooden shaft heated between slightly trembling fingers. That was a good sign, right? Delta's face, when I risked a glance, said no.

Chanting at it didn't work, either. Or blowing on it. Infusing it with balefire turned the wood dark and the stone made a crackling noise. By then, Delta was staring at me over crossed arms, and her toe tapped out her frustration on the ground.

Still holding the wand, I waved my hand at her and said, "If you have any ideas, now would be the time to trot them out. I'm standing in a puddle of suck here." The waving turned into a little angry flourish at the end. The stone hummed and flared like a beacon.

"Guess it needed the old swish and flick." Delta grasped my shoulders and turned me in a circle until the humming increased. "There, now we follow."

An hour and seven turns later, we popped out of the gray area and found ourselves on a sunny street lined with moss-draped oak trees that looked like ancient brides standing in a row. "Where are we?" I shouted over the engine's roar.

"Savannah."

"Georgia?"

Delta nodded and we followed the wand a mile or so out of town to a ramshackle house on a back road that almost blended into the trees. If not for the wand, I'm not sure we'd have noticed it. Or maybe it was the wards on the place that made our attention pass right by. As it was, Delta didn't stop.

"Where are you going? That was the place."

"I know." She slid the bike into a graceful U-turn and putted back toward town. Halfway there, she yelled for me to hang on, gave the throttle a vicious twist, and plowed us right back into the gray flatlands between realities.

Now that Delta had a lock on her quarry, the return trip went by in a blur that ended with me back in front of my house, shivering on the sidewalk. "I'll be back in an hour, two at the most. This is a job best done alone," she said when I pressed her for a reason why she hadn't just approached the Fate Weaver the first time around. "Go back inside, Lexi."

I'd have asked her who died and made her my mother, but she'd ripped the quiet to shreds and was already roaring into the void before the words could form on my lips.

TWENTY-THREE

I paced the parlor for much of the duration of Delta's absence, and the Balefire snapped, cracked, and popped along with my mood. Kaine seemed to enjoy its activity, if the giggles rising from his playpen were any indication. It seemed Kin wasn't planning on heading back to his place anytime soon, and we fell back into our old routines quickly. Even though nerves were at an all-time high, I couldn't help but take comfort in the fact that things were getting back to normal.

With all the witches, including my mother and Salem holed up in the sanctum talking shop—I was shocked to see my grandmother and mother had patched things up —and the faeries cooking an elaborate dinner in the kitchen, there wasn't much left for me to do. I wasn't yet ready to deal with Sylvana, so I tended to the baby, with pleasure, while I explained our current predicament to Kin in more detail.

"Diana got to you while you were gone on your tour, but she covered her tracks so well I had no idea she was behind the spell until it was too late. The woman came to my office and shook my hand, and I still didn't realize she was a supernatural. Neither did Flix, for that matter. She's duplicitous, and ruthless. I believed I had her number—that I had her under control. Following her around, neutralizing her cards—I thought that would keep her at bay. I should have known better."

"Lexi," Kin said gently, "You might be a Fate Weaver with magical powers and a cosmic weapon of love—but you're not all-knowing and nobody expects you to be able to foresee every detail of the future. Stop being so hard on yourself. You made a difference to those people you saved from Diana, and the countless others you've matched over the years. I'd say you're still in the black."

"Maybe," I allowed, "But I should have known she had more tricks up her sleeve than just the cards. Now, not only do I have to worry about her, but I have to worry about the Balmorrigan and they've already attacked me twice. How much longer can I keep outrunning them?"

"As long as you need to. You've got a veritable army at your disposal, Lexi. We'll win. We have to." Kin's confidence in my abilities was cute and all, but something in my gut told me the plot was about to thicken. And my gut is never wrong.

"Not only that, but little Kaine here needs help. If anything happens to me, and that Fate Weaver slips Delta again, he'll be alone, and Serena will probably go really and truly insane. I don't understand why he doesn't seem to affect you the same way he does everyone else, but most people find him completely irresistible, and his magical acumen is off the charts." I told Kin about my experience at the coffee house and the concerning result of Kaine's fate weaving that day.

His response was a grim smile and a head shake, "I certainly do find him irresistible, for the record. It just doesn't seem to result in an unshakable desire to talk gibberish the way it does the rest of you. I—" Just then, there came a knock at the door— "I think you're about to get some answers."

By the time I'd handed Kaine to Kin and made it to the foyer, all the witches and faeries in the house had begun to peek their noses out of their respective rooms. I could feel the energy of nervous anticipation. No, I'm not that intuitive, it's just that when the faeries get nervous they tend to leak magic. Vaeta's wind crossing with Soleil's fire charged the air with static electricity.

Delta stood behind two men, her hair having been whipped into something resembling a messy bird's nest, her face contorted into an irritated and impatient expression.

"This is Garrick, and this is Fritzroy, the owner of the wand we found in the Nexus. Now, can we come in? They're feeling a bit exposed out here." She stopped short of an eye-roll and only widened her eyes when she glanced sideways at her two companions.

"Of course," I ushered the three of them inside and into the parlor where everyone had gathered and made introductions.

Fritzroy and Garrick were polar opposites.

Where Fritzroy was short and stout and clean-shaven,

Garrick was lanky and thin to the extreme, with a Gandalf-worthy beard that spiraled almost to his belly button. Great, now I'd made the comparison, I'd probably end up calling him Gandalf at some point.

Fritzroy's khaki trousers and collar buttoned up to his chin screamed *uptight office manager* and not *demi-god of love*. The skin-tight jeans Garrick wore contrasted starkly with his wizard-like appearance. Both, however, seemed curious and friendly. At first.

"It's very nice to meet you, Lexi Balefire, and I'm grateful you found my favorite wand," Fritzroy said, bowing toward me slightly as though I were the Queen of England.

"We're both sincerely sorry we haven't been able to contact you before now, little sister," Garrick interjected. "We weren't sure it was safe."

Fritzroy shot his companion a scathing look, "Don't mince words, Garrick," he warned with more fire than I'd thought him capable of based solely on his appearance. "We were so concerned with protecting our own skins, we failed you in your time of greatest need. We hope you'll be able to forgive us."

I sensed that this argument was an old one, but didn't have time to try to figure out the relationship or history between the two Fate Weavers. Not when they were right to be concerned, and with Diana's minions breathing down our necks.

"What's done is done." My tone suggested the matter

was closed to discussion. "I have a lot of questions and no time for apologies."

"I agree. We can discuss it later. I believe, given the assemblage of supernaturals in this house," Fritzroy glanced around the room. "We're quite safe for the time being. It's imperative that we're all on the same page, which means we need to get down to business. Any chance you've got a pot of tea at the ready?"

He had no idea he'd pressed the right button with the faeries.

Before I could answer, rattling sounds came from the kitchen. A full service including a steaming pot of water and an array of cookies and cakes appeared on the dining room table, which had grown to a size more accommodating of such a large group. In fact, I think the entire dining room expanded by a couple of feet. I shot Terra a grateful glance, and everyone settled in with cups and saucers. I took my place at the head of the table, flanked by Gran and Aunt Mag, while Serena chose a spot next to Delta at the other end.

Settling next to Kin with Kaine in her arms, Evian conjured a set of dancing bubbles over the baby's head to keep him occupied.

The four remaining Balefire witches had never been in one room together as adults for more than a few minutes, and despite the tension rolling off each of us, a feeling that this is where we belonged settled into my gut. I wondered whether the rest of my family felt it too.

Once the chairs stopped rattling as everyone scooted

up to the table, I introduced my new family to the rest of the group. We made quite the interesting picture: four elemental faeries, three Fate Weavers, two powerful witches, Kin, and a Fiach. I had no idea where Salem had gone, but I imagined he was canvassing the neighborhood for impending threats, and the thought made me feel that much safer.

Still hungry after three days in a magical coma, I snagged a plateful of food, and waited for the idle chitchat to peter out.

"Fritzroy, Garrick," I said, "I'm sorry we dragged you out of relative safety without much warning, but we're kind of in a jam here, and we needed another Fate Weaver to help fill in the blanks."

Garrick waved away my apology, "Of course, of course. Now, Delta tells me you've come up against the Balmorrigan and survived. I'd be interested to hear what happened."

Keeping it brief, I gave him the finer points of the story, which sounded a lot less dramatic in retrospect. Fritzroy seemed to disagree. He looked at me as if I'd managed some marvelous feat, and his tone went all formal when I asked him to tell us what he knew of our most current enemy.

Someone was also going to have to tell me what happened between Sylvana and Clara to make them seem so warm toward each other, but that would have to wait. One mystery at a time.

Fritzroy drained his teacup, rested his elbows on the

table, and steepled his fingers against his chin. "It's a long story, and I'll need to start at the beginning. As far as I know, the three of us are the last of the full-blooded Fate Weavers. There may be others of lesser heritage." I heard Serena snort, but she stayed silent. "But we are a dying breed."

Swallowing a bite of sandwich, Garrick took up the story. "However, we lost contact with father a few years back." Whoops. That was sort of my fault, but we'd trot out that piece of the story later. "So we have no way of knowing if he sired more of our kind since then, but he did tell us of your birth."

The look that passed between the two men was one I couldn't quite read, but I hoped it had nothing to do with latent jealousy. The last thing I needed was more family drama.

"Garrick and I shared a mother, and also a sister. She was barely in her thirties, a mere baby when the Balmorrigan took her soul." Fritz paused, and his eyes went glassy with unshed tears.

"For goodness sake, Fritz," Garrick said, keeping his tone free of any real malice—with some effort, I surmised. "That's *our* beginning, but it's not the beginning of the story."

Giving his brother a reprieve, Garrick took over the story. "It all started when the woman you know as Diana Diamond did what no true seer should ever do—she tried to foretell her own future."

I almost choked on a bite of gherkin. "Oh, I know this

part." Taking a ride through Diana's past in vision form hadn't given me nearly enough insight, but I explained what I knew.

Garrick continued, "Unfortunately, that wasn't the only time she broke the cardinal rule. It's a rookie move, really. A mistake I have no doubt she's still making to this day. No one ever sees the good of it when they look into their own future. Best case, they spend a lifetime chasing after an idealized vision. Worst case, they see just enough to bring about their downfall."

Aunt Mag broke in to confirm Garrick's assertion by telling a story about a near-sighted young witch who saw a pimple in her future and ended up shrinking her nose to half its regular size for a month trying to avoid the blemish. The young witch probably didn't see the humor in the situation, but we all had a laugh at her expense.

Turning serious, Garrick confirmed some things I already knew. "Diana saw how she could kill the human half of her soul, and thereby ascend to the status of the gods. All she had to do was eat the darkness created by altering the course of true love."

Having watched that particular devilry firsthand, I shuddered at the memory of the seething, oil-slicked blackness sliding between Diana's lips. It was enough to make anyone's stomach turn.

"The trouble started when she also saw her plans, her hopes and dreams, her single-minded goal, ruined by a god-blooded child. One who would grow into a woman who bore the mark of Cupid and carried a wand."

Well, at least her vendetta against me wasn't entirely personal.

Taking up the narrative, Fritzroy's voice shook. "She wasn't stupid enough to take on our father, so she decided to kill all his children."

Kin called Diana a name that made Serena put her hands over little Kaine's ears.

"Why go after Kin? He's not a Fate Weaver. Why didn't she put on her big girl panties and attack me instead? She's certainly taunted me enough times and tried to ruin my life."

Aunt Mag had the answer to that question. "She hit you where she could hurt you the most in order to make you weak and easier to kill because she's too intimidated by her own vision to come at you any other way."

Garrick waved a toast point, lost control of his fingers, and launched it across the table. He was so excited, he barely noticed its loss. "I think you're right on the money because Diana never had the nerve to do her own dirty work. She never once targeted any of us directly."

I don't have the sight. Okay, that's not entirely true, I sort of do because I can occasionally see the possible futures of certain matches. It's not something I can access at will. Salem insisted I could develop more skill if I took my training seriously, blah blah blah. He was probably right, and because of those few experiences, I had an inkling of how easily Diana had been tempted.

Better to let the visions come as they chose, I decided,

than actively pursue them. Too dangerous. Too easy to fall into the wicked darkness.

While I enjoyed my little epiphany, Fritzroy reached into an inside pocket and produced an item wrapped in a white cloth covered with warding sigils. He whipped the parcel open before I got a close enough look to confirm the designs had been drawn in blood, but I'd have still bet the farm they were. When he revealed a playing card—the two of clubs, to be specific—no one seemed surprised.

"This is the card she used to pair a witch and a demon with the hope of creating an anti-Fate Weaver. It worked, and the union bore a terrifying fruit. The Balmorrigan you've been dreaming about—they're twins, a powerfully talented brother and sister whom Diana later kidnapped and raised to fulfill a single-minded goal. Killing Fate Weavers. Mostly the female ones, but she didn't take any chances with the males."

I already knew part of the story, but there was one piece that came as something of a shock. "Diana raised them?" A few pieces of the puzzle fell into place. "As tailor-made weapons." Somewhere underneath the burning desire to carve off a pound of Diana's flesh was a hint of sympathy for any children unfortunate enough to call her mother.

"That's why father continued wooing the most powerful witches he could find."

The way Garrick spoke of Cupid, calling him father in such an affectionate way, stirred up a tempest in my gut, which caught me off guard. Why on earth was I suddenly pining for a pat on the head from a fatherly figure? It couldn't be jealousy, because that would be ridiculous. And nobody uses the word woo anymore.

Looking up, I caught the expression on Aunt Mag's face and figured she wasn't any too thrilled with that word choice, either. Her mother, my great-grandmother, must have known the danger, because she'd flat out refused my father's attentions and had taken great pains to instill the same distaste in her daughters.

"It wasn't just pleasure-seeking, though that's his reputation, and it's certainly well-earned, but father was stuck with an untenable dilemma. He could stop trying to create a Fate Weaver capable of defeating Diana, and hope that by proving that part of her vision wrong, she'd assume the rest was also a tissue of fiction. Or he could play into her hands by bringing forth the chosen one: a woman who could put a stop to the whole problem. We all know which he chose."

Garrick paused to let the implication sink in.

Oh, sweet Hecate. He meant me. I'd already known, but hearing Garrick put it so baldly was a shock to the system. Not just mine, either.

"No. You will not throw Lexi to the wolves. What kind of men are you?" Kin answered his own question. "Wimps, that's what you are. Sniveling crap weasels. And you call yourselves family? You have got to be kidding me. In my family men protect—" I'm pretty sure he was about to say the word women, but then thought the better of it considering the balance of power at the table.

Still, now that he was on a roll, I had to admire the fire in Kin's eyes. He'd learned his ranting skills from me, and that made me inordinately proud. "I won't allow it. Do you hear me? This is not happening. You won't put Lexi in danger, not after what she's just been through."

I don't think I'd ever loved him more. Even if he was dead wrong.

TWENTY-FOUR

Sometimes, I envy smokers their ability to exit any uncomfortable situation with a simple phrase, and for a moment considered taking up the habit just so I'd have an excuse to spend a few quiet moments processing what I'd just learned. Instead, I claimed to be in need of a trip to the restroom and scurried upstairs to my bedroom.

Looking around, I noticed the vestiges of my time as Alexis Balefire, Demi-Goddess Extraordinaire. Several shades of red lipstick lined the top of my vanity, my pink polka-dotted beanbag chair had disappeared, and my closet leaned heavily toward all things black. I remembered, of course, procuring all of these items; I even remember relegating Salem to the dormer room, beanbag chair and all. It was a good thing I'd kept my job, because it was going to take a month's salary in lobster to satisfy Salem's ire for the way I'd treated him.

I sank down into my cushy new mattress (the old one had carried the faintest whiff of Kin's aftershave) and took a deep breath. Yes, I was glad to be whole, free from the Balmorrigan's spell, and back in my family's good graces. I was elated to see Gran and Aunt Mag after months of avoiding them, and I was over the moon about Kin. Had those been my only concerns at the moment, I'd have asked Gran to hold down the Balefire duties, transported with Kin to some remote sandy beach, and insisted neither of us put on clothes for a solid week.

But there were more pressing concerns, like taking out my arch-nemesis before her evil spawn got to me or Kaine, and then of course there was the big dark cloud that had been hovering over my head ever since Garrick and Fritzroy explained what our father had been up to for the past several centuries.

The fact that they seemed to revere him didn't surprise me; he was, after all, a god. He also acted like a misogynistic pig toward women, at least from what I'd seen during my trips to the past, but I couldn't deny that I may have been somewhat mistaken in his intentions. Maybe. A little. But did the *why* of his intentions outweigh the *how* he went about fulfilling them?

Which also meant that I might have misinterpreted my mother's intentions as well. As if summoned by my thoughts of her, I heard a soft knock on my door, and a moment later, Sylvana poked her head inside. "May I?" She asked in a small voice.

I nodded, and she came over to perch next to me at the foot of the bed. "We need to talk. Get past this rift. I...I owe you an apology. Several, in fact," she said, looking at me expectantly.

Even though I knew it was cruel, I didn't say anything and allowed her to sweat it out. "Your father isn't the villain you want to think he is. Your grandmother wouldn't have approved of any man I brought home, and I'm sure Grandma Tempest had her reasons as well. Cupid didn't always come across as a nice guy, but that didn't mean his heart wasn't in the right place. A lot of what we just heard was news to me as well, and it was quite illuminating."

"You're still just trying to get me to help you find him. And I'm not sure if I'm ready for another family reunion. I'm also not sure how I feel about you. Kin says you saved him when the riders came. That you put his safety ahead of everything else." I looked my mother square in the eyes so she would know just how serious I was. "Did you do it just to make up for nearly letting him die before?"

She sighed. "I'm not perfect, Lexi. Not by a mile. And you're right, choosing the bow over him was not the right choice. Your father would be ashamed of me. I'm ashamed of myself. I knew you'd save him, and it would work out in the end. But it was selfish, and I've spent enough time being selfish. It was the second time I didn't take your well-being into account, and considering I had twenty-five years to mourn the first time, you'd think I'd have learned my lesson."

My mother's words struck a chord. How many times had I tried to mend my halves together? First, in the woods on the way to Shadow Hold where the Bow of Destiny had been kept. That had been too simple; an acceptance of what I considered my split personality, and easily forgotten the next time the question of exactly who and what I was had come up.

Then, again, when I repaired the bow and it became a part of me. The alien presence of a sentient weapon had me second-guessing myself, and I let the uncertainty pull me into its undertow. That was nothing compared to my reaction to Kin's absence in my life, which, thankfully, had finally helped me come to terms with what it meant to be a Fate Weaver. But just because it had worked out for the best didn't mean I was proud of my actions.

Tears shimmered in eyes so like my own that looking at my mother was like looking in a mirror. She'd gone to prison when she wasn't much older than I was now. Had I made the best decisions since major life events kept coming up? Probably not, and I kept expecting her to have more experience as a mother. How fair was that?

Would it be fun to spend the rest of my life trying to live down my choices? Again, probably not. My family had forgiven me without even requiring an apology. They should have been ashamed of me for my treatment of my mother, and it was time for me to let go of yet another emotional albatross, and just forgive her and move on.

"I understand." I stated simply, noting the look of surprise on Sylvana's face. "Nobody's perfect. Not me, not you, not Gran. Not even Aunt Mag," I added wryly. "But don't tell her I said that. She'd probably shrink all my underwear or something equally annoying."

We exchanged a look and burst out laughing. Every time I'd wiped the tears from my eyes, Sylvana's lip would twitch and it would set me off again. When we were finally able to control ourselves, my mother wrapped her arms around me in a hug so fierce it caught me completely by surprise. I blinked back tears that had nothing to do with laughter, and clung to her like a life raft.

"From now on, we behave like a team. Understood?" She spoke with the tone of a mother, and it almost made me start back in with the hysterics.

"Understood. And Mom?"

"Yes, Lexi?"

"I kind of stole the ritual tools you used to keep in the closet."

"That's okay. I stole them from Aunt Mag."

TWENTY-FIVE

Gran gave me a nod and a grin when we returned to the table and the discussion of just how bad Diana Diamond wanted to be. While I'd been upstairs with my mother, the faeries and witches had taken the opportunity to fill in a few more details from our history, including my embarrassing trip to the weird side of my personality.

Standing now, and pontificating in somewhat florid tones, Fritzroy lectured. "Love makes the world go around. It's not just an old standby, but an utter truth. If she has her way, Diana's meddling with dark fates would bring about the end of love in the world, and that's only the beginning."

I had to give him credit for passionate speaking.

"Oh no, if that horrid demi-god succeeds in opening the gate to Olympus, she could rip apart the veil between all the worlds." His voice fell to just above a whisper. "A void that might open up and swallow us whole."

Fritzroy paused, and I was grateful he stopped talking for a moment so I could get a handle on the implications. He'd said would and could and might, and I had a feeling he was one of those who always expected the worst-case scenario. With half his face covered in beard, Garrick's expression offered no enlightenment, either.

Before I had a chance to ask Fritz to define any other possible outcomes, the table erupted into chaos, and I let the noise reach a crescendo while I looked to see who was talking and who stayed silent.

Serena, Evian, and Kaine were no longer present, so I assumed they'd gone to the faerie's quarters to get the baby down for a nap. Terra and Soleil argued against Diana having the power to end the world. Kin, Gran, and Aunt Mag cursed my father's name for intentionally dropping this weight on my shoulders. My mother pressed her lips together during the Cupid-bashing, but was vocal enough about not wanting me to be in danger.

Vaeta, as per usual, watched everyone, but said little.

Eventually, Garrick had had enough. "Hush, all of you."

Their concern warmed my soul, but I needed to think. Silence fell, but I could literally see steam pouring out of Soleil's ears from the effort of keeping her lips zipped.

"You should be flattered that Cupid realized he could provide the world its best chance by getting on the good side of a Balefire witch. Unfortunately, none of your ancestors wanted anything to do with him." Garrick hit that nail squarely on the head. Thanks to my little jaunt through time, I'd seen exactly what my great grandmother thought of my father. If witches were buried instead of burned on a pyre, she'd be spinning in her grave right about then.

"I'm guessing it was his vanity that turned them off. Father never bothered wasting time on humility. I think it galled him a little to produce son after son when he needed daughters."

Gran and Mag exchanged a glance, one it seemed held an entire silent conversation, and then Gran spoke. "Our mother might have been somewhat short-sighted, but she did what she thought she had to do to protect our family line. It may be flattering, in a somewhat condescending way, but did it ever occur to Cupid that putting a Balefire witch in danger also put the fate of *all* witches on the line? Taking liberties with the fire keeper's life—well, that was probably far too risky for a woman and a mother like Tempest."

Is it okay to think your father might just be a total jackass?

Pouring out what he thought was the last of the tea, Fritz cocked an eyebrow at the pot when it refilled in his hand, and I knew Evian, wherever she was in the house, was still tuned into the conversation. He dosed his cup liberally with sugar and milk, then took a big sip while Garrick continued.

"We certainly don't blame Tempest for feeling the way she did. While father focused his efforts on creating a daughter powerful enough to take on the scourge, those of us who were old enough to understand the situation knew we had to do something. Some of our half-brothers went out into the world to test the boundaries of our heritage." Garrick's face went about half a shade pinker. Only someone watching closely would have seen it.

"What does that even mean?" Testing the boundaries of their heritage? I didn't get it.

Aunt Mag did, though. "It means they romanced a few witches in case a second-generation Fate Weaver might prove equal to the task."

Garrick flushed again while his brother gazed so deeply into his cup I wondered if he was trying to read the tea leaves. I couldn't begin to work up a mental image of Fritz bird-dogging the babes, and that was probably a blessing. Unless someone had perfected brain bleach, I'd rather not put anything else in my head that, once seen, could not be unseen.

No one said anything for a full minute until Garrick cleared his throat and went on with the story.

"Diana's dark power continued to grow, and because of her blood connections, father could not terminate her without repercussions. There was, however, nothing to stop anyone else from acting. When a member of the Inter-Magical Alliance approached with an alternative, father decided if he couldn't dispatch her completely, we'd just have to settle for neutralizing the threat."

Vaeta's head snapped up at the mention of the Alliance and she threw me a look before interrupting, "Which member?"

"A demon named Rhys." Fritzroy replied.

Vaeta and I exchanged a meaningful glance, but let him continue without explaining.

"Rhys offered up the location of a little-used Nexus leading to the underworld. Of course, in those days, this area was nothing more than a few scattered settlements. This happened in the 1770s, not too long after the Balefires relocated from Ireland. Father approached Tempest and begged for assistance, but at first, she demurred." He might be my half-brother, but after giving me the side-eye, it looked like old Fritz could be a bit of a snot.

Assistance. Who was he kidding? My father hit on my great grandmother like a hammer on a nail. While she was married and carrying Aunt Mag. Nothing like slapping a little whitewash on a broken fence and calling it new.

"Eventually, she agreed to forge us a cage made of iron and magic and living gold, but on one condition. Father had to promise to leave the Balefire women out of his romantic plans—which he did, for a time, but I guess you already knew that."

Five or six sarcastic answers popped into my head, and while I set about choosing one, Garrick picked up the story. From the way Fritzroy jumped and winced, I suspected our brother delivered a not-so subtle kick under the table.

"We lured Diana to the Nexus and trapped her in the unbreakable cage."

We all waited for him to tell us how, but it seemed that information would not be forthcoming.

"Anyway, things were quiet for a time, and for some

reason, even the twins kept their distance. But then the city began to grow up around the Nexus, and people started getting too close. The legend of the Darkest Heart was born. Diana seized the opportunity, summoned her minions, and lured two of our brethren to their deaths."

I held up a hand to halt the explanation. "Beatrice and Reginald, I presume?"

"Yes." Fritzroy frowned, but confirmed.

Months before, Mag had given me a ring that allowed me to go back in time. I'd seen many things I never should have had the opportunity to witness, including the events that had orphaned me. During the altercation between my mother, my grandmother, and my father, Gran had thrown Cupid's failure to protect his kin right in his smug face. Given what I'd just learned, it might have been somewhat harsh, but I wasn't sure if she had known the whole story at the time. Even if she did, there was no way I was going to say that to Clara Balefire.

"We realized we needed to close off the Nexus because it wasn't enough that Diana couldn't get out. We had to make sure nobody else could get in. That's when I lost my wand." Fritzroy squirmed uncomfortably in his seat, and glanced at his brother, who gave a subtle head shake.

What was that all about? Maybe Diana scared the wand off of him.

"The portal worked until—" Garrick trailed off.

"Until we"—I indicated myself and my godmothers—"came along and undid all your hard work. We didn't plan to let Diana out, but it happened, and there's no time to debate or disparage ourselves for the mistake. All we can do now is clean up our mess, starting with the Balmorrigan."

Garrick cleared his throat. "Well, we should be able to kill them by regular means. I would assume, as you are in possession of the Bow of Destiny, you have some weapons training. Their horses are fast, the scythe cuts the soul from the body so it can be trapped by the lantern, but they're flesh and bone, just like us."

Ignoring the question about weapons training because I didn't want to admit my best weapons were people, I asked, "How did you get past them to trap Diana the first time, and why didn't the twins come after me while I was magic-less?" When both men seemed confused, I had to explain how I'd come into my power rather late life. Almost too late, actually. When I finished, I repeated the question and waited for Garrick to explain.

"If I had to guess, I'd put it down to you being under your godmother's protection, but going radio silent for long periods of time is part of their pattern, from what I understand."

The word pattern struck a chord and I remembered what Carl had said about the Balmorrigan disappearing and then reappearing throughout history. Something niggled at the back of my mind, and I searched for some fragment of information that might make all the pieces fall into place, but came up empty-handed.

"As for Diana, putting her in a cell took a great deal of magical cooperation. And, of course, we had Father on our side." His voice dropped lower. "She fears him more than she fears a female Fate Weaver."

Now, that I could believe. She'd never shown me an ounce of fear, at least not in person, and that made me wonder if my brothers had the right of it.

"This is all very interesting." Now that it seemed the men were winding down with their story, Terra finally spoke. "But what is it you think Lexi is supposed to do? If I've heard you correctly, you've said Diana believes a female Fate Weaver will be her downfall, yet you've never said how she's supposed to make it happen."

"I say we mount up and go take the—" Vaeta jumped when Evian jabbed an elbow in her side.

"Watch your language in front of the baby." On any other day, those might have been fighting words.

Instead, Vaeta merely shot her sister a sideways look and continued, "—take care of the problem."

"A slipshod plan will never work." Fritz lectured. "And I suspect we don't have the luxury of time on our side. She's had three days unchecked by Lexi to get closer to her goal."

Scanning his face for signs of censure, I found none, but for all I knew, Fritzroy was a consummate actor. "About that. Why doesn't she just leave Port Harbor? She must know I'm tied to the Balefire enough to keep me from traveling much. She could go anywhere, wait for me to have to leave, and fling her cards every which way."

"I have a theory on that." I'd forgotten Delta was still there when she piped up from the other end of the table.

She proceeded to lay out a Harry Potteresque theory about how Diana was tied to me because she'd used one of her cards on Kin. A cardinal mistake she might not even realize she'd made. "Or, she's just arrogant enough to want to shove her victory in your face."

While I contemplated whether I was Harry or Voldemort in her scenario, Fritz speculated. "You said she's skipped town, so your theory only holds water if she's still in the area. Either way, it seems the ball is in her court."

"So what are you saying? That all we can do now is prepare and wait, like ducks in a row? Fabulous." I tend to get snarky when someone tries to put me on the sidelines.

"You're putting words in his mouth, Lexi." Gently, Garrick chided me. "Diana won't fall for the same tactics a second time, so erecting a new prison would be a fool's errand. Even if we had the resources, we'd need help, and since my brother and I've been in...seclusion," he was going to say hiding, but opted for a more manly sounding word, I was certain, "we've lost contact with the Alliance. It would take too long to reestablish our good standing, even if we knew how to locate the demon Rhys." Again the shared glance between the two brothers.

I caught Vaeta's eye, but she shook her head, so I didn't mention Rhys was sort of on our friends-and-family list. He'd also been on another one of her lists lately, though I knew if he was needed, she wouldn't hesitate to call on him.

Thankfully, Serena interrupted that thought when she

stomped back into the dining room with Kaine in her arms. I could tell she hadn't had much rest lately based on the bags underneath her eyes, and she looked like she was about to burst into tears. Instead, she just plain burst, "I'm really happy you're all enjoying your Earl Gray and everything, but what about me? What about Kaine? You might not be defenseless, but he sure is."

"I'm sorry, Serena, you're right." She was, and even if she hadn't been, I wasn't about to cross a cranky, sleep-deprived single mother.

I told my half-brothers all about Kaine's unusual birth and his extreme effect on just about everyone he met. "Is that normal for a Fate Weaver baby or did we mess him up during the birthing ritual?"

I'd been hoping for reassurance, but none was forth-coming. Garrick scratched his chin and Fritzroy feigned sudden interest in the drapes while I exchanged worried looks with Serena.

"We did the best we could under trying circum-stances," Clara reminded me, and I felt a twinge of guilt at dragging the Fate Weavers into such a large group. My family was a lot to take all at once.

"An unprecedented birth, so I can't say for certain if there were other choices to be made, but surely it can't be as bad as all that." Garrick wasn't quite stupid enough to say we women were overestimating the situation, but he didn't need to because his tone said it for him. "All babies are charismatic."

Giving the male Fate Weaver an arch look on her way

by, Serena retrieved the baby from Evian in the faerie wing of the house. I couldn't keep the smirk off my face when she deposited the baby in Garrick's arms and Kaine's unique brand of magic went to work.

Hearing Fritzroy singing the witch equivalent of the Alphabet song in a high-pitched tone was fun, but not half as much as watching the little bugger wrap Garrick—and that long beard—around his little finger. Or in the beard's case, his whole hand.

The kicker came when Kaine screwed up his little face and filled his diaper with what Fritzroy described as a charming mess. With the lesson sufficiently driven home, Serena gently pried Kaine away and waited for the men's sanity to return.

"Still think we're exaggerating?" Garrick watched Evian's retreating back as she carried the baby away to change him, and Vaeta whirled a finger to freshen the air. Repeated contact had let us develop enough immunity to keep from spending hours besotted by the baby's face, but I still fought the urge to kiss his little cheeks every time I laid eyes on him. "Or do you think he doesn't need your help?"

Pink-faced with chagrin, Garrick allowed the situation might be a little more serious than he'd thought.

"Oh, I think we got the point, and help him we will. We're family, after all," Fritzroy said gently. For a few moments, I'd managed to forget these were my half-brothers and Kaine's uncles. Suddenly, the term Fate Weaver took on a new aspect. Should I have hugged them hello? What was the protocol when meeting long-lost family you never knew you had?

Awkward!

"In the meantime," Garrick approached the fireplace. "It's been years since we've attended Beltane." He held his hands out toward the warmth of the crackling balefire. "Warms the heart, and feeds the soul." He was a witch, after all.

While Garrick communed with the fire, Fritzroy got down to business.

TWENTY-SIX

Hours had passed while we drank tea and talked, and night falls early in the wintry northeast. What's more, days had passed while I was incapacitated and unable to counter Diana's match un-making. We might not have a plan, but at least I could go out and, if she was around, buy us some time.

Or maybe I just wanted to show the puffed up, evil-queen wannabe that she hadn't beaten me. Either way, I pushed back from the table and went upstairs to change into an outfit that made a statement—something along the lines of, *come at me, Diana. I dare you.*

The unrelieved black I'd worn as Alexis would work just fine for issuing a challenge, but I wanted to feel comfortable in my own skin, so I dug through the closet to unearth a cable knit sweater in white. Kin walked in just as I yanked on a red boot with a line of buckles running all the way up to the calf-high top, and the only thing I wanted to do was let him peel it right back off along with everything else.

"You're not going alone."

I loved him. From the fire that kindled behind his eyes

when he figured out what I was planning, to the feet planted so his body blocked the door. I loved him.

But he would not keep me from my work and I wouldn't put him in danger, so we were at an impasse. Or about to have our first fight and in less than twenty-four hours since getting back together.

"You'd be a dangerous distraction. I'll be safer if you stay here."

Arms coming up to cross over his chest, he repeated, "You're not going alone. It doesn't have to be me, but you're taking someone or you're not going."

Despite there being only one person in my skin, I had to bite down on an Alexis-worthy retort.

"Is Delta still downstairs?"

If it came down to the physical, she'd be my best ally in a fight. Lightning fast, deadly with her weapon—of all the people in my life, she was the one I considered indestructible. Kin might as well have saved his bravado for another time, because when I hit the bottom of the stairs, there was an entourage at the ready, and they were all packing magical heat. Even Aunt Mag, bundled up in a vintage polyester snowmobile suit that made her look like a toddler, had her fierce face on. Diana would have to be unbelievably stupid to think she could take us all on and walk away unscathed.

Notably absent from the outing were Garrick and Fritzroy. According to Terra, the two men were in the sanctum "doing research" (her air quotes, not mine) to see if there was something they could do to tone down Kaine's effect on the unwary.

"You know it lessens the impact of shoving my fearless lack of deadness in Diana's face if I'm surrounded by a posse, right?" I selected a puffy white jacket with fake-fur trim on the hood from the coat closet and resigned myself to the inevitable. It was easier to let them all come along than it was to deal with the flack if I ditched them.

Still, it put a whole new spin on the concept of girl's night out.

Spinning back at the door, I grabbed Kin and soundly kissed him just because I could.

"Will you wait for me? We have some catching up to do."

He returned the favor, left me breathless and wanting, and then whispered an answer in my ear that made my face flame along with a few other parts of me.

Diana never showed her face, and neither did her minions, but two of my arrows unlocked hearts while my companions discussed all the things they'd do to her if she did. My personal favorite came from Gran, because the mental image could not be beat.

"I'll curse her so hard her boobs will wrap twice around her neck and still drag on the ground."

Laughing in the face of danger does great things for the body. It's impossible to remain tense while doubled over and wheezing. Plus, if the Balmorrigan were skulking around, they'd be able to go home and tell her we weren't running scared.

"Remind me to stay on your good side. I'd rather let age and gravity run their course if it's all the same to you." I scanned the area one last time for symbols and, seeing none, directed the troops back home.

I made it up all of three stairs before Fritzroy called my name.

"Can it wait?" I gazed longingly toward the top of the staircase, pictured Kin in my bed, gloriously naked, and shivered. "It's been a long day."

The man tsked at me. Who does that to another adult?

"You did indicate the situation with Kaine was of the utmost importance, did you not?"

Of course I had, so I sighed and followed him into the sanctum behind the fireplace. During my time as Alexis, I had avoided going in there, and now that I was my whole self again, it felt like returning home after a long absence. The sanctum, built by my grandmother Tempest, had been hidden until I gained my powers. When I'd found it, all those long months ago, I'd been in awe of the huge casting circle inlaid with what I now knew to be living gold—the same material used to create the Bow of Destiny.

Above the dais rested a domed glass roof encased in an elaborate wrought iron frame. Three stories of shelving lined the walls, and at night, you could climb up a complicated ladder system and gaze at all the stars in the sky surrounded by the musty scent of thousands of old books. Since my Awakening, the space had reconfigured itself to my preferences, with sections suitable for alchemy, meditation, and research. In my absence, it appeared to have become somewhat disheveled, and it seemed as though the coven-worth of witches currently taking up shop within it hadn't helped matters much.

When this was over, I was looking at two days' worth of cleaning and reorganizing, since half the contents of my bookshelves had been emptied to form piles on the floor.

"What are we doing? Recreating Stonehenge out of books?" I asked

My little joke teased a grin out of Garrick. "I think we found something," he said.

"You did? You mean this kind of thing has happened before?" Had it happened to me? No, I didn't think so. The faeries wouldn't have seemed so surprised by Kaine if his behavior was similar to mine as a baby.

Round, wire-rimmed spectacles perched low on Garrick's somewhat long nose as he peered over them, and somehow, I knew I'd failed to live up to his expectations. Again. Seemed like a pattern.

"Not exactly. Such a pity we were dragged out of the house without ceremony. Your book collection is lacking in the areas of inter-breeding, specifically among deities."

Considering the hours I'd spent futilely scouring the musty old tomes for useful information about my own abilities, I couldn't even argue the point. Besides, I didn't want to argue, I wanted to go upstairs and finish making up with my boyfriend.

Maybe that's why I was a little short with the brothers. "Look, until just after Beltane, I had no idea there was such a thing as a Fate Weaver, let alone that I was one. The only people left in the world who could fill in the gaps of my knowledge are the two of you, and we all know where you've been all my life. So if I didn't pick up the nuances by osmosis, you'll just have to forgive me for not being as nifty as you'd like me to be."

That shut them up, but then I felt bad. "Look, just tell me what I need to do to help Kaine, and I'll do it. Gladly."

My sincerity diffused a situation well on its way to becoming a family squabble.

"We found this balancing spell," Fritzroy brandished a book that just happened to be my family grimoire; the one book in the sanctum he should have asked my permission before opening. I had to bite down on my tongue to keep from saying so. "It's meant to—"

"I know the spell." I'd used it to level out a few magical bumps in the early days of gaining my powers. "It's self-oriented, which means it can only be performed by a witch who has gained his or her majority. Even if Kaine's already exhibiting powers, he's too young to speak the spell."

"If you'd let me—" Fritzroy's mouth snapped shut when Garrick jabbed an elbow in his side. He winced and then continued in a less strident manner. "We think we can adapt it into a charm. I hear your grandmother has a knack for crafting them. Is it a talent she passed on to you, by any chance?"

I allowed I could probably get the job done, and if not, Gran would be only too happy to help. "How do we go about adapting the spell?" If Salem were here, he'd be grumbling about my lack of focus on basic spellcasting, but I'd come late to the magical party, and he'd never offered to teach me about going off-book with spells. A stickler for protocol, was my familiar.

"It's a simple matter, really. Shouldn't take more than a jiffy once we have a suitable item of focus. The child is too young for jewelry unless you think his mother would allow us to pierce—" I held up a hand to stop Garrick right there.

"No."

"Okay, then a toy perhaps. Something he'd carry with him at all times."

I had a mental image of my nephew carrying a teddy bear to high school, and shook my head. We wanted to protect Kaine, not set him up for the sort of ridicule that would scar him for life. My fingers fiddled with the row of buttons on the sleeve of my sweater, and that was what gave me the perfect idea.

"Wait right here." Leaving them staring after me, I went to retrieve a glass canning jar filled with buttons in all sizes, shapes, and colors. "Couldn't we use a handful of these? Then Serena can sew them into his clothes."

Even Fritzroy had to admit the buttons were a stroke of genius.

Ten minutes later, a pile of buttons occupied the center of the casting circle, and the ritual candles flickered merrily at the four corners. It was time to cast the spell.

Except for one minor hitch—my Fate Weaver brothers

pulled out their fancy wands, and all I had was the one I'd borrowed from Gran.

"You can't use that thing." Substitute piece of poo for the word *thing*, and you'll have an idea how much revulsion old Fritz aimed at me.

"What?" I held up the polished wood. "It's not as fancy as yours, but it will get the job done."

"Where's your Fate Weaver wand? You can't cast a spell meant for a Fate Weaver with that thing." There was that tone again. Fritzroy was bucking for the position of my least-liked brother. "Don't tell me you don't have one. You're supposed to be powerful enough to take on Diana and you don't even have the proper wand?"

Calming breaths, Lexi. In through the nose, out through the mouth. He lost his sister, just remember he's hurting.

"Clearly not, and if it's something I can only get from our father, then the chances of me ever having one are smaller than...well, they're small." At the last moment, I figured a comparison to his anatomy would be unkind.

"Wands are witch tools, our father is not a witch."

What was it with Cupid anyway? I'd never met the man, or god I guess, but I was beginning to wonder what everyone saw in him. I wanted to ask why, if I was the best hope for saving the world from Diana Diamond, our father had walked away from me without a backwards glance. But Fritzroy wouldn't have an answer to the question.

No, that wasn't entirely true, Fritzroy was the type to

have an answer for everything, but it wouldn't be the right answer, it would only be the one that pissed me off.

Garrick shot his brother a dirty look. "Your mother would need to complete a ritual to create your wand."

Seemed simple enough, so why was he looking at me like this was bad news? "Okay, I don't see a problem with that. Do I need to call her now, or can she come back in the morning?"

"Lexi, it's blood magic." Again with the weird tone.

And again, I wasn't seeing the problem, but then, I hadn't done a lot of blood magic, so maybe I was missing some key piece of the puzzle.

"What am I missing? You both have one, right? So your mother did the ritual at least twice. Sylvana will do what she needs to do." Being certain of that gave me a case of the warm fuzzies, but Garrick just stared at me like I'd said something stupid. I knew that look. It was the same one I got from Salem when I didn't know some nuance of magic.

"We're in the waning phase of the moon."

Like that explained everything.

Sighing, Garrick elaborated. "Blood magic should always be done under a full or at least a waxing moon or it costs the spell caster more power and strength. It would take an inordinately strong witch to complete the ritual during this moon phase."

If that was all, my brothers were in for a surprise. Balefire witches kick butt.

Grinning, I asked, "How long do you need to get everything ready? I can have her here in half an hour."

"No. No need to call tonight. It will take a day to assemble the ingredients for the spell, and we need to charge the wand-stone under running water for a full twenty-four hours. You do have citrine points of a suitable size, right?"

The waning moon rode high enough to shine down through the glass skylight before we had assembled all the necessary items. "Are you okay to bunk in here for the night? We're a little short on beds at the moment."

With a smile, Garrick pointed a finger at one of the sofas, and converted it into a nice, four-poster bed complete with privacy curtains. It was a sweet piece of magic. "We'll be fine, and thank you for your hospitality."

I left them to it, and finally made my way upstairs to get reacquainted with Kin. Naked-style.

TWENTY-SEVEN

During the time it took for my new wand to be assembled and properly charged, I fought the urge to return to the streets and simply take Diana out once and for all. I'd started to wonder if killing her would also neutralize the twins, or maybe somehow weaken them enough to minimize the threat they posed to me and the rest of the remaining Fate Weavers.

Salem deigned to speak to me long enough to tell me that was a stupid idea, and remind me that he was on his ninth and final life, and if I happened to die during the battle he'd also be headed straight for kitty heaven. Or, wherever it was familiars go to meet their maker. I'd heard his diatribe before, and I let him know in no uncertain terms that it was beginning to lose its effectiveness. After all, if I were dead, and he as well, there wasn't much either of us could do to retaliate against the other.

Not that I had any intention of dying, mind you, but I did heed Salem's advice and decided to wait until I had all possible weapons at my disposal. And that meant I had to endure long enough for my mother to complete the ritual for my Fate Weaver wand.

With two rituals to complete including the one for Kaine's balancing, the sanctum was packed with witches and faeries. Evian stood by Serena's side while she completed the relatively simple task of charming the jar full of buttons that she'd later sew into all his clothes. As she spoke the words, I remembered my last experience with the same spell.

Serena held Kaine in her arms, stroking his cheeks while she chanted,

> *You have Seen*
> *And now you know*
> *Where the Balefire burns*
> *Your powers grow*
>
> *You listened well*
> *And braved the flame*
> *But still must work*
> *To earn your name*
>
> *When at last*
> *You know your way*
> *This spell you cast*
> *Shall fade away*
>
> *If balance be*
> *Your heart's desire*
> *Then speak your wish*
> *Unto the fire*

Kaine couldn't speak his own wish, but after mouthing along to the words I murmured my own into the flame. I'd found balance, finally, and no longer needed the assistance of a spell to dull my powers. With a silent whoosh, I felt the vestiges of it trickle away, leaving me feeling fresh and clean and completely in control. Just the way I liked it.

Serena spoke for her son, and for a moment the buttons glowed with magic before returning to their former appearance. Whatever Fritzroy and Garrick had done to alter the spell seemed to work, and the overwhelming charisma Kaine possessed lowered a few notches until he felt more like a regular baby. An inordinately adorable, and still quite compelling baby, for sure, but I doubted he'd be able to affect anyone like he'd affected Katie in the coffeehouse.

"Will he still be able to weave fates in this state?" I asked. It seemed unfair to take away all of his abilities without giving him a choice in the matter, even if it was the right decision for his and Serena's safety.

Garrick's smiling face turned from Kaine to me, "He still possesses power, yes. Just to a lesser degree. It should take the edge off and allow Serena to live a relatively normal life until he's old enough to make informed decisions. And I promise we won't disappear again. We'll assist you both to the best of our abilities." Garrick turned to his brother, who nodded in agreement.

"Now, for your wand." Fritzroy announced. "We'll

need everyone except Lexi and Sylvana to clear out for this one."

My entourage filed out of the sanctum, leaving the four of us to complete the process of making me an official Fate Weaver wand of my very own.

"Lexi, the bowstring?"

Garrick held out a hand, and I pulled the bow from my flesh and into its solid form. "If I give you the string, I won't be able to shoot." The thought hadn't occurred to me before that very second.

"No worries," He replied, "Just give it a tug, you'll see."

I did as instructed, and pulled on one end of the string. A low keening noise assaulted my ears, but the string turned all glowy and grew to an appropriate length before snapping in half and reattaching itself to the bow. The piece I held in my hand was dull and nicked in a few places, evidence of the work I'd done since acquiring it.

"This will work, right? It's not bright and shiny anymore."

Garrick nodded, "There's powerful magic in that piece of string now, and it's only going to make your wand that much stronger. Sylvana, it's your job to bind the citrine. Your godmother fetched us the perfect length of a willow branch from the backyard. Willow signifies intuition and femininity, and of course citrine is—"

"An element of power." Sylvana cut in impatiently, "We are all witches here, and we do know the basic properties. It's the perfect combination, and the bowstring will act as a conduit. Let's not waste any more time."

With that, she ran a fingernail down the middle of her right palm, drawing a line of glistening blood to bind the spell. A few chanted phrases later, and the wand fused together with a somewhat anticlimactic click. My mother's face paled, and for a moment she looked shaky on her feet, but in typical Balefire fashion she composed herself almost immediately.

I hadn't been lying when I said we were powerful witches, and I think even Garrick and Fritzroy were surprised by her hardy constitution.

Sylvana handed the wand to me, and I gave it a little wiggle just to make sure it worked. Sparks flew from the end of it, erupting into a shower of fireworks, and that's when the climax came.

Raw power surged from within me, making my teeth chatter and my bones vibrate. The undulating wave arced outward, and then reverberated off itself as a pulse of dark magic pushed back against my light. I recognized Diana's essence, and felt certain she'd been touched by my own.

I was also certain that she was furious, and that it wouldn't be long before she'd send the Balmorrigan to retaliate.

Call me Kreskin, because in under an hour my prediction came to pass.

Imagine you're standing in the middle of several concerts at once—orchestra, heavy metal, show tunes, rock, and country—all playing different songs at top volume. I swear I heard the *shark is coming* tune from Jaws in there somewhere, too.

Now, imagine the concerts are in your head.

I was polishing my arrows—which if I were a man might have been a euphemism, but I'm not—when a wall of sound radiated from the bow and took me to my knees.

"Something's wrong," I heard someone say, but the cacophony in my head distorted and nearly drowned out the words, so I wasn't sure who picked up on my distress. Slapping my hands over my ears did nothing to reduce the thunder between them.

If I ever managed to get in a room with my father, the man was going to get a piece of my mind. Well, if the bow left me any pieces to give away.

Hands lifted me from the floor while I shrieked into the booming void. "Tone it down a notch." The bow listened, barely, and took the sound down from brain-melting to a volume still loud enough to set all my bones vibrating, but not enough to actually pop my eyeballs. Thank the goddess for small mercies.

"Enough." Yanking the bow out from its more nebulous form to its solid one, I watched the faces in the room go from worried to pained when they got a taste of what it felt like to be a Fate Weaver. Not so glamorous a job as one might think. "Message received." Singing bow. Who ever thought that was a good idea, I ask you?

The sudden silence seemed to hum. Sylvana sounded like she was talking from the bottom of a well when she said, "What the hell was that?" She shook her head and poked her little finger in her ear as if to clear out the last of the sound.

"That was my father's legacy." It wasn't the aftermath that flattened my tone. Proud as I was to carry on the work, the tools of the trade came with a learning curve and no instructions. When my mother only stared at me, I felt like I was missing something important.

"What?"

"Nothing. I just never heard it do that before."

Of course not, because the bow saved its most annoying aspects for me. I felt so special. All warm and fuzzy inside.

Or maybe that was just the aftermath of being hollowed out by sound. "Didn't the bow communicate with...um...him at all?" Having never met the man, I still wasn't sure what to call my father. Dad seemed a little informal. Cupid? Eros? Daddy? Um, no.

"You'll have to ask him when you get the chance."

I'd add that to my list of questions, sure. It was only about as long as Santa's naughty list at this point anyway. In the meantime, I assumed the attention-getting volume had been meant to warn me of something. Probably impending doom, since that tended to be the go-to problem in my life.

The living gold weapon quivered in my hands as if gearing up for another blast of chaotic noise. "Don't even think about it." There's no need to point out the absurdity of my talking to what should have been an inanimate object. I'm already aware. "If Timmy fell down the well, giving me a headache isn't the most useful way to help. Do better."

After a blast of frustrated instrumentation, the bow settled in and told its story through music. Sort of.

First, it hit me again with the Jaws da-dump da-dump sound. Simple enough to interpret. Danger headed my way. Next up was a song I didn't recognize.

"Anyone know what that is?" I looked around the room for willing participants in musical charades since my gut wasn't pinging anything to do with impending matches, but all I saw were blank faces until Aunt Mag walked into the room with my grandmother in tow.

"Hey, that's classic Floyd," she started to hum along.

I had a moment of stupidity. "Floyd who?" I racked my brains for anyone we knew named Floyd and came up dry.

Mag, whose musical and wardrobe tastes ran to the 60s and 70s but preferred Victorian decor, tilted her head and gave me a pitying look. "Pink."

For crying out loud, was the old bat going senile?

"Floyd Pink? I don't know anyone by that name." Sometimes it takes me a minute.

She looked at Gran and then back at me. "The song is Shine on You Crazy Diamond, by Pink Floyd." Then she shocked me even more by breaking into a nicely resonant contralto and singing along for a few bars with the bow.

Crazy diamond, and danger. I had to hand it to the bow for choosing topical references, even if one of them was well before my time. As far as codes went, this one was easy enough to break. Diana Diamond was up to something dangerous.

So, basically, it was Tuesday.

Except, the bow had another song or two to play, and when it launched into a lullaby that sounded like it came from a child's music box, my blood froze. Then it shot up to boiling.

Kaine.

Evian figured it out about a half second behind me, and when I turned to warn her, it was to see the twinkling motes she left behind as she shifted directly to Serena's with Soleil right behind her. Fire and water normally don't mix, but when those particular elemental faeries decided to work together, watch out.

Before the sparkle died out, they were back. Evian with the baby carrier, and Soleil with a hand wrapped around Serena's arm.

"What is wrong with you?" Indignant, a towel-draped Serena still had shampoo in her hair. "Dragging me out of the shower like that. I barely had time to grab a towel."

"We got word Diana might be headed to your place."

Soleil's hair lifted in the heat of her emotion. "She wasn't there, but I can promise she'd have been in for a surprise."

But then, so was I. The next tune from the bow of destiny was Riders on the Storm. An oldie even I recognized. Riders had to refer to the Balmorrigan, and what with the spate of reunions, I hadn't given enough thought to what we should do with them. Carl and the Fate Weavers had good information, but even knowing the supernatural predators could be killed wasn't enough. I needed to know how to get the jump on them.

"Salem, is Delta still around? Can you check the sanctum?" He was finally speaking to me without rolling his eyes every time, but if there was a championship for grudge carrying, Salem would be the poster boy. We hadn't had time for kitty cuddles or ear scratches yet, and I knew from past experience he wouldn't fully forgive me until I dragged his favorite bed out of storage.

In all fairness, he wasn't the only one who deserved some extra attention from me. I'd been quite short with the godmothers during my little break from dignity, and while they'd already forgiven me, I'd probably have to offer up penance and a few faerie game nights before they'd forget. All of which I was happy to do. If we all survived whatever was coming next.

"Don't bother, I'm right here." My hearing was returning, but even so, Delta's voice startled me from behind.

Heart racing, I turned to her. "Must you sneak around like that?"

She shot me a cocked eyebrow and a sarcastic answer. "Hello, my name is Delta. I track down supernatural beings for a living. I tend to be stealthy."

Flapping a hand at her because we didn't have time for a bout of verbal sparring, I cut her off.

"I think the Balmorrigan felt that burst of magic from

creating my wand." At the time, I was too busy to ask what put the frown on her face as she glanced at the bow and then back at me. Later, I'd wish for a do-over.

TWENTY-EIGHT

The Balmorrigan brought darkness with them when they thundered down our street. Not a true darkness—they weren't powerful enough to bring night on early—but a wind ill and dank that pushed clouds over the late-day sun. With the lowering gloom came a sense of dread, or at least a hint of it. It's a lot more difficult to scare someone when they're anticipating you, but the riders had no idea we'd been forewarned, so they came in hot.

Shock and awe.

Not even close.

I'm not saying we took the threat less than seriously, just that we were as ready as we could be, and we had the home-turf advantage. It would have been a slow-motion, wind-in-the-hair moment if we'd actually stepped down off the porch. Honestly, what were they thinking going up against four elemental faeries anyway?

Vaeta and Evian had already thrown up a fog barrier to keep the neighbors from seeing and hearing too much.

As if on parade, the horses passed by the house, reared, then whirled to speed back in our direction. Evian's face hardly twitched; her eyebrow raised only slightly as she called water from the snow to form an ice slick on the street.

Steam plumed from overheated nostrils. Later, Kin swore he saw a tiny flicker of flame shoot out as well, but we all saw sparks as metal shoes made short work of Evian's efforts. Round one to the twins.

A guttural shout of triumph went up from the one carrying the scythe. He swung a graceful leg over the pommel and slid gently to the ground just as Soleil went into action. I'd seen her perform a variation of this trick before, but not when her efforts were directed at an outside threat. This time, she added a little oomph.

Heat blew all our hair back on the way by to concentrate on the pavement at the end of the walkway. Snow melted with a crackle and hiss, turning a three-foot diameter spot just ahead of the cowled figure to a puddle of melted tar. Before you could say boo, Vaeta called the wind, and if he'd had time to stop before, she gave him no choice. A strong gust pushed him forward until he was knee-deep in the sticky muck. As an added bonus, the breeze pushed the hood away to reveal a face I recognized.

Mr. Tall Dark and Creepy from outside Driven glared back at me. "You'll die screaming."

"Nice comeback. Want to try for a new one? I've heard that one before."

The look on his face was priceless. Sort of *don't you know who I am* meets *how the hell did I get here*. The real question was what to do with him.

I'm not a murderer and even if I was, the man was half

witch. Killing him would turn me to stone. Or maybe only half stone, but either way, I wasn't taking that chance. The faeries would dance over the line, I was sure, and not lose a minute's sleep.

While I took half a second to contemplate our next move, the other twin forced the issue. Limber as a gymnast, she flipped off her horse, somersaulted through the air, grabbed the scythe on her way by, and fixed her gaze on the weakest prey. Fritzroy.

Not on my watch. One of the things Delta had taught me about physical combat was that the element of surprise only goes so far, but used properly can be a useful distraction. And sometimes, like this one, you hit pay dirt.

This was my fight, not the faeries, not Delta's, mine— and maybe Garrick and Fritz's—but mostly mine, so I reached for my two natural weapons, the bow and my magic. I'd had a theory about using the bow in a fight— that the instrument of love couldn't be used to cause physical injury. After all, the golden arrows struck hearts bloodlessly.

The theory turned out to be only partially correct. Stalking Diana through the streets of Port Harbor proved it. The first time I'd reached into my quiver, out of reflex more than intention, only one arrow came to hand: my arrow, the one I'd pulled from my own body to free Clara from her stone prison. Made from my flesh and bone and a tip of living gold, it was the only arrow to bend to my intent.

On that day, I drew it against the Balmorrigan, infused

it with my will, encased it in my new brand of goddess-enhanced pink witchfire, and let it fly. Straight and true, it winged toward my target while I cocked a hip and watched.

Like I said, I'm no killer, but Delta also taught me the best way to beat an enemy is to take out the source of its power. My arrow pierced lantern glass with a tone like a wet finger traveling around the rim of a crystal goblet. A tone so pure it vibrated against my skull and threatened to close my throat.

The lantern went off like a hand grenade, only instead of shrapnel, it spewed Fate Weaver souls to light up the artificial darkness. The Balmorrigan shrieked her fury as Delta, sword drawn, flashed past me to engage in hand to hand combat with the female half of the minion twins while the male struggled against the tar holding him captive.

Watching Delta fight was not too different from watching a good ballet. She leapt and pivoted with grace, her sword matching the scythe blow for blow. She had the Balmorrigan in fierceness, though not in weight or size, and still, she backed the cowled figure into the middle of the street and right up against her brother.

Delta's sword arced down to score a bloody line along the Balmorrigan's upper arm then lifted to flip the hood back.

"Let's see that pretty face. I like to know who I'm fighting with." Turns out, both the twins had been at

Driven that night, because this was the luminous woman I'd noticed on the dance floor.

Pure fury twisted the beautiful face into something ugly, and I couldn't help myself. "You keep making that face, it's going to freeze like that." Sometimes my mouth engages ahead of my brain and I hear the comment right along with everyone else. This was one of those times, and it goaded the Balmorrigan into action.

Lifting the scythe, she brought it down, and so quickly it blurred through my vision. I thought Delta was done for, but the Fiach executed a cartwheeling flip that took her out of harm's way. The blade sliced through cooling pavement and set her brother free.

Now, Delta stood alone with the rest of us too far away to help.

Except Delta wasn't the quarry, and since they were clearly outnumbered, the twins chose to retreat. I moved to follow.

"No, let them go." Delta flung out an arm to hold me back. I pushed against her, but it was like trying to shove a piece of grass through a rock.

"Have you lost your mind? They're getting away." Maybe stating the obvious would get through to her.

Instead, she just grinned at me, so I struggled harder. "What is wrong with you? Are you on their side or something?"

She shoved me back a few steps and her voice whipped out hard enough I knew I'd struck a nerve.

"Don't be an idiot." On any other day, I'd have had sense enough to shut up. Today I didn't even try.

"What am I supposed to think? We had them. It was almost over, and then you kicked over the cauldron. On purpose is what it looked like. Hence the question: what is wrong with you?"

It occurred to me that I'd never asked Delta anything about her personal life—like if she was married or if she had kids. Because if she did, the look she gave me then would have worked a treat to get them to stop acting out. Nearly made me think twice about my tone. Nearly.

Gritted teeth and a growl did it, though. "They're not working alone. You know that, right?"

Light dawned. "You gave them half a butt whooping so they'd run and we could follow them back to wherever it is Diana's hiding out and put the hurt on them all at the same time?"

"Look who's finally thinking."

That triggered round two of stating the obvious and I didn't even try to resist. "They're gone, so how's that working out for you?"

I got a dirty look and a snort out of her as she waved around a small piece of paper rolled up to about the size of my finger, then yanked a necklace out of her cleavage and showed it to me. Another living gold compass, but hers carried the winking fire of a flawless diamond and wasn't marked with the points of direction.

"What's that?" I tried not to ask and I tried not to have a Harry Potter Defense Against the Dark Arts moment.

"My next job and a tracker, what else?" Delta ran a finger over the bloody sword tip and then the leading edge of the tracker, a thing she'd done so many times the spot was burnished to a shine. Her touch activated a hidden mechanism—oh, who was I kidding, it was magic—and fire lit the diamond from within.

She unrolled the paper to show me a single word: Balmorrigan.

"Looks like I'm officially on the clock."

Fate Weavers, even me who finally got her marbles back in the case, are still the sum of their parts. Witch was one of my parts, and I was a damn good one even if I hadn't learned every spell Salem wanted me to learn.

My mother was better.

"Let's go." She took my arm. "My supplies are back at the apartment, but we can whip up few things here."

If it hadn't been for her, I'd have taken off after the Balmorrigan with nothing more than the clothes on my back and a new wand I wasn't sure how to use. With no plan, armed only with the knowledge that I was the only person alive who could stop Diana Diamond. It didn't matter if I was the chosen one not. I was here, she'd chosen the time, and that meant the job fell to me.

As with everything my father handed down, it would have been nice if I had a little more information.

"What am I supposed to do?" I'd followed my mom to

the sanctum where she, Gran, and Aunt Mag were already knee deep in spell crafting and directed the question to Garrick because he was the closest. "You know the lore or whatever, tell me everything, and make it snappy."

"Why, Lexi, you carry the Bow of Destiny. I should think it's obvious what you need to do. We will, of course, accompany you on this most noble of quests." Who did he think he was? Lancelot?

He might think the bow was the answer, but he'd never released the bowstring and launched an arrow at a heart not ready for its match. All that ever did was make things worse.

"So there's no strategy?" No advice from dear old Dad? Even second hand, it might have helped. But no, that would be too easy. Excuse me for being bitter, but I'd had just about enough of things dumped in my lap for one year.

Fritzroy couldn't hide his relief when I declined the offer of help, but Garrick seemed a little miffed to be dismissed, and there wasn't time to smooth things over. I had plenty of other ticked-off people to deal with. Salem was alternately not speaking to me because he thought I was going to deprive him of his last life, and threatening to go tell Kin what was going on so he could talk some sense into me. Terra was on his side. Soleil wanted to come along, and Vaeta wasn't speaking to anyone for some reason.

On the witch side of the family, Gran seemed resigned, but Balefire sparks shot out the tip of Aunt Mag's finger when she shook it under Delta's nose. "You just remember that with age comes experience."

Respectfully, Delta stood her ground. "Which is why we need you here to watch over the house in case the Balmorrigan don't lead us to Diana and she shows up here."

From the look on her face, Aunt Mag knew she'd just been handed a lollipop and sent out of the room to let the big kids play. I would probably pay for that later.

In the end, only my mother and Delta would accompany me in tracking the twins back to wherever Diana was holed up. If they even returned to her at all. We could spend a day tracking the wild goose back to its nest and still not find the golden egg.

That wouldn't be my luck, though. If I was chasing the wild goose, it would turn out to be some denizen of the Faelands that had sharp teeth, farted fire, and flew around dropping poison eggs everywhere. You laugh, but you haven't seen the things I've seen.

TWENTY-NINE

"Is it safe to ride triple?" Mom had a pack of spells on her back, so I would be riding in the middle spot. Delta looked at me like I was the biggest fool in the world. So sue me, I wanted to live long enough to get to Diana and risk my life against her minion twins. On second thought, a clean death against a tall tree might not be the worst way to go.

Something tugged at my hair as we pulled out onto the icy road, and an odd sense of calm washed over me. Diana wanted me dead, and I wanted her neutralized, whatever that looked like. One of us would not get our wish today. Her vision said I would be her downfall. It did not say how, or what would happen to me after, which was enough, normally, to induce a freakout. Yet, here I was, freakout-free.

The tracking device fitted into a holder mounted on the handlebars, where it blinked merrily as Delta followed it into her middle dimension. We whizzed along through the flat gray for a couple of minutes, burst out into the world of color and light on the edge of the industrial section of town, and pulled up in front of a warehouse building.

"They're in there." Delta pointed. "Wait here, I'll find a way in."

It felt like someone yanked a hank of hair out of my head right before I caught the flutter of motion in my peripheral vision. Vaeta, in a smaller form than I'd ever seen one of the faeries take, was the size of a large dragon-fly. "I didn't know you could get that small, but you're not supposed to be here."

She whooshed to full human size and shrugged off the censure.

"What, and miss all the fun? You need me." With that, she turned, assessed the building for a moment, then lifted her hands and blew the door in.

So much for a stealthy approach.

Beyond the opening where dust particles glittered in the sunlight slanting through the hole where the door used to be, darkness shrouded the interior. We'd be going in sun-blind.

"I guess we're going to make an entrance." Mom deadpanned.

As if they'd agreed on it ahead of time, Sylvana and Delta moved into protective flanking positions on either side of me while Vaeta practically danced on ahead.

Our plan, made on the fly, seemed simple enough. We each went in with a different method of containment. On the fingers of both hands, I wore eight rings, each one charmed with a variation of the same binding spell Gran tried to use on Mom the day they fought.

Walking behind Vaeta, I hoped it was enough.

All resemblance to Dorothy and her crew creeping down the wizard's shadowed corridor ended when my mother shot a ball of nearly white witchfire up to hover in the rafters and light the place up like a stadium during a night game.

Whatever I expected to see, it wasn't a huge, empty space with an open loft area jutting partway out from a glassed-in office at the top of a set of metal stairs. Actually, all that was fairly normal for a warehouse. Diana wearing a crown and sitting on a throne made from what might have been the bones of my brethren—that was not normal. The twins lounged at her feet, their legs hanging over the edge of the platform in a perfect Kodak moment of creepiness.

"Hello, Lexi. Did you come to die?" Diana's silvery tones echoed and turned harsh in the cavernous building.

I don't know why, but I tried reasoning with her. "You don't want to do this, Diana. Killing your soul, even part of it, won't make you a god." Based on my recent experiences, I thought I was safe in pointing that out. "It's not too late to turn back."

That might have been a lie. Dark veins traced winding paths under Diana's skin, framing her face in a delicate lacy pattern before disappearing into her hairline. They'd turned her lips and eyes obsidian black. She couldn't have much light left in her.

In response, she barked out a laugh. "Why would I ever want to do that?"

A hundred answers, but none that would sway her

came to mind. "Your choice, I suppose." I'd tried, and by trying, my conscience was clear. Whatever happened next was on Diana.

She placed a hand on each of the twin's heads and made the first move. "Go, my pets."

Her minions exploded off the platform to land lightly on the floor below, and the battle began.

The Balmorrigan fought in silence, which I found unnerving. Most of my fighting experience has been from the outside perspective. Between the smack talk and the magical chaos, watching the faeries go at each other was never a quiet affair, so the slither and slide of sword over scythe seemed almost tame.

Vaeta and my mother worked surprisingly well as a team. Devoid of her lantern, the female twin produced a length of pipe from under her cloak, which she swung one-handed while casting spells with the other.

After the fourth time his scythe missed me narrowly, I began to wonder how the male Balmorrigan got his reputation. Delta's sword blazed toward him and he sidestepped it easily, even though she moved at blurring speed, yet he missed me and I barely had to dodge.

"What are you waiting for?" Delta hissed as she countered the scythe with the edge of her blade.

"For you to get out of the line of fire." I hissed back. Binding our best fighter in the middle of a battle was not part of the plan.

I heard the slither of steel sliding over steel, smelled the coppery tang of blood, but couldn't tell who'd been cut until Delta sprang back and left me the perfect opportunity. Anticipating his speed, I activated three of the rings in rapid sequence.

The ploy worked. He dodged the first, barely managed to slap the second out of the air with his weapon, but couldn't bring the heavy scythe back up in time to stop the third. Ropes made of fire and light slammed into him at mid body, and though he strained, the bindings held. Long enough, anyway, for Delta to slap on her version of magical handcuffs, and suddenly, we were down to a four-against-one battle.

From her bizarre throne, Diana's laugh echoed across the empty space, but she never lifted a finger to try to help the Balmorrigan. Some mother she turned out to be.

Ten minutes can seem like nothing or forever depending on what you're doing to occupy your time. Fighting supernaturally strong creatures for that long had begun to put a strain on us all. Delta's breath came in short gasps, Vaeta's whirlwinds were slowing, and even my mother's spellcasting aim had weakened. I needed to bind the second twin before it was too late.

She fought like a demon, but since I'd used the rings once, they'd lost the element of surprise. Nimble as a cat, she dodged the first one and kept coming for me, and because the others were still trying to protect me, they kept getting in my way. There was a lesson in that somewhere, but I didn't have time to think it through.

This would have been a great time to use a few of Evian's tiny shell communicators, but none of us besides Vaeta had one handy. I'd have been able to whisper to my companions without telegraphing my intent to the Balmorrigan.

Another minute passed, and I realized I'd have to bull my way into the middle of the fray, or someone on my team was going to get hurt. Vaeta was closest, so I hip-checked her out of the way and took aim. I'd chosen the wrong moment, and the next few seconds seemed to happen in slow motion.

Caught in the middle of sending out another mini tornado, Vaeta couldn't pull it back in time, and the blast of air hit me instead. I felt my feet sliding across the concrete and saw the pipe coming toward my face at a speed that would probably knock it clean off my head.

I activated two more of the ring charms.

Several things happened all at once. My binding took the Balmorrigan just as Delta's sword jumped between my face and the pipe that was about to obliterate it. The force of Delta's upward thrust went awry as the binding shoved my attacker backwards, and the sword plunged into the Balmorrigan's middle.

Diana screamed in fury, and without even thinking, I launched the rest of the bindings toward the sound. Even if I'd hit her with all eight, they wouldn't hold her for long.

"Arabella, no!" Brother screamed for sister, but she never fell because Diana was there. Not five feet from where I stood, helpless to do anything but stare. Cold and black were the eyes of the wannabe goddess who held the woman she'd raised by the neck as casually as if she were nothing more than a bag of groceries.

"Now, now. Mustn't let all that lovely darkness go to waste."

No one moved while Diana bent her head as though to kiss her daughter, and instead, consumed the darkness that was the Balmorrigan's soul.

My skin crawled, and my stomach tried to climb up into my throat.

"That's where you're wrong." The first time she'd spoken since we arrived, the female's voice rasped with pain and conviction. "You think because you made us, you control our thoughts, but you only control our actions. I hope you choke and die for all you've made us do."

Her eyes fell on me. "She told us witches were the evil ones. That we were bred to be strong and to fight against those powerful enough to bring darkness to the world. We believed we were on the side of good until she was imprisoned by a demon named Rhys who showed us what she really was."

Sneering, Diana let her talk. "Isn't that nice, a deathbed confession."

"Kill me. I beg of you, set me free. She forced me to darken my soul, and now that she's taken what she put in me, there's nothing left but a soul-killing stain. All that ever was good in me is dying, and if you don't finish me now, the demon will be all that remains. A demon she can control. Kill me now while I can die knowing there was love and not only hate. Please."

The terror, pain, and desperation in her voice made my heart constrict. Her words rang true, even without my witchly powers of truth parsing, and I knew someone had to do something. I just really didn't want to be that person now.

None of us heard him move, nor did we realize he'd broken free of the binding, but when the scythe rose and fell, neither were we its victims as the male dealt his sister the killing blow. "Blessed be, sister. Blessed be." When it was done, he did the totally unexpected and handed the weapon to me.

"I cannot repay the debt I owe your blood, but I will give myself in service for what I owe."

Before I could process the meaning of that, he'd shucked off my binding along with Delta's, and launched himself toward Diana.

"Be thou the most perfect version of thyself."

Salem has always maintained that a novice witch can funnel only so much of her power into a spell, or it will arc back and consume her. I'd thought him overly cautious, but I'd never expected a full-grown witch could do the same thing on purpose.

The Balmorrigan's power struck Diana like an avalanche rolling down a mountain. It caught her in its ferocity, and she began to shriek as she felt the change coming on. I saw her reach into her cleavage and pull out one of her cards. I saw her throw it, but I was too busy watching what came next to see where it went.

As his magic poured into her, the Balmorrigan began to shake, and then to burn. He went up like a torch, leaving the smell of burning flesh behind until he turned completely to ash.

Tendons popped with sickening sounds, and Diana's skin blackened, turning leathery while she howled in pain. I couldn't tell you what she became because I'm not sure there's a name for something that's part bird and part human. Either way, she wouldn't be throwing any more cards until she figured out how to turn herself back. The process took mere seconds, and then she took flight and busted out through one of the multi-paned windows.

Only the sound of the wind whistling through broken glass could be heard until a groan sounded behind me and I turned just in time to catch Delta as she fell.

Diana's weapon had not been a card made of paper, but one fashioned from razor-edged metal, and it was now lodged in Delta's chest.

"Help her." I screamed at Vaeta and my mother. "Do something." But I could tell by their stricken faces, it was too late.

While I held her and begged for it not to be so, Delta died in my arms.

EPILOGUE

I don't know what happens to the Fiach when they die. Witches go to the Summerlands, though with my mixed heritage, who knows where I'll end up. Of course, humans can't seem to agree on their ultimate resting place, and some believe they'll be reincarnated into another person, or a butterfly, or maybe a rock.

What Delta had hoped her afterlife would hold, I couldn't have begun to guess, and our friendship had been cut too short to reach the point of me finding out.

I also don't know if the Fiach erect gravestones for their dead, but by the goddess, I made sure this one did. It held nothing but the date of her death, her name, and an etching of her face. Kneeling to place a bouquet of flowers at its base, I traced a finger over the rendering and made a promise to Delta. I would defeat the woman who had stolen her from this world, or die trying.

And I wouldn't do it alone. All Diana had accomplished was to royally tick off a veritable army of powerful supernaturals, and every single one was willing to go to the ends of the earth to avenge Delta's death.

If that meant I had to swallow my pride and give my mother what she wanted, so be it. If going straight to the source and seeking out my father was necessary, I'd do it. And if choking the life out of the evil Diana with my bare hands was what it took, I'd happily pay whatever karmic debt the act incurred.

But I would get justice.

Lexi's journey isn't over just yet.

Keep reading for a sneak peek at the final book in the series, Heaven or Spell, where her past collides with her future, unexpected alliances are forged, and a life-changing decision could alter the course of the Balefire legacy forever.

QUICK AUTHOR'S NOTE

If you weren't already aware, ReGina and Erin are a mother/daughter writing team, and yes, that means we mix family and work—with all the ups and downs you might expect. But since we're best friends too, we let that stuff roll right off our backs.

When we began writing A Cold Day in Spell, we knew Lexi's journey would continue to surprise us. After the revelations and challenges in Spell Hath No Fury, Lexi's struggle to balance her powers as a Balefire witch, her family ties, and her love life reached new heights. We loved exploring her growing confidence as a Fate Weaver and her resilience when the magical and mortal worlds clashed. Her encounters with new allies—and more dangerous enemies—forced her to redefine what it means to trust, love, and lead.

This book allowed us to unravel secrets about the Balefire legacy while introducing twists we couldn't wait to see unfold. But even as Lexi finds her footing, the stakes in Heaven or Spell, the final book of the Fate Weaver series, will push her to her limits. Old friends will return with new agendas, and Lexi will face decisions that could either heal her broken heart or shatter it entirely. With the balance of magic in question, every choice she makes will matter—and not just for her.

Anyway, if you've come this far with us and not decided we're complete and total whackadoodles...and especially if you have, we're offering a chance to sign up for our newsletters— the best place to get new release updates, sales notifications, and other fun content.

You can sign up for ReGina's newsletter and/or Erin's newsletter, and as a thank-you gift for hanging out with us, you'll also get a FREE novella that isn't available anywhere else. And of course, we promise not to SPAM your inbox!

Love, hugs, and happy reading,
ReGina & Erin

P.S. If you enjoyed this book, it would be great if you could leave a review or recommendation at your favorite store, GoodReads, or BookBub.

Your reviews help indie authors sell more books!

P.P.S. If you loved Mag & Clara, there's a spinoff series where the two of them solve mysteries in the sort-of fictional town of Harmony, Maine!

EXCERPT FROM HEAVEN OR SPELL

FATE WEAVER - BOOK SEVEN

Heat and the weight of Kin's arm slung across my hip brought me slowly out of sleep. Well, that and the sandpaper tongue sliding along my cheek.

"Salem," I slit one eye open, tilted my head back slightly to bring his face into focus. "Lay off."

In response, he turned and flicked his tail in my face. An eloquent gesture, which he repeated until I finally groaned and dragged myself out of bed.

"I hate you."

Not true. Mostly.

But enough to take my sweet time getting dressed before I joined him in the hallway with one last, lingering look at the man in my bed. There are better ways to wake up in the morning than a cat kiss. I'm just saying.

"You're not supposed to be in the bedroom when Kin's here," I said. "You know the rules."

Between one step and the next, Salem's feline shape gave way to his human one. "I'm not supposed to sleep in the bedroom when Kin's here." Salem's voice was as silky smooth as the eggplant-colored shirt that billowed back from his muscular shoulders. "I didn't sleep there."

"It's too early to argue semantics. I need coffee."

When I moved to detour into the kitchen for some, he blocked the door.

"There's coffee in the workshop." Under a cocked brow, his blue eye dared me to argue while the green one glinted with amusement. I don't know how he does that, but I find it unnerving at times. "And your mother's already there."

"Great." I didn't remember making plans with her, but I followed him toward the fireplace, steeling myself as I reached into the flame to activate the handle that opened the secret door to the sanctum. I know the fire won't burn me, but a lifetime of conditioning takes a while to overcome.

"Get in here," Sylvana said when she saw me. "We're burning daylight."

"It's ten minutes after dawn." I'm not a morning person.

"It's after eight. Drink your coffee, eat your pancakes, and stop whining."

Pancakes?

"I wasn't whining," I mumbled, wondering why even a mother who hadn't been there for my formative years could bring out the rebellious child in me. "And the pancakes are probably cold by now."

Sylvana slapped her hands on her hips and gave me a look that could wither dandelions. "You are a fire witch. Heat them up, for Hecate's sake, Lexi. Didn't those faeries teach you anything?"

She turned away, and I did not roll my eyes and make a face at her.

"I saw that."

Okay, maybe I did.

Two hours later, curled on the sofa with a stack of musty old books on the floor beside me, and Salem sprawled across my feet—which would have been more comfortable for me if he'd been in his feline form—I came across something interesting.

"You lied to me," I cast a glare at Sylvana.

"Not that I'm aware."

"Don't give me your innocent face, you lying liar." Heat rushed across my skin. "According to *Pembroke's Treatise on Tactical Potions*, I didn't have to poke that flame fowl in the backside. There were other ways to scare it awake."

It didn't help my mood when she smiled and nodded. "All of which would have been far less entertaining for me. But you wouldn't have fallen for it if you'd taken time to study your craft."

"Very funny, Mother."

"Anything useful in there?"

"Not so far," I said. "Do you think we're looking at this the wrong way? I mean, we've been looking for a tracking spell all this time. Should we have been looking for one to summon him instead?"

Sylvana frowned, and began to offer an automatic dismissal, then stopped and thought about it a bit more. In the end, she shook her head.

"Too dangerous and probably wouldn't work unless we found a way to reverse the spell that banished him. The whole thing could boomerang on us."

Spell that banished him? What was she talking about?

"Mom, there was no spell. He chose to walk away."

Balefire witches have an affinity with fire, but we don't actually shoot it out of our eyes. If we could, I'm pretty sure Sylvana's would have burned me to ash where I sat.

"I was there, Lexi. Your grandmother banished him." She paused, her eyes widening, then narrowing craftily. "Now that gives me an idea. If I cut off the power to her spell, he'll be able to come back on his own."

"Cut off the power? What does that even mean?" I blinked back the dire image forming in my mind. "I thought you were getting along better. You're not thinking of hurting your own mother?"

Salem had reverted to feline form at the beginning of the conversation. I glanced in his direction and then toward the exit. I had no problem using him to tattle if Sylvana decided to do something drastic.

"Un-bunch your panties. I'm only talking about binding her powers for a minute. Just long enough to break the spell. Nothing major."

Nothing major, she said. Clara would not be amused. Someone would get hurt.

"You're out of your mind."

Sylvana ignored me while she pondered possible ingredients for a binding spell.

"I'd need a length of gallows rope. Not something you find just lying around the house."

"You'd need your head examined, and it wouldn't work because he walked away of his own accord."

"I'm sure that's what my mother told you, but I was there, Lexi, and I'm telling you he didn't."

"There was no spell. Your beloved walked away. I saw it happen."

"You were a baby. You couldn't possibly—"

"Yes, I could." Hadn't I told her the story of my trip back in time? "I thought I told you about this already, but I wasn't a baby when I saw it, and I can prove it."

I grabbed the book I'd been poring over, turned back a few pages to a spell I'd read earlier. All I needed was a bowl of water or, better yet, a large mirror. Something shiny to cast the spell against. Something shiny. I knew just the thing.

"Follow me."

Books scattered as I launched from my place on the sofa. I let them lay where they fell because I'd had an idea that might just rival one of Aunt Mag's impressive feats of magic. Passing through the sanctum, I gathered what I'd need for the spell, then led the way back up to my bedroom.

Sylvana said little with her mouth, letting the sardonic arch of her left brow do the talking while I set up candles, sprinkled some herbs, and inscribed a circle on the floor.

Ignoring her, I pulled a DVD out of my movie collection.

"Sorry, Ferris Bueler, you're getting sacrificed to the cause."

Magic welled inside me—something I hope I never take for granted—as I focused on the memory of my trip back in time, then rushed out to bind with the shiny plastic.

"Here goes nothing." I popped the DVD into the player, turned on the TV, and hoped for the best.

In white against a field of deep blue, the words A Balefire Production appeared. The spell—it seemed—had worked. I grinned until the theme music kicked in. You know the song, the one they played when the witch showed up in Wizard of Oz. Probably didn't bode well.

"Should we have popcorn?" Honeyed sarcasm dripped from her tone as the camera panned across treetops before zeroing in on a grassy clearing where two women stood off against each other.

"Get away from him." Sylvana's scream shot out of the TV speaker, her voice sharp and edging toward hysterical. "You vicious old witch. Leave him alone."

White fire lanced from her fingertips, arrowed toward her mother's body. Clara batted the sizzling flame away with as much attention as she would have paid a fly buzzing around her ear.

I watched my mother watching herself as she threw a temper tantrum on screen. Her jaw clenched, but that was her only reaction.

My voice coming from the TV called my attention away from my mother.

Calm in the face of Sylvana's rage, Clara's attention remained focused on the man who was at the crux of this fight. Or, technically, the minor deity: Cupid. The one and only god of love who carried a bow and heart-tipped arrows but was as far from a winged cherub as a donkey is from a goose.

Chiseled perfection from head to toe, there was nothing baby soft about him. It was no wonder Sylvana had fallen for his...charms. She stared at him now, her face carefully blank but for the occasional twitch at the corner of her mouth.

I'm Lexi Balefire, daughter of Sylvana, granddaughter of Clara and Cupid? Well, he's my dad. I know; it shocked me, too, when I found out. And not in a good way.

Apparently, I would be the narrator for this little piece of cinema.

Oh, goodie.

Heaven or Spell, the final book in the Fate Weaver series is available now. Keep reading for a preview of the free novella you'll get for joining our newsletters.

A FREE STORY FOR YOU

Enjoyed meeting Lexi? Not ready for her story to end?

Sign up for either or both of our newsletters and you'll receive *A Snowball's Chance in Spell*, a prequel novella featuring characters from the *Mag & Clara Balefire Mysteries*, the *Haunted Everly After Mysteries*, and the *Psychic Seasons* series.

Christmas is canceled! Lexi Balefire's faerie godmothers didn't mean to knock Santa Claus and his sleigh out of the sky, but now his reindeer are missing, and it's up to Lexi to find them all before time runs out and Christmas is ruined!

EXCERPT FROM A SNOWBALL'S CHANCE IN SPELL

Lightning flirted in shadows of the dark clouds hovering over my house when I came home from work the afternoon before my twenty-second Christmas Eve. Nothing unusual there. With three elemental faeries living in the house, weird weather happened all the time. Or rather, every time my temperamental godmothers mounted some sort of snit.

The godmothers idled at snit.

Going back to work wasn't an option. I'd cleared the last match of the year—a lovely couple with a shared affection for online gaming—and I was no coward. When it came to diffusing faerie fights, I consider myself an expert, and this one didn't look like it rated more than a two on the volcano scale.

Yes, you heard right. I measure faerie fights on the scale of whether or not a volcano might erupt in my backyard. Living with faeries is never boring. Occasionally dangerous—especially because I have yet to come into the magic that is my birthright, but never boring.

A quick check proved they'd contained the madness to the inside and/or the backyard. The two feet of snow on the front lawn was still there and still white—you try explaining black snow to your neighbors sometime. I didn't see any winged denizens—fae or otherwise—dotting the roof ridge, or hear any ominous sounds. If not for the fact that lightning is rare in Maine during the winter, and rarer still when confined to a single area, I'd have thought it was a quiet day in the household.

In my head, I downgraded the threat to a level one, and went inside.

For the most part, my place looks like an ordinary, New England style home. Built by my great grandparents, it's the oldest house in a neighborhood that grew up around it when the suburbs expanded into what was once a rural area. Because, I think, the faeries wanted to give me a normal upbringing, they left the house in mostly the same condition it was in when they came to take care of me and only added on a wing for their own use.

I stepped into the front hall expecting...well, just about anything. Did I mention the faeries love holidays? Maybe they don't have them in the faelands, or maybe they do and go overboard there, too. I can't say since I've never been, but I could tell at a glance there were more decorations than there had been when I left.

"Terra!" I yelled, but got no answer. Terra, faerie of earth, held sway over all the flora and fauna found on dry land. She would be the one responsible for the pine boughs twining over anything that held still long enough. Fire faerie, Soleil, contributed by setting sparks of faerie light to twinkle inside the delicate ice bubbles crafted by her sister, Evian, mistress of water. The effect was lovely, but not as lovely as the three women could be when their faces weren't twisted, as they were now, with rage.

I came upon them in their favorite fighting grounds: the kitchen. It looked like I'd caught this one early since there was relatively little damage done so far. Steam rose from a puddle of water at Soleil's feet which I assumed had come from Evian. Vines snaked from between the kitchen tiles to twine around Evian's ankles, and there were a few smoking embers dotting Terra's hair. Nothing more than a minor spat.

Keeping it casual, I asked, "What's going on?" There's no rhyme or reason to what will settle a fight or send one into the red zone.

Terra turned one granite pink eye in my direction. "This doesn't concern you." The fingers of her left hand twitched and the vines slithered from Evian's ankles to her knees.

Retaliating, Evian conjured a gush of water from thin air, and doused the smoking embers. The scent of pine boughs couldn't compete with the stench of burnt hair, or the pungent funk erupting from the flowers that burst into bloom near her feet.

"Now look," I pointed out to Terra before she conjured something worse. "Evian is trying to help."

"Was not." Evian snapped her fingers and turned Terra's wet hair white with frost, except because the vines were now questing higher, she overshot the mark and doused a few of Soleil's decorative sparkles.

That was the moment I lost control.

Oh, who am I kidding? I never had control.

Soleil let out a screech and lobbed a fireball at Evian, who encased it in a ball of water and batted it toward Terra. I felt scoured clean when Terra called all the dirt and dust in the house to form a layer over the bobbing ball of doom which now resembled a small planet whizzing back toward Soleil.

It might have ended better if I'd have kept my mouth shut, but I didn't.

"You're going to put an eye out with that thing."

The ire of three faeries is a potent thing, but not as potent as a flaming mudball. I ducked, rolled, and hit the latch on the patio door in what I'd like to think was a graceful move. Probably looked like a seal rolling off a rock.

The flaming fireball arced over my head, its warm breeze tossing my hair, and rocketed off into the sky.

Crisis averted. Except, it wasn't. I should have known.

A Snowball's Chance in Spell is only available by signing up for one of our newsletters here:
https://reginawelling.com
https://erinlynnwrites.com

OTHER BOOKS

If you'd like to meet more people who live rent-free in our heads, here's a list of other series we've written. Our books are all set in fictional towns in Maine, and some characters like to flit back and forth between series. The cast of Psychic Seasons hangs out with Everly and also with Lexi Balefire from the Fate Weaver series. Mag and Clara Balefire are Lexi's grandmother and aunt!

The Psychic Seasons Series
Four women, four love stories, and a whole lot of supernatural surprises. In the quaint town of Oakville, Maine, psychic visions, ghostly whispers, and fate itself conspire to change lives—and hearts—forever

The Haunted Everly After Mysteries
Everly Dupree came home for a fresh start—not a full-time gig solving ghostly murders. But when the dearly departed start demanding justice, what's a reluctant medium to do?

The Ponderosa Pines Mysteries

Nothing bad ever happens in the weird little town of Ponderosa Pines...until someone dies. Now it's up to best friends Chloe and EV to solve the mystery—before the town's secrets bury them too.

The Mag and Clara Balefire Mysteries
Sister witches Mag and Clara Balefire move to a sleepy Maine town for a fresh start—only to find themselves conjuring up trouble, solving murders, and keeping their magic under wraps in this charmingly witchy cozy mystery series

Laurel Haven Witches
Four witches, destined by blood and magic, must embrace their power, battle a dark legacy, and surrender to the love that could break the curse—or bind them to it forever.

Nell Page: Accidental Investigator
Nell Page owns a bookstore, drinks too much coffee, and has a habit of noticing things she probably shouldn't. With warmth, wit, and an accidental talent for investigating, Nell tackles mysteries that don't always involve murder—but always matter.

www.ingramcontent.com/pod-product-compliance
Lightning Source LLC
Chambersburg PA
CBHW061059190726
48286CB00006B/1805